THE HITLER DECEPTION

ALLAN LEVERONE

Braveship
BOOKS

Aura Libertatis Spirat

THE HITLER DECEPTION

Copyright © 2015 by Allan Leverone

Braveship Books

www.braveshipbooks.com

Aura Libertatis Spirat

Cover Artwork & Design by Elderlemon Design
Print edition formatting by JD Smith Design

ISBN-13: 978-1-939398-94-9

Printed in the United States of America

Special thanks to:

Elderlemon design and Kealan Patrick Burke for the outstanding cover art, to editor Dan Persinger for ensuring I dotted all my i's and crossed all my t's, and to JD Smith Design for the formatting and design of *The Hitler Deception* print edition.

Prologue

April 29, 1945
7:10 p.m.
Führerbunker, Berlin, Germany

The young soldier was afraid.

His position on Adolph Hitler's personal security detail for the past three years had allowed Klaus Newmann to witness the tide of war turning against his country even as he developed a personal relationship with the man whose life he was sworn to protect.

By April, defeat for the Thousand Year Reich was imminent. It seemed obvious, even to a common soldier like Klaus. The Soviet Union's Red Army had by now fully encircled Berlin, and relentless Soviet bombing runs were pounding the capital city into smoking ruins.

The Führer's behavior had become more and more erratic, even as wild rumors of impending coup attempts and assassination plots swept through the bunker. Klaus had observed first-hand some of the Führer's near-incoherent rages, as Hitler spent hours and days developing elaborate defense plans, only to scrap them abruptly and begin work on new plans.

Meanwhile, the Wehrmacht's supply of ammunition was dwindling, defense of the capital city falling to the elderly, and women and children.

Time was running out, and Klaus knew Hitler knew it, even if he refused to acknowledge the obvious.

But none of that was why he was afraid at this moment. He was afraid because of the look on his fellow soldier's face when the man—Hirtzel, his name was—approached him in the flickering half-light of a bunker hallway and said, "Klaus, your presence has been requested by the Führer, for a meeting in his personal quarters."

Hirtzel's face was pale, his lips set in a tense line. Of course, by now everyone was tense. A black sense of despair filled the bunker. This had been a very bad day, even in comparison to the series of bad days that had piled up, one after another, over the past several weeks and months.

The morning had begun with Hitler's marriage to his longtime companion, Eva Braun. What should have been a joyous occasion was offset by a series of steadily worsening developments that poured in hour by hour over the course of the day.

First came the news of SS leader Heinrich Himmler's offer of surrender, presented to the Allies and immediately refused. Capitulation had not been authorized by the Führer and word of Himmler's treachery sent Hitler into an apoplectic rage. The mood in the Führerbunker turned even darker with word that Italy's leader and close Hitler friend Benito Mussolini had been executed, his corpse then defiled by an angry Italian mob.

Time was running out for Adolph Hitler and everyone inside the Bunker. The steady stream of visitors coming and going throughout the day made it clear the Führer recognized as much. High-ranking Nazi Party officials, Army generals, diplomats, they all came and went, convening in Hitler's office and then departing with uniformly grim looks on their faces.

But what possible reason could Hitler have for wanting to speak with a common foot soldier right now, even one he had begun to treat almost like a son?

Hirtzel cleared his throat. "Klaus," he said softly, almost apologetically. "It would be a mistake to keep the Führer waiting."

Klaus recognized the wisdom of his fellow soldier's words and he chuckled nervously. The stress of counting down the days—perhaps the hours—of precious freedom was wearing on him, as it was wearing on everyone inside the bunker. Soon they would all be prisoners of war.

Or worse.

"Of course, you are right," he said. "I do not want to keep Adolph waiting for our evening game of whist and our snifter of brandy."

"How can you joke at a time like this?"

"How can I not? It is either laugh or break down, and I don't see how breaking down would help my situation."

"I hope not to break down," Hirtzel said, "but laughing is beyond me at this point. Now, go, before the Führer begins to doubt whether I passed along the order. I do not need to try to deal with that problem."

A trembling Klaus Newmann double-timed down the drafty hallway. Although it by now had become crystal clear that the Thousand Year Reich was doomed to fall well over nine hundred fifty years short of completion, Adolph Hitler was still the leader of the country and the party, not to mention an obviously unstable man operating under almost crippling stress levels.

Keeping him waiting meant risking two slugs in the head from the Führer's own Walther. And although Klaus would have preferred almost anything to facing Adolph Hitler at this moment in time, disobeying a direct order was something he would never consider.

Klaus Newmann was a man to whom honor mattered.

* * *

Newmann was escorted to the Führer's quarters by a pair of guards. Klaus had served with both men for months. They weren't exactly friends, but had shared beers and laughs on more than one occasion, and he assumed they must be as curious regarding the unexpected summons as Klaus himself was.

Neither man said a word, however. They simply flanked him as they walked, and when the small group reached Hitler's private office they turned, one on each side of the door, and began scanning the empty hallway.

For what, Klaus did not know. Soviet troops, perhaps.

He took a deep breath and then knocked, two quick raps with his knuckles. From inside the room came a muffled command to enter, the response clipped and curt.

One more deep breath—almost a sigh, really—and then Klaus pushed open the door and slipped into the small office. Even as close as he had gotten to Hitler over the past few months, he had never been inside this room. No one he knew had ever been inside it.

The Führer sat behind a desk. A security guard had been stationed just inside the doorway, and the man immediately spun Klaus around and forced him up against the wall next to the door. He slipped Klaus's service weapon out of its holster and quickly patted him down.

"Any other weapons?" the man said, and Klaus shook his head.

"Any other weapons?" the guard repeated.

"No other weapons," Klaus said.

The guard took him by the elbow and turned him around once more so that he was facing the Führer. Under different circumstances, Klaus might have chuckled at the irony of being assigned to this bunker to protect someone, and then not being trusted enough to be left alone in a room with that very same man.

But these were not different circumstances. These were extraordinary times.

At the desk, Adolph Hitler seemed not to have noticed his visitor's entrance, nor the frisking that had taken place immediately afterward. His eyes were focused downward, toward a sheaf of papers on top of the desk, and in his hand he clutched an ink pen. Even from across the room, Klaus could see the Nazi seal—a black eagle with wings spread, clutching the iconic swastika insignia in its claws—wrapped around the pen's barrel.

Rumors had been flying all day, and one of those rumors was that the Führer had dictated his last will and testament this afternoon. Klaus wondered briefly whether he had been called to the office to act as a witness to the document's signing.

Then he realized the thought was absurd. It would not be left to a lowly soldier to serve as witness to such a historic document. The Führer did not operate in a vacuum. Adolph Hitler had a longtime personal valet, as well as a team of secretaries and the constant stream of high-ranking German Army officers and other officials that had been entering and leaving the bunker all day.

Any of them would make a more appropriate witness than Klaus Newmann.

Klaus had snapped out a salute the moment the guard released his elbow and he waited motionless inside the door, holding his arm at an angle, palm out. Eventually—ten seconds that felt to Klaus like ten years—the Führer raised his eyes from his document and returned the salute lazily.

"Thank you for coming, Klaus," the great man said with a smile. "It does my heart good to see that some German soldiers still understand the concept of duty." For all his angry ranting and raving earlier, Hitler's eyes appeared clear and bright, captivating. Klaus was reminded how this man had been able to unite a German population beaten down after the devastating loss of World War I and the humiliation of being forced to accept the Treaty of Versailles.

"Of course, Mein Führer," he said. He started to add that he couldn't imagine anything being more important than meeting with the leader of the Third Reich, but his tongue would not cooperate and after a moment he simply closed his mouth and waited.

"Please, sit down."

"Yes, Mein Führer." Klaus moved to a single chair placed in front of the desk and sat. The guard who had frisked Klaus moments ago had moved to the side of Hitler's desk and now stared unflinchingly ahead.

Hitler cleared his throat. "I must apologize for the lack of comfortable seating," he said. "Our accommodations down here are far more...rudimentary...than above ground. On the other hand, they are much safer, eh?"

The Führer chuckled and an uncomfortable Klaus Newmann responded with a hesitant smile.

After a moment Hitler continued. "I am sure you are aware our situation here is...tenuous," he said, his eyes glittering as he held Klaus's gaze steadily. Klaus felt the first stab of real panic, a cold vice gripping his insides as he realized the Führer was waiting for an answer and he had no idea what the man expected him to say.

"Of course," he said, feeling stupid and waiting for the

tongue-lashing he so richly deserved. Surely the leader of the Third Reich expected something more out of Klaus than "of course."

But no rebuke was forthcoming.

"Of course," Hitler repeated, nodding, arms crossed as he cupped his chin with one hand. Klaus noticed that the Führer's eyes had left his own and were now focused—or perhaps unfocused—on something over Klaus's right shoulder. They had a faraway look and the soldier wondered what he was thinking.

"I am sure you're wondering why I've called you here."

"Well…yes, Mein Führer."

"You have been selected for a great honor, Herr Newmann. You will serve the Reich in a very unique manner."

Hitler paused. He seemed to be awaiting a response, and Klaus shook his head in confusion. "I am very sorry, Mein Führer, but I do not understand."

"Things will be changing very soon, and not for the better. The war effort is failing, as I am sure you are well aware. The Reich teeters on the very brink of extinction, with the Allies overrunning the Fatherland and poised to take our historic city and country. Defeat seems imminent."

Hitler paused and gazed at the young soldier, who was again overcome by a terror worse than any he had ever experienced. What response was the Führer expecting? How could Klaus possibly know? Surely the leader of the Thousand Year Reich was not requesting tactical advice or war planning from a lowly foot soldier?

He was saved from having to say something when the leader continued. "Defeat *seems* imminent," he repeated. "But appearances to the contrary, all is not lost. This stinging downfall will not stand. It is temporary. The Third Reich has *not* been defeated and *will not* be defeated. Not now, not ever!"

The Führer's voice had taken on the shrill, persuasive quality Klaus recognized from listening to dozens of the man's speeches on radio. He seemed poised to launch into a soaring rhetorical soliloquy. Already had, really. But then he reined himself in, taking a moment to regain control of his emotions before continuing.

"The Reich has not been vanquished," he insisted quietly. "Full implementation has merely been delayed. For quite some time, in all probability, I will admit. But still, it has only been delayed. However, given the circumstances in which we find ourselves, eventual implementation will depend heavily on people who may not ever have expected to play such a critical, historic role. People who may consider themselves unprepared for what will be asked of them."

Adolph Hitler focused his steady gaze on Klaus Newmann. His eyes burned with the glow of righteous fanaticism. "People like you," he said dramatically.

"I-I'm sorry, Mein Führer. I am afraid I still do not understand. How can I possibly—"

"It is very simple," the Führer replied. "You must safeguard this key."

He reached under his collar and grasped a gold necklace between his thumb and forefinger.

Pulled a pair of ornate-looking gold keys from beneath his undershirt.

Held them up for Klaus's inspection.

The first thing Klaus noticed was that the keys were oversized, larger than any keys he had ever seen. They were nearly twice as large as he would have expected them to be.

They resembled skeleton keys in design, but even from across the desk Klaus could see they were different in very significant ways. Each key featured a series of odd-looking appendages fused to its teeth, tiny squares that looked like gold boxes, with what appeared to be microscopic wires threaded through the gold.

The keys were exotic-looking. Bizarre, even.

At last he shook his head, mystified. "I am so sorry, Mein Führer. I still do not understand."

Hitler smiled. "Don't worry about that, Klaus. You will."

1

November 12, 1987
7:30 a.m.
Wuppertal, Federal Republic of Germany

Klaus Newmann's day started out exactly as had nearly every other day for the past forty-two years: a cup of black coffee and a Danish, followed by a shower and a hike.

Klaus completed his hike every day, no matter the weather, no matter his mood, no matter his physical condition. He had hiked through blinding snowstorms, through brutal heat. He had hiked the day after an appendectomy and hours after the death of his beloved wife.

In forty-two years, Klaus had never taken a day off.

Now sixty-four, he did not hike because he loved the outdoors, and he certainly was no physical fitness buff. Klaus was much more at home in his study, feet propped on a divan, reading from the collected works of Nietzsche or even *Mein Kampfe*—although bitter personal experience had taught him to keep his love of Adolph Hitler's biography to himself, except among a handful of very close friends—than trudging through the thick forest surrounding Wuppertal, risking a sprained ankle or worse navigating the rugged terrain.

He hiked because he had made a pledge as a young man, a pledge to someone he admired more than anyone else in the world. He knew now, with the benefit of years—decades—of reflection, that he had been caught up in the fever of nationalism that swept his country during his teen years and immediately after.

Over time, that fever had subsided, even in a true believer like Klaus. But although his passion for the cause had waned and his body had grown old and increasingly frail, deep down inside he was still the wide-eyed optimist he had been once upon a time, and he was no more likely to forget his pledge or ignore his duty than he was to put a gun to his head and squeeze the trigger.

Klaus was under no illusions. He knew his limitations, knew he was nothing special. He was neither physically gifted nor particularly intelligent. He was a quick learner and a hard worker, but so were millions of other Germans. There was nothing about him that would have set him apart from any other young Nazi male in the waning days of World War Two.

But responsibility had been thrust on Klaus Newmann, regardless of his lack of worthiness to accept it. Many Berliners had been called to sacrifice once the tide of the great war began turning against their country, and Klaus knew that the sacrifice asked of him could not begin to compare with what had been asked of many of his fellow citizens.

The difference, of course, was that Klaus was in a position to *make* a difference. He had waited decades for the payoff that had been promised, faithfully discharging the duties assigned to him that horrible night so long ago in a cramped underground bunker, with stale air and faulty wiring, lights flickering almost constantly from the relentless Allied bombing raids on Berlin.

His youthful enthusiasm had waned, of course it had, but Klaus had never once doubted the sagacity of Adolph Hitler's words, spoken as the Red Army closed in and Germany's situation went from dire to hopeless. He had also never doubted the inevitability of the Third Reich's return.

And now, after so many decades of waiting, forty-two years of it, during which Klaus had given up hope of ever living long enough to see the Reich's triumphant rise from the ashes of defeat, it was finally going to happen. Whispered rumors had begun circulating among his band of aging true believers nearly a year ago, months before Klaus received official notification.

The time was right. The Soviet Union was collapsing under the weight of mismanagement and a more open world, and citizens trapped for generations behind the Iron Curtain had begun to get tantalizing glimpses of just how much they were missing out on under the jack-booted rule of their Russian masters.

The dissolution of the Soviet Union was only a matter of time, so the rumors went, and the collapse of Soviet rule would throw open a power vacuum that must be filled. Citizens conditioned over the course of eighty-plus years of hard-line Soviet rule would be ill-prepared for the freedoms enjoyed by so many in the West, indeed by Klaus himself in West Germany.

Some other system of government would be necessary.

Something besides old-style Communism.

Something like Nazism.

Klaus quickened his pace as he picked his way through the forest. The odd-looking key given to him so long ago had been stored for decades in a bank vault, the location of which was known only to Klaus. His lawyer had received explicit instructions that upon Klaus's death the location of the key, along with the code to access the vault, would be given to one member—and one member only—of the secret Third Reich group to which so much had been entrusted.

But nothing had ever happened to Klaus. No accidents had befallen him, no serious illnesses, and one after another the decades had passed with no reason for him to retrieve the key from the secret bank vault.

That had all changed one morning two weeks ago. Klaus's phone rang, and when he picked it up he was greeted with the coded message he had memorized in April 1945, and had given up on ever hearing again. The message meant he was to retrieve the key and keep it on his person at all times.

Operation Phoenix had begun.

At some point in the near future, a courier would approach Klaus, a man unknown to him. The courier would greet him with a separate coded message. Upon receipt of the message, Klaus was to hand the key over to the courier, who would carry it to another representative of the Reich, a man who well understood the key's significance.

That man would use the key to unlock the vault.

And the Third Reich would rise to power once again.

* * *

Following Germany's surrender, Klaus Newmann had moved immediately to Wuppertal per the Führer's explicit instructions, issued April 29, 1945. Using capital supplied by investors sympathetic to the cause, he opened a machine shop in his new hometown and went to work fabricating parts for the industrial boom that would immediately follow the Allied victory. Great swaths of the countryside had been leveled and required rebuilding, and as the victorious Allies—most notably the United States—poured hundreds of millions of dollars into the reconstruction of West Germany, a small but significant portion of those funds found their way into Klaus's pocket.

He grew comfortable, not quite wealthy but nearly so, expanding the machine shop several times over the years and eventually employing several dozen fabricators and machinists.

No matter how busy the shop got, though, he never sacrificed his daily hike. It was, after all, the reason he was living and working in Wuppertal to begin with.

He wiped the sweat from his brow with one sleeve as he stepped around a large boulder. He was breathing heavily and perspiring freely despite the chill in the air. The objective of his daily hike was surveillance—to observe a munitions factory that had been abandoned with the defeat of the Nazis at the end of World War Two.

The factory stood in a remote area, accessible by car only via a long-since abandoned and crumbling access road. The condition of the road was irrelevant to Klaus, though, since he never approached by car. To do so might cause the wrong people to ask the wrong questions.

Instead, he exited the back door of his home—chosen so long ago for its specific location rather than style or comfort—and set out through an area as forbidding as the Black Forest. Over the years, Klaus had memorized dozens of different routes, all mapped out to avoid wearing down a path or establishing any kind of trail that could be followed.

This surveillance of the abandoned munitions factory was as

important a part of his mission as was safeguarding the special key, and Klaus took it very seriously. Should the wrong people—meaning anyone not involved in Project Phoenix—begin to take notice of the building, advance warning would be critical. Klaus would pass word to his contact, who would ensure the necessary measures be taken to eliminate those people.

By any means necessary.

Including murder.

But it had never come to that. It had never come close to that. The factory was simply too far off the beaten path, and too much a relic of a past most Germans wanted to forget, for anyone to care about. Klaus doubted many people were even aware of its existence now, so long after it had been shuttered.

He plodded forward, his route taking longer to complete now than it had even just a few years ago. He breathed heavily but easily, swinging his arms and daydreaming about the mug of hot cocoa he was planning to make upon returning home. He would enjoy the drink and then leave for work.

But the satisfaction brought on by the image of the drink was tempered by a growing uneasiness. His sense of caution, developed out of necessity decades ago and honed to a razor-sharp edge, was telling him something was wrong.

Alarm bells were ringing in his head.

Someone was here. He couldn't see anyone, hadn't heard anything, but he knew, nevertheless. His subconscious had observed something out of the ordinary, something his conscious mind had missed.

It wouldn't be the first time he had stumbled across another hiker, even out here in the middle of nowhere. It was unusual, yes, but it had happened before. Germans were not intimidated by thick forest, and a goodly percentage of them were fond of the kind of solitude that a walk through the woods could provide.

Still, this was different. Perhaps it was the muffled snap of a twig underfoot, or a glimpse in his peripheral vision of someone hiding behind a tree.

Could it be his contact, coming to relieve Klaus of the tremendous burden he had carried for more than four decades as he aged from young man to middle-aged, and now as he approached elderly?

13

A meeting here, in the middle of nowhere, would make sense. And that meeting was bound to happen soon. It was why he had retrieved the bizarre-looking key from its secure location in the bank vault to begin with.

But Klaus didn't think that was it; it just didn't feel right. The other presence felt too...stealthy, which was why Klaus was suddenly so aware of his extreme isolation, deep in the forest outside Wuppertal. He had hoped for a secluded place to turn over the key, but the fact of the matter was that isolation was a double-edged sword. Lack of witnesses to a key exchange meant lack of witnesses to a mugging as well.

Klaus froze in his tracks. Spun very slowly in a three hundred sixty degree circle. Examined the surrounding area, searching for movement, for a flash of color, anything that would pinpoint the location of the person stalking him.

Because he *was* being stalked.

He knew that.

He reached under his windbreaker and eased his Walther out of its shoulder holster. Then he turned to the left, and—

And felt the cold, hard steel of a gun barrel press against the side of his skull.

Where the gun's owner had come from and how he had managed so completely to get the drop on Klaus were issues he would have to address and resolve moving forward.

Assuming he survived.

A voice, calm and in control, said, "Very slowly, you will extend the hand holding the pistol straight out in front of you. You will not attempt to discharge your weapon or you will die. Do you understand, Herr Newmann?"

The accent was not German, although the phrasing was accurate and the words clear. The speaker was a foreigner, but one with considerable experience in the German language.

And the man to whom the voice belonged had not uttered the code words Klaus had waited so long to hear. Had not even come *close* to uttering the code words.

This was not his contact.

For a split-second Klaus considered cocking his wrist and firing semi-blindly in the direction he knew his assailant was standing:

slightly behind him and to the left. He calculated the odds at slightly better than fifty-fifty he could squeeze off a shot before the mystery man could react and fire his own weapon, blowing a hole in Klaus's skull.

But almost as if reading his mind, the assailant said, "Do not shoot, Herr Newmann. It is not worth the risk. Even if you succeed in killing me, the chances are good my gun hand will spasm reflexively as my muscles contract, and then you will die right alongside me. And even if not, I did not come into these woods alone. There are two other weapons trained on you even as we speak. Do as I say or you *will* die."

Klaus blew out a breath in frustration. Adrenaline pounded through his body, the fight or flight instinct was almost overwhelming. Still, he forced himself to remain calm and hold his ground.

Consider the man's words.

It was extremely unlikely his assailant was telling the truth, at least where the existence of two other gunmen were concerned. Klaus knew his instincts were not what they once had been. Age and comfortable living had eroded them years ago. But he simply could not accept the notion that three men could have tailed him successfully this far into the forest without him noticing.

One man, perhaps—*well, okay,* he thought. *One for certain, obviously*—but not three.

But the assailant's point was still a valid one. Klaus must acquiesce or die. And as long as he was breathing there was always the chance he could turn the situation around. He couldn't imagine how at the moment, but that was irrelevant. He would accomplish nothing dead.

There's always the chance this attack is unrelated to the key. The thought flashed through his mind but the likelihood of that being the case was so slim as to be laughable.

Not that he could manage to laugh at the moment.

He considered all this in a half-second, and then did as he was told. Extended his arm and held his Walther away from his body, barrel pointed at the ground.

A hand snaked under his arm and plucked the gun away. A man Klaus had never before seen stepped out from behind him and into his line of sight. The man held Klaus's Walther in his left hand. With his right, he lowered his own weapon and trained it squarely on Klaus's chest. It did not waver.

"Excellent decision," the man said.

"What is this all about?" Klaus asked. He had envisioned this scenario and his potential responses to it hundreds of times over the years. Thousands. He had imagined himself remaining calm and collected, analytical almost, coolly considering his options and then selecting the most appropriate one.

Now that the thing he had dreaded most was happening, Klaus discovered it was all he could do to keep his voice steady.

"You know what this is about," the man said.

"I am certain I do not. I was out for a hike and now I find myself accosted by a hooligan with a gun. This is outrageous. Unacceptable."

"A hooligan," the man repeated. A trace of a smile ghosted across his bland face and then vanished. "Let me ask you a question. If you are simply a man out for a hike, why were you carrying this very nice Walther? Why was it necessary for me to disarm you?"

"Look around you," Klaus said without hesitation. "This area is wild. Untamed. I carry the pistol for protection. I had assumed it would be for protection against wildlife. Little did I realize."

The man smiled broadly now. He nodded. "I applaud your manufactured sincerity," he said. "Or I would, if I weren't holding a pair of guns in my hands. Now, let us dispense with the charade. We are alone out here, it is just you and I, so please give me what I require and I shall be on my way."

"I thought you said there were two other assassins pointing weapons at me."

"You caught me in a lie. Oops. Now, give me the key."

"I told you already, I do not know—"

"Enough." The man stepped forward and shoved his gun roughly against Klaus's ear. "This game has grown tiresome. I did not simply stumble across you out here in the middle of nowhere, kilometers from Wuppertal, Herr Newmann. You have been under surveillance for quite some time. I, personally, have followed you on your daily hike more than a half-dozen times. So your protestations of innocence are wasted on me, regardless of how sincerely

you are able to repeat them. Drop the act and give me what I came for. Hand me the key."

Fear mushroomed in Klaus's belly, hot and sickening. He had always known this moment was a possibility, in some ways was surprised it had taken this long to arrive. But in the thousands of times he had envisioned the scenario, he had always managed to convince himself there would be an escape. A way out.

Now he knew there was no way out.

He sighed heavily. Realized he was shaking, and not just from the adrenaline. "You are going to kill me."

"Give me the key and I'll let you live."

"You're lying."

"All I want is the key. I have no interest in harming you."

"You can't afford to let me live. Even if you take possession of the key, you could not possibly move the contents it protects before I could alert my superiors to the situation. That would create complications you do not need, and probably could not handle."

"You are too perceptive for your own good, Herr Newmann. It is no wonder Hitler chose you as custodian of the merchandise." He shrugged. "Fine. Your analysis is correct. You will not leave this forest alive."

"If you're going to kill me anyway, there is no benefit to me to hand over the key. And you will never find it if I do not give it to you."

"But there *is* a benefit. If you give me what I came for, your death will be quick and painless. You have my word on that. If you do not, well…" He dragged out the last word and let it hang in the air between them.

Klaus had by now formulated a plan. It was born of desperation and unlikely to succeed, as the gunman had stepped back two paces, placing him out of reach. But there was no downside to making the attempt. Klaus placed his hands on his hips and leaned back as if stretching while considering the merits of his attacker's argument. He slipped his right hand under his windbreaker and grasped his backup gun, nestled under the waistband of his trousers at the small of his back.

He looked into his assailant's eyes and saw a twinkle of amusement. The corners of the man's mouth twitched upward.

There would be no taking this man by surprise. No getting the jump on him as he had gotten the jump on Klaus.

There was no point even in trying.

He tried anyway.

He yanked the Walther out from behind his back, the movement as smooth and polished as any sixty-seven year old man could accomplish, and drew down on the assailant.

He never saw the shot coming. Never felt the bullet enter his skull.

He was dead before he hit the ground.

2

Dobromir Victorovich spat on the ground. He had started out the day hung over and things were only going downhill from there. Now he was annoyed and hung over.

He holstered his weapon and tossed Newmann's to the side. He had had no alternative than to gun down the German fool once he went for his second pistol, but that fact was small comfort now.

Dobromir had hoped for a smooth, stress-free transaction: key for him, two bullets to the cranium for Newmann. Had counted on it, in fact, given the element of surprise and the old Nazi's advanced age.

But he should have known better. The KGB operative had seen even the easiest of assignments blow up unexpectedly, and here was a perfect example. Instead of intimidating Newmann and taking possession of the damned key, he had allowed a gun battle to erupt. *Although, to be fair, it was more of an execution than a battle.*

Either way, the result was the same: dead Nazi and no key.

It was his own fault. He should have frisked Newmann the second he took the old man's gun away. He had almost done so, too, but overconfidence had gotten in the way. Overconfidence and the fact that Dobromir's head was pounding from too much vodka last night. He had just wanted to get this over with.

Who could have predicted the old fool would be carrying a backup weapon? He'd been making this hike every day since the end of the Second World War, more than four decades ago. He should long since have become lazy and careless.

Instead it was Dobromir who had been careless. And it had damned near gotten him killed.

He spat on the ground again and sighed. Recalled Newmann's words: *…you will never find the key if I do not give it to you.*

He was so close to completing his mission successfully. He had been in West Germany for weeks, surveilling the old man and verifying the truth of the rumors that had circulated throughout the KGB—and all of Mother Russia—for years, rumors involving Adolph Hitler, and buried treasure, and millions of rubles' worth of Russian heritage that had been stolen from St. Petersburg during the darkest days of World War Two.

Through his surveillance Dobromir had discovered to his immense surprise that the rumors were all true. And they were all tied to this anonymous elderly factory owner, an old man who had been hiking these woods outside Wuppertal for more than forty years.

But none of it would matter without the key. If he returned to Moscow empty-handed, Dobromir knew he might just as well kiss his job—and probably his life—goodbye. The best he could hope for would be a one-way train ticket to Siberia.

He needed that key.

And he had just killed the only man who knew its location.

All was not lost, however. The key was here. Dobromir knew for a fact that the old man had kept the key in his possession for more than two weeks now. He had never let it out of his sight.

Which meant the key was here.

All Dobromir needed to do was find it.

And he would not leave until he did.

* * *

He checked all of the obvious places first. Dug through the old man's pockets. Frisked the body as it lay face down in the decaying autumn leaves. Didn't find the key, but did discover that not only had the old Nazi been carrying a second gun, he had also strapped a *third* pistol into an ankle holster above his right foot.

The man had been a walking armory, and while he had been no match for a trained KGB operative and was now lying dead in the spot where he would soon be buried, his stock rose just a bit in Dobromir's eyes. He had been a worthier opponent than Dobromir realized while he was alive.

But, while interesting in a professional sense, none of this had gotten him any closer to finding the key.

He began removing the old man's clothing, piece by piece, using his combat knife to cut the material into thin strips, searching for hidden pockets or double seams large enough to hold something as small and thin as a key.

Found nothing.

Now he sat on the forest floor, the damp chill leaching into his body, surrounded by ribbons of material littering the ground and a nearly naked dead old man lying next to him. He had decided to leave the man's underwear on him for now. Removing it and searching the anal cavity of a cooling corpse could wait until there was no other option, as far as Dobromir was concerned. He would do exactly that if necessary, but *only* if necessary.

He had expected to be finished by now, had assumed the key would be readily accessible. His head was pounding and his tongue felt scratchy and he didn't think he had ever wanted anything as much in his life as he wanted to find the damned key and get the hell back to Wuppertal.

Right now.

He ran a hand through his hair and shook his head. Stared at the body. The old guy looked ridiculous, all dignity gone, and for just a moment Dobromir felt ashamed of himself. He wondered what his mother would think if she could see him now, digging through a dead man's clothing as he lay on the ground with his pasty-white skin exposed to the chilly afternoon air, the body clad only in a pair of yellowing boxer shorts and well-worn hiking boots.

Hiking boots.

Of course. The key was in the boots.

All thoughts of Dobromir's mother vanished as he kicked himself for his stupidity. Of course the old man would store the key in his boots. It was the one way he could be sure he could always access it when he needed it. Who goes for a hike without wearing his boots?

He bent down and unlaced the left boot. Slipped it off the corpse's foot. Felt around the interior, searching for a telltale bulge or secret compartment.

Found nothing. Poked and prodded the exterior with his fingers, massaging it, willing the key to be under a hidden flap of leather.

It was not.

Dobromir turned the shoe over, examining the sole. This was where the key would be found. He was so certain of it that allowed himself a small smile and forgave himself his sloppy performance thus far. None of it would matter in the end, and all it would have cost him was a little lost time.

His fingers explored the sole, paying close attention to the seam where it had been fastened to the boot. There had to be a release here somewhere, probably in the heel, a spring-loaded mechanism that would open and reveal the key.

It should be easy to find, but he was getting nowhere. Dobromir felt his frustration level rising. He was wasting time, getting cold, and he could feel his muscles tightening and becoming stiff. All he wanted was to locate the key and get the hell out of here, and he still had a body to bury once he found the damned thing.

He was getting nowhere. Maybe the key was in the other boot, but Dobromir didn't think so. Newmann had held drawn his backup gun with his right hand, meaning that unless he had learned to shoot ambidextrously—highly unlikely; most people hadn't had KGB training—he must be right-handed.

And if that were the case, Dobromir theorized it would be much easier as a practical matter to access the bottom of his left shoe than his right.

He muttered a curse and reached for his combat knife. Began slicing horizontally through the sole of the boot at the heel. He should have done this from the start, rather than wasting time searching for a release mechanism he might never find, but he had always loved a good puzzle and hadn't been able to pass up the chance to try solving it.

Now he no longer cared about puzzles. He worked quickly but carefully, and within ninety seconds had removed the heel from the rest of the boot.

And there it was.

*   *   *

Dobromir's excitement mounted as he hiked through the woods to where he had parked his rental car. It had taken longer than he anticipated to bury the old man's body without a shovel, and he had done a mediocre job at best of concealing the corpse. But it only needed to stay hidden long enough for the Soviets to figure a way to smuggle the treasure out of West Germany and back to its rightful home in Leningrad. Or Moscow, or wherever.

That would be someone else's problem. Dobromir's assignment had been to recover the key and deliver it to his superiors, and after a few bumps in the road, he was well on his way to completing the mission successfully.

He examined the prize curiously as he walked. An ornate gold key, glittering in the dim light filtering through the forest canopy. It was big, considerably bigger than an average house or car key. It had the look of a skeleton key, topped with a wide round handle in the shape of the Nazi swastika. And there were boxes with a vaguely electrical look fused to the key's teeth.

It was a strange-looking key, but still just a key. It was hard to imagine this small piece of molded gold—if that's what it was— was worth killing a man to retrieve. But that was the way of the world, particularly the espionage world, and Dobromir felt little remorse. Klaus Newmann had demonstrated his readiness to die to protect the key, and more importantly, he had demonstrated his readiness to *kill Dobromir* to protect it.

Dobromir had been quicker than Newmann, and thus was still alive. It was no more complicated than that.

The rutted cow path that passed for a road leading to Wuppertal loomed in the distance; Dobromir could see the day's brightness radiating outward from the clearing that had been hacked out of the forest to support it. He felt a surge of excitement. His mission was complete, and now he could relax.

Technically, his next move should be to depart Wuppertal, and as quickly as possible. Return to Moscow immediately and hand the prize over to his superiors. He would be sent off on his next assignment and West Germany would become just a memory.

That was what he should do.

That was not what he was going to do, however.

Dobromir had discovered during his Wuppertal assignment that he rather enjoyed the West German nightlife. The alcohol was of the highest quality, and so were the women. The KGB would have no way of knowing how long it had taken to secure the key, and thus there was no reason to hurry back to Russia.

What the KGB didn't know wouldn't hurt them. He decided he would return to his hotel. He would stash the key in a safe place and then take a few more days to fully enjoy the Wuppertal experience before returning to Moscow.

It was the least he could do for himself. The KGB certainly wouldn't allow him any time off, and he hadn't had a real vacation in years.

Sometimes he loved his job, and this was one of those times.

3

"Tell me what you know about the Amber Room."

Tracie Tanner had barely settled into the chair placed—as always—directly in front of CIA Director Aaron Stallings's home office desk, when he hit her with the challenge. There was no "good morning," no "nice to see you," no "how is your day going?"

No greeting at all.

Just, "Tell me what you know about the Amber Room."

Tracie rubbed a palm absently over her left thigh. The bullet wound she had sustained a few weeks ago in a fight to the death with a domestic terrorist deep in the Florida Everglades still throbbed and burned on occasion, but she wasn't about to admit to feeling any pain. Not even any discomfort.

Not in front of Stallings. Not ever.

She had assured the CIA director by phone earlier that the injury was fully healed. It was the only way to be reinstated to fieldwork, and she thought if she had to spend one more day pacing her apartment and watching ridiculous soap operas on her tiny black-and-white TV she might go completely, batshit crazy.

Her fitness to return to duty had been verified—reluctantly, but in writing, which was all that mattered—by a physician at Langley who'd wanted her to take another thirty days off but who seemed resigned to the notion of confirming diagnoses for operatives that may not be…fully…accurate.

The issue of why a young woman with no official ties to the agency was being examined by a CIA doctor had never been raised. Even company medical professionals understood that many questions were better left unasked.

"It's nice to see you, too, boss," she said drily. "And yes, I'm doing well. Thanks for asking."

Stallings raised his eyes from the paperwork cluttering his desk and peered at her over his reading glasses. It was the first time he had looked up since bellowing, "Come in," when she knocked at the door.

He spread his hands. "Well?"

"Thanks for starting me off with an easy question. The answer is, nothing. I know nothing about the Amber Room. I've never heard of it. Something tells me that's about to change."

"I see you haven't lost any of your superior sense of perception while lounging around on an extended government-sponsored vacation."

She gritted her teeth and said nothing. Three hours per day of physical therapy seven days a week, sandwiched between twenty-one hours per day of extreme boredom, didn't strike Tracie as anyone's idea of a vacation. And it certainly hadn't been "extended."

But she couldn't imagine anything positive coming from voicing that observation, so she smiled grimly and waited for the director to continue.

"Nothing to say?" he prompted. "No wise-ass comeback?"

This was too much, especially for her first day back to work.

"Okay, I'll admit it, the vacation was great," she said cheerfully. "Nothing like lounging around on the taxpayers' dime. I'll have to see what I can do about getting shot more often."

Stallings shook his head. He cleared his throat with what sounded like the growl of an angry German Shepherd, and she congratulated herself on getting under his skin. She had convinced herself on the drive here that no matter the provocation, no matter how badly he asked for it, she would be good. She would stick to business.

That vow had lasted all of maybe three minutes, but as always, he had insisted on pushing her buttons. It just wasn't in her nature not to push back.

And she had to admit she hadn't felt this pleased in quite some time. It wasn't even nine a.m., but no matter what else happened today, tweaking the CIA's pompous top man made it a good day. She doubted she wanted to know what that fact said about her, but there it was.

"Where were we?" Stallings rumbled, his face flushed red. The man's temper was legendary in Washington circles; he had made a career out of intimidating politicians and bureaucrats all over D.C. for decades. But after Tracie had been dismissed from the CIA and then rehired unofficially by Stallings as his blackest of black ops specialists, she recognized instinctively that she would need to demonstrate she was not intimidated by his bluster.

And she had been reinforcing that point ever since.

"You were referencing the Amber Room," she said, smiling like the teacher's pet.

"Yes. That's right. The Amber Room." He shuffled some papers around his desk as he gathered his thoughts and then said, "In the early 1700s, Russian Tsar Peter the Great was given a gift of a series of large, gold-encrusted amber panels by Friedrich Wilhelm I of Prussia."

"The panels made up the Amber Room," Tracie said. The smile was gone, the teasing over. She was all business.

"Correct. They were literally dripping in gold and weighed more than six tons. The panels were erected in the tsar's castle in 1716, covering the entirety of one room, where they remained for two hundred twenty-five years."

Tracie did the math in her head, adding 225 to 1716, and then said, "Until the Nazis invaded Russia in World War Two."

"That's right. Nazi troops looted the treasure from Catherine Palace in Leningrad in 1941 and removed it to Germany in twenty-seven massive crates. The Amber Room panels were transported to the city of Koenigsberg, where they dropped off the face of the earth prior to Germany's surrender to Allied forces in 1945."

"Fascinating story," Tracie said. "I assume you're getting to the part that involves me."

"You assume correctly. The value of the Amber Room, were

the panels to be recovered in their entirety, has been estimated at upwards of two hundred fifty million dollars. Or more."

Tracie felt her eyes widen involuntarily and whistled softly. "A quarter of a *billion* dollars?"

"Or more," Stallings repeated. "Some historians believe that figure to be overly conservative, that the actual value could potentially be as much as one hundred million dollars *higher.*"

"But nobody knows where the Amber Room panels are located."

"Correct."

"How could they simply vanish?"

"Germany was in chaos by 1945. Bombing raids had reduced Berlin and most other major German cities to rubble, and many German Army officers and civilian officials were out to salvage anything they could from what was left of the Third Reich."

"Whoever was in charge of securing the Amber Room panels hijacked them."

Stallings nodded. "That's been the prevailing theory since the end of the war. The most popular of a number of competing theories regarding the Amber Room is that an East Prussian Nazi leader named Erich Koch, who amassed a trove of looted treasure, stashed them somewhere in or around his home city of Koenigsberg."

"But no one's been able to find them in four decades of searching. And a treasure as valuable as that must have had its share of hunters searching for it."

"One would have to assume."

Tracie sat back in her chair and nibbled on her lower lip, thinking. She looked up and locked eyes with the CIA director. "They've been looking in the wrong place, haven't they?"

He smiled. "Very good, Tanner."

"You know where the Amber Room is, don't you?"

"More or less," he said.

"I don't understand."

"The history you and everyone else learned regarding the end of the Second World War is not accurate, at least not in its entirety."

"Meaning?"

"Meaning there was a small cadre of Nazi officials and

sympathizers that never abandoned the dream of Nazi world domination."

Tracie shrugged. "There are fanatics who cling to any cause, no matter how horrific, and no matter how unlikely. A few wild-eyed Nazis would never be able to accomplish much, regardless of how dedicated they were to their cause. Especially now, more than forty years after their infestation was eradicated."

Stallings eyed her closely. "What if the wild-eyed fanatics had access to three hundred million dollars? Would that change your opinion of their prospects?"

She felt her jaw drop in momentary surprise, but then shook her head. "I can see where it would be cause for concern, yes. But even with access to that kind of cash, it would be almost impossible to organize any serious revolution without a central rallying point, someone all the fanatics could get behind. And in this day and age, who the hell would want to be the face of a resurgent Nazi movement?"

"Does the name Adolph Hitler sound like one the fanatics could support?"

4

"What are you talking about? Hitler committed suicide in his bunker in April, 1945." Tracie felt like Alice falling down the rabbit hole. A day that had started with coffee and a return to the job she loved had somehow taken a ninety-degree turn straight into the realm of the bizarre.

"I told you already," Stallings said. "The history you think you know about Adolph Hitler's death does not necessarily reflect the truth of the matter."

"You expect me to believe that Hitler is alive, forty-two years after supposedly putting a bullet in his own head? And that not only is he alive, he's poised to take three hundred million dollars in stolen treasure and fund a Nazi revolution?"

Stallings chuckled, something Tracie wasn't sure she had ever seen him do before. The sight was a little disconcerting, like suddenly discovering dogs could talk. Or long-dead Nazi leaders might actually be alive.

"I know it sounds farfetched," he said. "But the agency has known Hitler was alive almost since the day he escaped Germany."

"But what about the bodies?" Tracie said. "The Soviets discovered the corpses of Hitler and Eva Braun in a shallow grave. They had been wrapped in a Nazi flag and burned, but enough of the bodies remained that Soviet troops were able to positively identify the remains."

"Exactly," Stallings said, nodding. "Enough of the bodies remained. That was the whole point. The corpses were *meant* to be found. Yes, a male with a bullet wound to the head and a female who had been poisoned with cyanide were found partially covered in dirt outside the Reich Chancellory buildings in Berlin. But the bodies were *not* those of Adolph Hitler and Eva Braun."

"I've seen pictures," Tracie insisted. "Photographs taken at the scene by Russian troops. The body had been burned but the face was remarkably well preserved. It was Hitler."

"Come on, Tanner, wise up. This was the leader of the Thousand Year Reich who supposedly committed suicide and was buried by Josef Goebbels and Martin Bormann. You don't think they would have treated the corpse of their revered Führer with a little more respect than to drop it in a hole and toss some dirt over it?"

Tracie narrowed her eyes in concentration. Stallings's point was a good one. It would be like a U.S. president dying and then being dumped in a shallow grave by the secretary of state.

The silence stretched on as Stallings, normally not the most patient of men, allowed her to work through the story.

Finally she said, "But, boss, those pictures. The likeness was striking."

"The end of the war didn't happen overnight, nor did it occur in a vacuum. The handwriting was on the wall for months, and even the most ardent Nazi supporter could see over the course of last few weeks that all was lost. It was only a matter of time. But there was more than enough of that time for Nazi leadership to hatch an outlandish plan to save the Führer."

"So you're saying the Germans located and sacrificed a man and a woman who looked enough like Hitler and Braun that the public and the media would accept it?"

"By 1945, the war had been going on for six years. The world was more than ready for it to be over. Human nature being what it is, people were only too happy to accept that Hitler was dead and the Axis threat was finished."

"Still," she said. "Those photographs, the resemblance of the face to pictures we've all seen of one of the world's most notorious men. The likeness was uncanny."

"It would not have been difficult to find a man with the distinctive Hitler mustache at that point in time in Germany. The Führer had restored German pride and brought the country back from the ignominy of their crushing defeat in World War One. You probably couldn't swing a dead cat in Berlin in the early 1940s without hitting a man wearing a Hitler mustache."

Tracie was silent and Stallings continued. "We have copies of dental records on file in CIA archives that were taken from Hitler and from the corpse recovered that day. The dental records prove *they were not the same person.*"

Tracie opened her mouth, but before she could speak, Stallings said, "And if you have any remaining doubts, the agency also has in its possession definitive DNA evidence that corroborates what we already know from the dental records. Have you heard of DNA?"

She nodded. "It's brand-new technology. I don't know much about it, but it's supposed to be very reliable."

"It's more than just reliable. It's almost foolproof. We don't know who was buried that April night in Berlin in 1945, but we *do* know it was not Adolph Hitler."

"So the Nazis kidnap a man who looks like Hitler and a woman who looks like Eva Braun. They wait for the right moment and then murder them, making it look like Hitler and his new bride had killed themselves. Meanwhile they spirit their leader out of the country to…where?"

"Argentina."

"So you expect me to believe Adolph Hitler has been living in Argentina for more than forty years, where he's now poised to rise to power once again on the mountain of cash provided by the missing gold panels of the Amber Room?"

Stallings returned her gaze steadily. Wordlessly.

"But I don't understand. Hitler would have to be, what, in his eighties by now?"

"Nineties, to be precise."

"And he's still alive."

Again Stallings gazed at her without speaking.

"Come on, boss, even if everything you've said is true—a stretch, to be sure—a man in his nineties would be frail and feeble. He wouldn't be up to leading a parade, never mind a Nazi revolution."

"He doesn't have to lead anything. All he has to do is be the face of the uprising. The populist focus of every misguided malcontent in Europe and South America. Appear on television and say a few words to exhort his followers, maybe snap off a Nazi salute or two. He could be on his deathbed and it wouldn't matter. He could plunge the globe into World War Three from a wheelchair. There aren't many people alive I would say that about, but Adolph Hitler is one of them."

Tracie felt numb. "Why is it suddenly a problem now? You said the agency has known Hitler was alive almost from the moment he escaped death or capture in Berlin more than forty years ago. What's suddenly changed?"

Stallings smiled again. "Excellent question, Tanner. Your ability to cut through the bullshit and get to the heart of complex matters at a moment's notice is why I keep you around. Why I put up with your attitude."

Tracie couldn't remember the CIA director ever offering her a compliment, and while this one was obviously of a backhanded nature, it still represented something of an earthshaking development. It was unlikely the Aaron Stallings she had come to know would ever say anything nicer to her than that.

But Tracie wasn't in the mood for anything besides puzzling through this bizarre scenario.

She shook her head and ignored his words. "What's changed?" she repeated.

"After the end of World War Two," he said, "it took quite a bit of time—years, in fact—to ascertain the approximate whereabouts of the Amber Room. Between rebuilding Germany and Japan, and monitoring Hitler's whereabouts, the location of what in essence was a cache of buried treasure, even one as massive as the Amber Room, was of secondary importance to the U.S. intelligence community.

"But then, in the late 1940s, one of our operatives learned of the existence of a secret group of Nazi loyalists led by a man named Klaus Newmann. This group was called Phoenix, and it was different from the dozens of similar organizations in East and West Germany at the time, because Phoenix had an actual plan for rebuilding the Nazi party. The plan was concrete and workable. And a major component of that plan involved—"

"The Amber Room."

"Yes. The Amber Room. The agent insinuated himself into the

organization and learned that while the entire membership of Phoenix was aware they had access to a mountain of wealth that would aid them in building their revolution when the time was right, only one man actually knew what specific form that wealth took and, more importantly, where it was hidden."

"The agent shadowed this Newmann and discovered his secret."

"Yes. Newmann was too careful to actually enter the storage site. Phoenix obviously feared their man might be under surveillance, and didn't want to risk the Amber Room's discovery."

"But…"

"But Newmann's daily forest constitutionals always took him to the immediate vicinity of one single, secluded location. Always. It was a crumbling, abandoned building. There was no legitimate reason for him to visit this location, especially with that kind of single-minded consistency."

"So you know the location of the Amber Room treasure."

"Presumably, yes."

"How can you be sure it's even still there?"

"We don't know for sure, which is why I say, 'presumably.' The agency has maintained occasional surveillance on the site for the last four decades. The panels are massive and heavy, and would require eighteen-wheel flatbed trucks to be moved. They are being stored in a location where the use of such trucks would be obvious. We're as certain as we can be that no trucks have visited the location. The treasure is still in place."

"Presumably."

"That's right."

Tracie leaned back in her chair, thinking. "How could Newmann resist the temptation to check out the treasure? To show it to other Phoenix members? How could they resist the temptation to *force* him to show them?"

"These guys were—are—true believers, Tanner. They're Nazis through and through. Their entire focus was on maintaining organizational integrity and waiting until the proper moment in history to put the master plan in motion. Undoubtedly they were curious—who wouldn't be?—but they had been ordered to follow Hitler's precise plan, down to the letter, and that's what they did."

"So this Klaus Newmann was the only man in Germany who

knew the location of the Amber Room treasure."

"As far as we know, he was the only person alive who knew the location, besides Adolph Hitler himself."

"And he guarded that secret for…"

"Forty-two years."

She whistled. "So he's still alive. He must be getting up there in years, as well."

"Late sixties."

"That's quite a story. But you never answered my question, and it remains the same. What changed?"

"Klaus Newmann vanished yesterday."

Tracie sat back in her chair, thinking hard. "So you believe his disappearance means the Nazi plan is finally being put in motion."

"That was my initial reaction, yes. But we dispatched one of our operatives to Wuppertal, West Germany—the approximate location of the Amber Room treasure—several weeks ago after receiving intel that the Soviets were exhibiting unusual interest in the area. Our man has been maintaining surveillance on Newmann ever since."

"Obviously, given the sudden Soviet activity, you believe Newmann was murdered."

"Yes I do. Klaus Newmann held what we believe to be the only key in existence to the Amber Room storage site. That key has now disappeared, along with Newmann. Our current working theory is that the CIA was not the only entity to learn the location of the treasure. We believe the Soviets either knew the location all along, as we did, or somehow learned of it recently."

"And they made a move on the key."

"As I said, that's the theory."

"But from the standpoint of U.S. self-interest, isn't it a good thing that the key is now out of the hands of the Nazi loyalists? I understand with the crumbling of the Soviet Union a power vacuum will be created that makes this the perfect time to set some Third Reich revolution into motion, but if the Nazis no longer have access to the treasure, that will shut them down before they can even get started."

"True," Stallings answered. "But there are two reasons it's a problem. First off, the only thing more potentially dangerous than three hundred million dollars falling into the hands of people determined to reassert Nazi dominance, is three hundred million dollars falling into the hands of an unknown group with unknown intentions. That was why we allowed this Newmann character to possess the key for as long as we did. The Amber Room in an underground storage facility wasn't hurting anyone."

Tracie nodded. What Stallings was describing sounded exactly like the CIA she had worked for going on eight years now. Rather than taking action to recover the artifacts and return them to their rightful owners, they had waited for an opportunity to use the treasure as leverage.

Now the plan had come back and bitten them in the ass.

"What's the second reason?" she said.

"Excuse me?"

"You said there were two reasons why the lost key presents a problem for the United States."

"Yes. The second reason. If our theory regarding the Amber Room is correct, and the Soviets have gained possession of the key, that development is unacceptable. It cannot be allowed to stand.

Tracie tilted her head, thinking. "It makes sense that the Soviets would go after the Amber Room," she said. "If the treasure was stolen by the Nazis out of Russia in 1941, the Russians would have the greatest interest in recovering it."

"It may make sense, but as I said, it's not a good thing. The Soviet Union is on its last legs. The president knows it. You and I know it. Undoubtedly even Gorbachev knows it. If they are able to add three hundred million dollars to their treasury in one fell swoop, it will allow the Soviet machine to stagger along indefinitely. For months, if not years, depending on how they utilize the influx of capital. The money won't save them, not in the long run, but it will prolong the Cold War at a time when we're within a handful of years of finishing the Russians off for good."

"There's an obvious solution," Tracie said, "and it's so obvious I'm sure you must have thought of it already. You said the CIA knows the location of the treasure. Why doesn't the president simply send U.S. troops into Wuppertal to recover the Amber Room panels before they can be removed by whoever has taken possession of the key?"

Stallings sighed heavily. "And *this* is why you annoy me to no end," he said. "You're like a bull in a china shop sometimes, Tanner. Sending American troops into a West German city to break into West German property would require the permission of whom, Tanner?"

"The West Germans."

"Exactly. And securing that permission would require us to inform the West Germans exactly *why* we want to break into the hidden storage facility. And once we did that—"

"The West Germans would claim ownership of the treasure, based on the fact it's been stored there for the last four decades."

"That's right. And then we would be right back to the Russians demanding the treasure be returned to them. Nobody can know about this, Tanner. The treasure might belong to the Russians," he finished, speaking firmly, "but it is *not* in the best interest of the United States—or the free world—to allow the Amber Room to find its way back to Moscow or Leningrad."

"I think we're finally getting to the reason you're telling me all this. I know it's not because you love to spin an interesting tale."

"You are correct. Your assignment is to travel to Wuppertal, West Germany and pick up the trail of the key to the lost Amber Room treasure. You will recover the key and return it to Langley."

"I thought you said we have a man in Wuppertal. Why send me to Europe when there's already an operative on-scene?"

"Tanner, I don't want our man in Wuppertal anywhere near that key. He's already screwed the pooch so badly we're going to yank him home to the states the minute we can replace him. Think about it: he allowed a KGB operative to shadow Newmann for more than two weeks before likely assassinating him and stealing the key. Meanwhile, he did nothing. He's in over his head. The only reason he's still in West Germany right now is because he has intel that will help you when you get there."

"What intel would that be?"

"The KGB's man didn't leave Wuppertal following Newmann's disappearance."

"What?" Tracie thought she must have misheard Stallings. "He's still there? What is he waiting for?"

"That's right, he's still in Wuppertal. Apparently he's become rather fond of the West German nightlife, and he's taking the opportunity to enjoy a little mini-vacation before returning to Moscow."

"That's an idiotic decision."

"Obviously. But it's clear he doesn't realize we had Newmann under surveillance. He thinks nobody knows he's there. Anyway, our man is your contact when you land in West Germany. His code name is 'Matthias Gruber,' and he's to update you on the whereabouts of the Soviet operative—assuming the man is still in Wuppertal by the time you arrive—and then provide logistical support and assistance to you as long as you're there. After that he's coming back to Langley and will never work in the field again."

Tracie felt a stab of sympathy for the operative she had never met. She was very familiar with the feeling of being in Aaron Stallings's crosshairs, and it was not a pleasant experience. Still, she had to admit that at least in this situation, Stallings was right. The agent had screwed up, big-time.

Stallings continued, "I want you to go home from here and grab your go-bag. The agency Gulfstream is being fueled and prepped for departure even as we speak. A driver will pick you up at your apartment within the hour to transport you straight to Washington National, where you'll depart immediately for West Germany. The driver will have an information packet for you that will bring you up-to-date while you're in the air."

She nodded and rose without a word. Turned toward the door and reached for the knob.

"*Tanner!*" he said sharply.

"Yes?" She turned around and kept her tone neutral.

"This assignment's important. Don't fuck it up."

Thanks for the pep talk, she wanted to say, but instead settled on, "They're all important to me."

Then she turned and walked out the door.

5

November 13, 1987
10:30 p.m.
Wuppertal, Federal Republic of Germany

The driving beat of the techno-pop music blared from massive speakers suspended at strategically-place intervals above the dance floor. The room throbbed with a sensual rhythm Dobromir Victorovich had never experienced before coming to West Germany, and he was pretty sure he had checked out every dance club worth visiting between Moscow and Leningrad.

As much as Dobromir loved Mother Russia—and it was a lot; he had wanted to be a KGB agent for as long as he could remember, not just to experience the travel and excitement of covert intelligence work, but also to play his own small part in expanding the Soviet Union's reach around the globe—the clubs at home were different. Less…exciting.

It wasn't that there was any shortage of beautiful girls in Russia with whom to dance, and even occasionally bring home to his apartment. But Russian music was heavy, somber, somehow less joyful and overtly sexual than what he had discovered in Wuppertal.

He had become intoxicated by the nightlife here and wanted more. He had already stayed longer than he should have. If his superiors at KGB headquarters in Moscow were to discover he had lingered in West Germany rather than returning immediately with their precious key, there would be hell to pay. He could face demotion or suspension, possibly worse.

But how would they ever find out? His assignment had been to shadow Newmann for as long as it took to discover the whereabouts of the key, and then to kill him and take possession of it, but only when he was able to do so with no potential witnesses and no risk of capture.

And that was exactly what he had done. How could the pencil pushers back in Moscow know he had completed his mission in slightly more than two weeks instead of, say, three weeks?

The fact was that they would never know.

Dobromir was virtually certain he was the only KGB operative stationed in this region of West Germany, and he had seen no evidence of an American presence. As long as that remained the case, there was no way his mini-vacation would ever be discovered.

And it wasn't like he was taking unnecessary chances with the key. Officials back at the KGB's Lubyanka headquarters would disagree with that assessment, of course, but it was perfectly safe in his possession. Nobody in the world knew he had it, so it would occur to no one to try to relieve him of it.

So a couple more nights in Wuppertal would be no big deal. No one would be hurt by it. No one would ever know. He downed his vodka and slammed the empty glass onto the rickety wooden table, his eyes scanning the crowd for a suitable dance partner.

He caught sight of a blonde out on the dance floor. Short skirt. Nice legs. Big boobs. Decent moves. She was finishing up a dance with a short, skinny guy who looked like the type of pencil-necked wimp Dobromir could chew up and spit out without even breaking a sweat.

He checked his watch. There was definitely time for one last dance before he had to leave to meet his "date."

He signaled the overworked waitress in the leather skirt and black lace bustier to bring him another vodka, and then sauntered across the floor to rescue Big Boobs from Pencil Neck.

* * *

Big Boobs turned out to be a major disappointment. She could dance okay but she was dumb as a stump and only interested in convincing some sucker to buy her next drink.

Dobromir was no sucker. And striking out with the blonde was no great loss as far as he was concerned, because he was only in the club to pass the time before his "date," anyway. And now that time had arrived. He blew off the blonde, went back to his table and downed his vodka in one long swallow, and then made a beeline for the door and the short walk back to his hotel.

Toward the end of his first week in Wuppertal, Dobromir had had the good fortune to buy a drink in a different dance club for a loud man dressed in a loud suit. He wasn't sure at the time why he had bothered, but a few drinks later, Dobromir was glad he had.

It was the best purchase he had ever made.

Because the loud man in the loud suit turned out to be a major runner of prostitutes, and the man hooked Dobromir up that night with a girl right out of his wettest dreams. She blew Dobromir's mind—among other things—and after that he was hooked.

Each evening since, the loud man had sent another girl to Dobromir's room. Same time, different girl. They didn't come cheap. It was costing Dobromir more money than he cared to think about, but the "dates" were worth every bit of cash he spent. The girls were clean and beautiful, and there wasn't a kink invented they weren't willing to execute, and with incredible skill.

All of which meant he was anxious to sample tonight's merchandise. Would she be a blonde, with big boobs like the dumb stump back at the club? Or maybe she would be a petite brunette with a pretty smile and great imagination.

It didn't much matter to Dobromir. By now he knew two things: she would be great company, and she would give him the ride of his life. He strode briskly along the sidewalk, the night chilly but not at all uncomfortable to a man accustomed to bitter cold and biting winds.

It was still early, and Wuppertal's entertainment district was in full swing.

Music blared through closed doors, men and women strolled the sidewalks in various stages of drunkenness, and hookers plied their trade on corners near dark alleys, keeping one eye out for local law enforcement and the other for potential customers.

Two weeks ago, Dobromir would have been one of those

customers. In fact, prior to meeting the loud man in the loud suit, he *had* been one of those customers. But no more. He was like an alcoholic who had gotten his first taste of Jameson Irish Whiskey. Suddenly the rotgut he had been drinking his whole life—and perfectly happy with—was no longer quite up to snuff.

He wanted the good stuff.

He walked into his hotel, barely slowing as he shoved open the front door. Crossed the lobby and moved immediately to the stairs. He would have much preferred the added comfort and personal attention offered by one of the many small, family-run inns dotting the countryside, but personal attention meant…well, *personal attention,* and the last thing a field operative needed while working an active mission was to become memorable. So he had chosen to take a room at a large hotel chain's six-story lodging center and thus remain as anonymous as possible.

Of course, the argument could be made that he had done the opposite of blending into his surroundings by availing himself of not just one West German call girl, but by now close to a dozen. Dobromir felt confident that back at Lubyanka, had his superiors learned of his amorous activities, at least three handlers would suffer heart attacks and probably drop dead onto the floors of their offices.

But he was the one in the field, and he looked at the situation a little differently. What could possibly help him fit into his sur-roundings better than to drop a little cash into the local economy? What western businessman would travel to Wuppertal and *not* do exactly that? By hiring a posse of the loud man's hookers, Dobromir was doing nothing more than cementing his cover.

That was what he told himself.

He crossed the lobby, which at this time of night was almost but not quite empty. The bored desk clerk eyed him and then looked away. Had Dobromir been paying attention, he might have noticed a man he had never seen during his stay in Wuppertal sitting in a stuffed chair in front of the fireplace. The man held a newspaper in front of his face, but his eyes tracked Dobromir's progress over the top of the paper.

Dobromir was not paying attention, however, and thus did not notice. He had consumed a half-dozen glasses of German vodka back at the club—and in a remarkably short time—and his mind was focused on other things at the moment, anyway. Things that seemed to be growing in importance the closer he got to his room.

His "date" for the evening would be knocking on his door in a matter of minutes. He really should have left the club sooner, and he mentally kicked himself for wasting his time on Big Boobs when he should have been starting back to the hotel.

He took the elevator to the fourth floor and hurried down the hallway. By now he was nearly running, moving faster and faster, like a metal ball bearing being drawn toward a large magnet. He wanted to clean up and change clothes before his guest's arrival, not that his appearance would really make any difference. He was paying for his date's time, and thus it wasn't like she was going to turn around and march out of his room if he opened his door and she didn't like what she saw.

Still, Dobromir had his pride, and he wanted the rest of the night to go smoothly. He had paid plenty for this upcoming visit. Might as well at least wash his face and get the most bang for his buck.

6

November 13, 1987
2:40 p.m.
Somewhere over the Atlantic Ocean

The CIA's Gulfstream IV was roomy and comfortable, with a passenger compartment that featured thickly padded leather captain's chairs, plush carpeting and a walnut wood-grain finish that struck Tracie as more appropriate to a wealthy banker's study than an airplane. She wasn't about to quibble, though. This mode of transportation was infinitely preferable to riding in the back of a C5 cargo plane, something she had done more than once in her career.

She smiled as she pictured Aaron Stallings sitting in this very chair, sipping whiskey from a cut crystal tumbler as he jetted across the Atlantic to meet with his MI5 counterpart in London. It was easy to visualize. Stallings was intimidating and overbearing, brusque with allies and enemies alike, but he made no secret of his love for the finer things in life. His beautifully appointed home in McLean provided ample evidence of that fact.

Stallings's estimate of "within the hour" for her agency driver to arrive at her apartment had been accurate, but Tracie hadn't needed much time to prepare. One of the first things she had learned during her training at The Farm nearly eight years ago was to be ready to depart at a moment's notice for a destination anywhere in the world. So by the time the driver rolled into her apartment parking lot, she was standing in her front door tapping her foot impatiently.

The agency transport was a silver Dodge Caravan, the very essence of anonymity, and the driver slid the side door open and waited while she ducked into the vehicle. She dropped her duffle on the floor next to her seat and accepted a thick information packet offered by the driver—undoubtedly another agency case officer—before he closed the door and returned behind the wheel.

The trip to Washington National Airport went smoothly—for D.C.—and less than thirty minutes later the Caravan pulled to a stop directly beside the idling Gulfstream. The CIA jet was parked off by itself, outside a hangar located far from the commercial passenger terminals, and far from any other private planes or prying eyes. Tracie climbed aboard, her bag slung over one shoulder, information packet in her hands.

Moments later she was seated and buckled for departure. Almost immediately the high-pitched whine of the G4's twin engines increased in intensity and the Gulfstream began taxiing. They bumped and bounced along the taxiways at a high rate of speed, much faster than would have been acceptable on a commercial jetliner, and Tracie knew the flight crew had been briefed on the time-critical nature of their passenger's mission. They wouldn't know what that mission was, or why it was so important she get to West Germany as quickly as possible, but they were clearly prepared to do everything in their power to fulfill their own mission parameters.

The taxiing plane arrived at the departure runway in what—to Tracie at least—felt like record time, and it never stopped moving. They made a ninety-degree turn onto the runway and then the pilot poured the coals to the engines. The high-pitched whine became a throaty roar, and Tracie was pressed back into her seat as the jet leaped into the sky.

The Gulfstream turned left almost immediately, and then quickly back to the right. Noise abatement departure procedures required every jet leaving D.C. to make turns that, to the uninitiated, might seem random and nonsensical. In reality, the flight paths were carefully scripted and choreographed, not just to minimize noise to the surrounding community, but also for security reasons.

The G4 climbed at a rapid pace, and soon D.C. fell away as the jet turned northeast and continued climbing out over the ocean. Soon they leveled off, and Tracie wasted no time opening her information packet and spreading files and photographs out on a small cocktail table.

Stallings had told her the soon-to-be-disgraced CIA field operative in Wuppertal—"Gruber"—would fill her in on all details relevant to the case when she arrived in Germany, but she wasn't about to leave anything to chance. The flight would take a little over eight hours, and Tracie was determined to use as that time wisely, to familiarize herself with the particulars of the assignment before touching down on West German soil. If any there was any time left over, after studying her intel and learning all she could from it, she would nap.

Tracie guessed she would not be sleeping on the plane.

* * *

She was deep in thought, head bent over the table, poring over a thick file when she became aware of the presence of a figure standing a few feet away. The person was at the outside edge of her peripheral vision. She glanced up to see the younger-looking member of the two-man flight crew standing quietly, holding his cap in both hands. It was obvious he wanted to get her attention but was concerned about disturbing her.

She scowled, annoyed that the man had been able to get within ten feet of her without her noticing. Situational awareness was critical for an operative, and the knowledge that she hadn't seen him leave the flight deck and walk down the aisle grated on her. It was the sort of mistake that could get her killed in the field, and the fact that she had been absorbed in the intelligence packet was no excuse.

The man misinterpreted her annoyance with herself as anger at being interrupted, and he grinned sheepishly and raised his hands in apology. "Sorry to bother you," he said. "I'll get back to the flight deck. The captain said I should leave you the hell alone, but I wanted to welcome you aboard and make sure you were comfortable."

Tracie blinked. Her attention was still on Russia's Catherine Castle and three hundred million dollars' worth of missing treasure, and it took a moment for her to figure out that he thought she was upset with him.

Then she smiled. "No," she said. "You don't have to leave. I was just…ah, never mind, it's not important."

"That's a relief. For a second, there, I thought I was about to get shot and tossed out of the airplane at thirty-five thousand feet."

Tracie raised one eyebrow and the young pilot laughed. "Just kidding," he said. "Although you did look a little angry. I've flown enough missions to know not to ask too many questions, so I'll simply leave it at this: please don't hesitate to let the captain or me know if you need anything. We have a mini-fridge with drinks and some light snacks, and there is very little for us to do now that we're in the en route portion of the flight. There's no flight attendant on board, so you'll have to make do with one of us, but we're more than happy to help with anything you need."

"That's very kind, thank you," she said. "And I'm sure I'll take you up on your offer in a little while. For now, though, I need to get some more work done."

The pilot nodded and returned her smile. "Very good," he said. Then he spun on his heel and returned to the flight deck.

Tracie watched him walk away and smiled again. She decided she liked traveling on her own private CIA jet. The service was friendly and professional—not to mention quite handsome—and discreet. The young airman had made a point to stay far enough away that Tracie didn't have to worry about protecting the classified material from his gaze. It was obvious he had kept his distance intentionally, so as not to invade her work area.

I could get used to this, she thought, and then laughed out loud, all alone in the passenger cabin. The notion that she might ever see the inside of this plane again was ludicrous. She was here only due to the time-critical nature of the mission, the fact that the Soviet operative who had likely killed Klaus Newmann and stolen the Amber Room key might disappear at any moment.

Still, it was fun to daydream.

7

November 13, 1987
10:40 p.m. local time
Hahn Air Base, Hahn, Federal Republic of Germany

Tracie blinked instantly awake as the Gulfstream touched down with a jolt at Hahn Air Base. She had spent virtually the entire flight engrossed in her intel, stopping to use the lavatory and to eat a small snack, but otherwise determined to use the down time of a transatlantic flight productively.

With a little over an hour left in the trip, however, she had closed her eyes, intending to rest for just a moment. The next thing she knew, the jet was rolling out on the runway, the twin engines' high-pitched whine returning with a vengeance as the pilot hit the reverse thrusters to aid in braking.

The G4 exited the runway and taxied at such a high rate of speed across the airfield—moving even faster than they had on the ground back in D.C.—that Tracie guessed the pilots could probably get the airplane airborne again if they really wanted to.

But they didn't want to. What they wanted to do was get their passenger deplaned and on her way as soon as humanly possible. While the captain taxied the aircraft, the younger crewmember turned around and raised his voice so that Tracie could hear him over the ambient noise of a moving jet.

"We'll be coming to a stop momentarily, ma'am," he said. "As soon as we can safely do so, we'll lower the stairs and escort you to your ride, which I'm told is waiting on the ramp. It's been a pleasure having you aboard and Captain Stallworth and I hope you enjoyed your flight."

Tracie flashed once again on the dozens of overseas trips she'd taken over her CIA career. On virtually every one of them she'd been an extra passenger, often on military cargo flights were she was stuffed in among crates, or soldiers, or the plane's interior was too hot or too cold or noisy as hell or vibrating like the whole damned thing might just come apart at the seams.

One trip in particular had been an airborne scenario she knew she would never forget. She was aboard a C5, acting as courier, delivering a top-secret message from Soviet leader Mikhail Gorbachev to U.S. President Ronald Reagan. One member of the flight crew was being blackmailed by the KGB and had been instructed to crash the airplane into the ocean in order to destroy that message, and the man had very nearly succeeded.

After a desperate gun battle inside the plane, the crash had occurred, but on land instead of over the water. Tracie was the only survivor, pulled from the burning wreckage by a passerby with whom she'd promptly fallen hopelessly in love.

And who had then been killed just days later.

While saving her life.

Again.

She pushed the memories of Shane Rowley aside and smiled. "I think you can safely say this trip has been the highlight of my aviation experiences. When I get back to the states I'm going to let the brass know just how courteous and professional you were, and how quickly you got me here."

The young pilot touched his cap and then swiveled back around in his seat. In the distance a massive hangar loomed, doors closed, a single F-16 parked at an angle facing the taxiing Gulfstream. The fighter jet was part of the 50th Tactical Fighter Wing and was based at Hahn, armed and ready to be scrambled at a moment's notice in the event of Soviet/East German provocation.

The G4 rolled to a stop. A few feet away a nondescript gray automobile sat idling in the shadow of the hangar, its finish dull, bluish-grey exhaust leaking out the tailpipe.

The relentless whine of the engines abruptly ceased as the pilot in command cut the power. A moment later, both men turned and walked back to escort Tracie off the plane. A crewman chocked the wheels and the door opened and was lowered to the tarmac. Tracie had packed her files away while they taxied, and the moment the stairs hit the ground she was exiting the aircraft.

She shook the hands of both members of the flight crew and thanked them again, then hurried to the car. Slouched behind the wheel was a youngish man, maybe early thirties, with slightly shaggy hair and a face overdue for a shave. The man wore a tweed scally cap at a rakish angle, and he looked impatiently at his watch as she approached. She recognized him immediately as her West German contact.

The man made no effort to help her with her bag—not that she would have allowed him to handle it, in any event—and she opened the passenger door and tossed the duffel into the back seat. The files she kept in her arms. Then she dropped into the front seat and stuck her hand out.

"You must be Gruber," she said, knowing full well that whatever the man's real name, it most certainly was *not* Gruber.

"Indeed I am," he said, hesitating just a moment before taking her offered hand and giving it a shake. "Matthias Gruber. And you are…"

Tracie knew her contact's alias because she had studied her intel on the plane, but it was obvious *Herr Gruber* had not burdened himself with any serious preparation. It was easy to see why this man would soon be called home to Langley.

"Quinn," she said. "Fiona Quinn."

"Ah. It is indeed a pleasure to meet you, Fiona." He lingered over the pronunciation of her alias and gave her hand a slight but noticeable squeeze before letting go.

Wonderful. The operative whose mission in West Germany was about to come to an abrupt and undistinguished end—even if he didn't know it yet—not only demonstrated questionable decision-making skills, he fancied himself a ladies' man as well.

This is the last thing I need, Tracie thought, and stifled the urge to roll her eyes. She pursed her lips and cleared her throat as she withdrew her hand. Debated whether to tell her new friend to stick to business. Decided not to bother.

For the time being.

"How long's the drive to Wuppertal?" she said evenly.

"All about the mission, eh?" he answered. "Fair enough, I suppose, although I must say that when I received word I would be picking up a second operative, I had no idea it would be someone as…attractive…as you." He smiled widely for the second time, flashing a mouth full of pearl-white teeth.

"The drive?" she reminded him.

His smile faded away and he shook his head ruefully. "Can't blame a guy for trying, right Fiona?"

"Listen to me, Gruber. Unless you received a different mission briefing than I did, you know this assignment is important, and it's time-critical. Put this car in gear and aim it at Wuppertal, or get your ass out and I'll do it myself."

He scowled and raised his hands in mock surrender but did as she asked. The engine sputtered and the transmission caught and the car lurched forward. Gruber spun the wheel and headed for a gate in a chain-link fence topped by razor wire and manned by an armed guard wearing a U.S Air Force uniform.

"Okay, okay," he said. "Message received. We're co-workers, not friends. Got it."

Tracie was tempted to remind him they weren't exactly co-workers, either. Her assignment had made it crystal clear that Tracie was in charge and Gruber was to defer to her from the moment she landed in West Germany, and he was to continue to do so until the mission was complete.

She was certain he had received the same briefing. Still, she elected to hold off on that particular reminder.

She wouldn't hesitate to put pull rank if it came to that. But for all his shortcomings—and it was obvious there were several—the man behind the wheel was someone who had been in country for weeks and so must know the area nearly as well as the local players. He could make or break this mission simply by how forthcoming he chose to be with information. It would be to her benefit to handle Herr Gruber with care.

He mumbled something and she said, "Excuse me?"

"I said, we should be in Wuppertal in a little over two hours, as long as this marvel of German engineering doesn't let us down."

This was a perfect opportunity to extend an olive branch, and Tracie decided to take advantage of it. "Yeah, what is this thing? It's definitely no BMW."

She didn't get a laugh out of him, but Gruber did smile. "No, it's not a BMW. I didn't want to attract unnecessary attention with something flashy, so I picked out this beauty. It's called an Opel Kadett, and believe it or not"—he grimaced in distaste as he glanced around the car's interior—"it's only three years old."

By now they had left Hahn Air Base behind, and Tracie glanced out the rear window to see that most—but not all—of the blue smoke had disappeared once the car got under way. It didn't do much to increase her confidence the Opel would survive a two-hour trip. "Well, I could pick a lot of adjectives to describe this car, but 'flashy' would not even have crossed my mind."

Gruber chuckled this time and said, "Mission accomplished, then."

He maneuvered the little car to the motorway, and once they were up to speed Tracie said, "Tell me about Klaus Newmann and the Soviet operative."

Gruber shrugged. "I assume you've read the mission reports." A trace of bitterness crept into his voice. He may not be the best field operative, but he was perceptive enough to know he knew he must be in big trouble back in the states for the home office to send over a replacement.

He glanced across the front seat at her, a look of bland innocence on his face. She could see why he thought of himself as a ladies' man. His hair was just long enough to be sexy without crossing the line into unmanageable, and his teeth were as straight as his smile was crooked.

But he was delusional if he thought "Fiona Quinn" was here for any reason other than to complete her assignment and get the hell out of Germany.

"Yes, I've read the reports," she said. "But reports are written for the brass, and sometimes the real story gets lost in translation. I want to know everything that never made it back to Langley."

He returned his attention to the West German highway. In the left lane, cars passed the Opel in a more or less continuous stream. Tracie knew he was considering her point, trying to decide whether giving her what she asked for would result in even more headaches for him than he already had.

She remained quiet, allowing him his internal argument. She wasn't worried. Eventually he would give her what she wanted. One way or the other.

Moments later he cleared his throat.

Then he started talking.

8

November 14, 1987
10:50 p.m.
Kaminecke Hotel
Wuppertal, Federal Republic of Germany

Tracie adjusted her dress uncomfortably. It was red and formfitting and short, and it made her look like a hooker.

It was perfect.

The two-hour drive north from Hahn Air Base to Wuppertal last night had yielded little in the way of new intel, even though once "Gruber" started talking, it had been like opening the spigot of a garden hose—the information flowed freely. If he was leaving anything out about the part he had played in the Amber Room key fiasco, Tracie couldn't imagine what it might be.

Maybe he knew it was only a matter of time—and not very much of it—before he was called on the carpet back at Langley, and he was hoping "Fiona" would put in a good word for him with the handlers.

Or maybe he felt justifiably guilty about his role in allowing the key to disappear, instantly rendering his mission a failure and allowing some unknown entity—perhaps the Soviet Union, perhaps not—access to more than a quarter-billion dollars, an amount more than sufficient to further destabilize an already fragile world economy.

But whatever the reason, he started talking after the drawn-out silence in the car, and didn't stop until they arrived in Wuppertal. And while most of what he said was verbal white noise, designed to justify his actions and inactions, Gruber had said one thing that Tracie knew immediately was significant: the operative had demonstrated conclusively that nothing was as much fun for him as paid companionship.

With a different professional companion every night.

And Tracie had known immediately how she was going to recover the key.

* * *

One thing Gruber had managed to do without screwing up was to remain out of sight while tailing the Soviet. Tracie knew Gruber had not been made, because only a suicidal idiot would have stuck around town more than thirty seconds after completing his mission had he known he was under surveillance.

In the process of shadowing the Russian, Gruber had ascertained the location of the man's hotel room: number 417, which was located approximately two-thirds of the way along the corridor after exiting the elevator. And the Soviet's nightly routine was extremely consistent, varying only in the identity of the prostitute with whom he spent his evening.

Tracie's first move was to reserve Room 401. It was already occupied, but a small—relatively speaking—bribe convinced the desk clerk to relocate the couple already housed in that room to one on a different floor under the guise of room maintenance that was so critically important it simply could not wait.

Once inside the room, Tracie changed into her new dress and waited. Gruber told her that the Soviet always went out drinking early in the evening, returning to his room by eleven p.m. sharp. Shortly afterward, his companion for the night would arrive at the hotel, walk to his room and knock on the door. She would disappear inside and, in every case, not reappear until morning.

It was now ten fifty-five. The Soviet operative appeared right on schedule, stepping off the elevator and weaving his way drunkenly down the corridor. Tracie watched him pass by in the hallway through the peephole and then very quietly opened her door a crack and monitored his progress as he approached his room.

She had been careful not to give herself away, but realized after watching the man that she could probably have hired a brass band to play in her doorway and the Soviet would not have noticed, so drunk was he, not to mention focused on getting into his room and awaiting his nightly treat.

He disappeared inside his hotel room and Tracie waited.

And waited.

Eleven-fifteen. Nothing.

The elevator stopped on the fourth floor. Tracie stood with her door closed, right hand on the knob, one eye glued to the peephole.

False alarm. Three businessmen exited, dressed in wrinkled suits and loosened ties. They had clearly been drinking since Happy Hour. The men stumbled past, arguing drunkenly about which of them had left the biggest tip for the barmaid.

Silence descended on the hallway and she checked her watch. It was now nearly eleven-thirty. Where was the hooker? She should have appeared by now. The Soviet had demonstrated a discernible pattern of behavior, and barring unusual circumstances people did not tend to change their behavior patterns.

The bell at the end of the hallway dinged again.

The elevator door slid open.

And Tracie saw her.

The young woman was tall and blonde and willowy, with firm breasts stuffed into a short dress that looked remarkably like Tracie's. She wore lace stockings and six-inch spike heels, and adorning her lips was the reddest shade of lipstick Tracie had ever seen.

It couldn't have been more obvious she was a prostitute if she had worn a flashing neon sign. This was definitely Tracie's girl.

But there was a problem: the hooker wasn't alone. A young couple stepped out of the elevator right behind her, the woman wearing a scowl of distaste at having to share the car with their riding companion. The man was trying hard—and failing—not to be obvious about checking her out. At the moment his eyes were glued to her butt, and Tracie knew if she watched the man a little longer, his eyes would begin to travel down the prostitute's long legs.

But there wasn't time to watch longer. The couple was following the hooker down the hallway, and soon Tracie's chance would be gone. The young woman would enter the Soviet operative's room and disappear.

She opened her door and stepped out of her room.

"Oh!" she said, praying her German would pass muster. She hadn't worked in the country in nearly a year and despite her degree in linguistics from Brown University, German had never been her best language.

She slurred her words in an attempt to cloak the deficiency in the guise of drunkenness and carried on. "Gerda, I'm so glad to see you! You would not believe what the oaf in this room just tried to do to me."

She stepped toward the hooker with a wide smile on her face, conscious of the couple's attention shifting to her. She had to get rid of the elevator riders before the hooker voiced what her expression was already making clear: that she had no idea who this drunken prostitute was, or what her problem might be.

Or why she would care.

Tracie whirled toward the couple and stamped her foot. "This is none of your concern! How about a little privacy? Just mind your business and continue on your way."

The woman's eyes narrowed and it was obvious she was about to give Tracie a piece of her mind, but her boyfriend or husband took her by the elbow and spun her around. He whispered something in her ear and she shook her head in disgust but to Tracie's immense relief kept walking.

"What is this about?" the hooker said. "I do not know you, and my name is not Gerda." She kept her voice low, obviously looking to avoid a noisy confrontation that would result in her being removed from the hotel before collecting what was sure to be a significant payday from the horny young man waiting down the hall in Room 417.

And now it was too late for her. Tracie stepped behind the hooker before she could spin around. Her confusion and her six-inch heels practically stapled her to the floor.

In an instant, Tracie lifted her right hand and placed it palm side up on the woman's right shoulder, like a waiter carrying a tray of drinks. At the same time, she circled her left arm around the hooker's neck, nestling it into the crook of her elbow. Then she lowered her own head to her hands and clasped them together, squeezing as she did so.

The hooker's head was immobilized, and she had nowhere to go, and Tracie applied steady pressure to the woman's carotid sinus. The hooker lifted a leg in an attempt to kick backward at Tracie, but she was fighting a battle she could not win, already beginning to lose consciousness.

In seconds she went limp in Tracie's arms.

The young couple was still walking away down the hall. Their backs were turned but if one or both decided to look behind them there would be no way for Tracie to explain what had just occurred, so moving quickly was critical. Tracie kicked off her heels and hooked her arms under the prostitute's armpits. Then she dragged the unconscious woman into her hotel room.

Once inside, she eased the door closed with her foot. Her shoes were still on the hallway floor, but they were of secondary importance. An abandoned pair of high heels would arouse nothing more than curiosity from anyone exiting a room or the elevator.

Tracie had left the supplies she would need lined up in a neat row on the floor just inside the doorway. She ripped a long strip of duct tape off a roll and then picked up a hotel washcloth. She stuffed the washcloth into the hooker's mouth and secured it with the tape, wrapping it around the back of the woman's head twice and then slapping it down. She used a second cloth to cover the hooker's eyes, securing it with duct tape as well. Then she hogtied her with nylon cord before dragging her onto the bed.

The unfortunate hooker would awaken soon, utterly immobile but safe, if likely extremely angry.

Tracie double-checked her handiwork and then nodded in satisfaction.

"Sorry about that," she said to the unconscious woman. "But I'll take it from here."

She returned to the door and checked the peephole.

The hallway appeared empty.

She stepped into the corridor and closed the door behind her, double-checking the lock.

Then she strode down the hallway, running a hand through her hair and pulling one last time on the hem of the short dress. It was time to introduce herself to the horny Soviet operative.

9

The man's door was ajar.

Something was wrong. The situation stank to high heaven. Tracie supposed it was technically possible the Soviet operative had left his door cracked on purpose, to allow the prostitute to enter without knocking, but she knew that wasn't what had happened. Gruber had made it clear that the Soviet didn't know any of the women he hired; didn't even know what they looked like, in fact, until they showed up at his door.

And he was still a KGB professional, charged with getting a key worth three hundred million dollars back to Moscow. It strained credulity beyond the breaking point to think he would be that reckless, no matter how much he liked to party.

So this was bad.

She reached instinctively for her weapon before remembering that her dress was so skimpy she had had no place to put it.

She cursed silently.

Turned toward the fire door at the far end of the hallway. She hadn't wanted to leave her gun inside the hotel room with the hooker, no matter how securely she had trussed up the woman. So she had left it with Gruber, who was standing in the stairwell, providing backup.

Retrieving her gun from her new partner before returning to the Soviet's room would take several seconds of precious time, but entering without it under these circumstances was out of the question.

She kicked off her heels—again—and scooped them up into her hand, then trotted the length of the hallway. Where the hell was Gruber? Why wasn't he coming forward to meet her and pass her gun to her? He had to know why she was coming.

Within seconds she had arrived at the heavy steel door, annoyed and impatient. She glanced through the tiny, wire-reinforced window and the stairwell appeared empty.

She shoved open the door and stepped cautiously through it and found...nothing. Gruber had disappeared, and apparently taken her weapon with him.

And her backup gun was locked away inside the CIA safe house three blocks away.

Dammit.

Tracie raced up the stairs to the fifth floor landing, moving quietly in her bare feet. This floor was as empty and still as the one she had just left. She turned and reversed direction, taking the stairs three at a time, hurrying down to the third floor landing.

It was deserted as well.

Gruber was nowhere to be found.

Tracie blew out a breath in frustration. Her plan had come unraveled in near record time.

She returned to the fourth floor and looked through the tiny window.

The corridor was empty.

She slipped through the fire door and down the hallway, stopping once again just outside the Soviet's room. His door was just the way she had left it less than a minute ago, cracked slightly open.

And Tracie had no weapon.

She eased the door farther open with one foot, using its heavy metal construction to shield her body—as much as possible—from any hostile who might still be inside. It swung smoothly and slowly, revealing a room that had been trashed.

And a man lying on the floor.

And a lot of blood.

Tracie's pulse spiked. Her adrenaline had already been pounding, but now it flooded her system. Her hands shook and her breathing became shallow and ragged. She fell back on her training. Breathed slowly through her mouth and forced herself to think. Priorities would be crucial.

She needed to clear the room first, and then check the victim for a pulse. It was already obvious he was dead, but she could take nothing for granted.

She leaned back against the door and eased it closed with her hip until it latched with a heavy *clunk*. The room was a crime scene and she had no gloves, so opening and closing doors would be problematic. But there were always work-arounds.

The hotel room's layout was simple and open. With the exception of the bathroom it was nothing more than one big living area featuring a single closet. The closet door had been left ajar just like the entry door, and Tracie pushed it open fully using her foot, prepared to strike with a sidekick if occupied.

It wasn't.

The only place left to clear was the bathroom, and by now Tracie knew nobody would be inside it. Whoever had been here just a few minutes earlier was long gone.

Still, Tracie wasn't about to make an assumption that could get her killed. She dropped one shoe silently onto the carpeted floor. Grasped the other in her right hand. She slipped across the room, careful not to step in any blood.

Then she pressed herself against the wall adjacent to the bathroom door.

Took a deep breath.

Dropped into a crouch and gently tossed her shoe into the right side of the bathroom, hoping it would serve as a distraction in the event she was wrong and whoever had murdered the Soviet was hiding in there. It struck the side wall and before it hit the floor Tracie was moving, swinging around the door jamb and into the bathroom, staying low, left hand wrapped around her right fist, prepared to drive her hands under the jaw and into neck of any assailant.

She would crush his windpipe before he could squeeze off a shot.

But the bathroom was empty.

Tracie was alone in the room with the corpse of a Soviet spy.

"Dammit." She kept her voice down but couldn't stop herself

from uttering the curse. What should have been a relatively straightforward—if dangerous—assignment had come apart at the seams.

She stalked out of the bathroom and across the living area to the victim. He lay motionless on his side, a pool of blood surrounding his upper body, soaking into the carpeting and beginning to congeal at the edges.

Tracie knelt, contorting her body awkwardly in order to avoid the blood while still getting close enough to the man to examine his wounds.

His throat had been slit nearly from ear to ear.

It would be impossible to sustain such an injury and survive, but she pressed two fingers gently against his carotid anyway. The skin was slick with blood that was just starting to turn sticky.

The official murder investigation would reveal that someone had checked for a pulse, but she would smear the blood in order to eliminate fingerprints, and the investigators would assume the killer had wanted to be sure his victim was dead. There would be no reason for them to suspect someone else had been inside the hotel room.

She hoped.

Tracie located the carotid and was unsurprised to discover no pulse.

She removed her hand from the corpse's neck and shook her head in frustration. Her plan had not included killing the Soviet, only forcing him to turn over the Amber Room key. But she wouldn't lose any sleep over the murder, either.

What she *would* lose sleep over was that she had been too late. Someone had had the same plan as she—surprise the sloppy Soviet and relieve him of his valuable prize—but they had beaten her to the punch. The whole thing had gone down just minutes ago, too, because it had been no more than half an hour since she had watched this very man stagger down the hallway and enter his hotel room.

His body was still warm.

His attacker had probably been killing him even as Tracie was busy subduing the hooker.

She cursed again and glanced around the room.

Wondered whether anything would be gained by searching it.

Decided against it. The condition of the room—furniture overturned, television screen shattered—suggested the Soviet had fought hard against his attackers before succumbing. Whoever had surprised the man in his hotel room would not have made the mistake of killing him before getting what they came for, which meant Tracie could search until hell froze over and she wouldn't find the key.

It was gone.

She rose to her feet and retraced her steps to the bathroom. Picked up her shoe and moved to the door. Checked the peephole. The hallway was clear as far as she could see, but that didn't mean much. It was a long way from here to the elevators, as well as to the stairs at the other end, and it was entirely possible someone would be walking along the corridor when Tracie stepped out of the dead man's room.

But there was no alternative. The longer she stayed here, the colder the key's trail became.

She took a deep breath and slipped a hand under the hem of her dress, then raised it to the door handle. The dress lifted to her waist as she did so, but the man lying in a pool of blood behind her was beyond caring about seeing a naked ass.

Tracie turned the handle and pushed the door open an inch, then pulled her dress down. Eased her head out the door just enough to see that the hallway was deserted from Room 417 to the stairs at the far end. She had to poke her head a little farther out to see the other direction, and as she did she could see the elevator door sliding open.

Someone would be coming down the hallway in a matter of seconds.

She eased back into the room and counted slowly to sixty.

Tried again.

Now the hallway was empty in both directions. Tracie slipped out of the dead man's room, again using the material of her dress to avoid leaving fingerprints as she pulled the handle closed. It clicked crisply and she smoothed her clothing one more time before padding down the hallway to her room, high heels dangling from her right hand.

* * *

Tracie had expected the hooker to be angry, and she was. But she was mostly frightened.

The moment Tracie opened the door, the young woman began thrashing—as much as possible, which was not much—and trying to speak, presumably to beg for her release. Her words were muffled and indecipherable thanks to the gag, but her pleading tone conveyed the sentiment of her message quite clearly.

Tracie sat next to her on the bed and said in German, "If you do exactly as I say, you will live. If you do not, you will die quickly and will never see the kill shot coming. Do you understand?"

The muffled pleading stopped and the hooker nodded her head enthusiastically. The poor woman was terrified, and Tracie knew it would never occur to her that she could not see a gun.

"Good," Tracie said. "I don't want to hurt you, but I will if necessary, and without hesitation."

The enthusiastic nodding turned to equally vigorous shaking of her head.

"Remember what I said," Tracie finished. "You will not receive a second warning."

The hooker lay perfectly still. Tracie figured she couldn't decide on an appropriate response to her last words—whether to nod or shake her head—so she did neither.

"Here's what's going to happen," Tracie continued. "I'm going to untie you and escort you to the door. When we get to the door I will remove your gag and your blindfold. You will open the door and enter the hallway, turn right and walk to the stairs at the far end. You will take the stairs and exit the building, and you will continue straight ahead along the sidewalk for one kilometer. Do you understand me?"

Enthusiastic nods.

"Good. I will be directly behind you the entire time, gun pointed at your spinal cord. If you scream you will die. If you try to turn and look at me you will die. If you try to alert anyone that there is a problem you will die. Do you still understand?"

More nodding. The woman had already seen Tracie's face, but

that didn't matter. She was guessing that between the stress and the fear the hooker would recall nothing more specific about her assailant than her flame-red hair.

And the young woman wouldn't go to the authorities, Tracie was almost certain of that. But she *would* report immediately to her pimp and spill her guts, and the pimp would not be pleased about losing out on the income stream he had lucked into with the Soviet lothario.

That wouldn't matter, either. Whoever had taken the key was undoubtedly already in the process of leaving Wuppertal in his rearview mirror. If that was true, Tracie wouldn't be staying in town much longer, and what time she had remaining would not be spent anywhere near this hotel.

She untied the nylon cord and released the hooker's arms and legs. Took the young woman by the elbow and guided her to the door.

"Remember what I said," she whispered harshly, and then she used her combat knife to slit the duct tape securing the blindfold and the gag. Both cloths fell away, fluttering to the floor, and Tracie said, *"Move."*

She followed the young woman out of the building and just far enough along the sidewalk to satisfy herself that the hooker was following her instructions. There was no way in the world she would make it a full kilometer before succumbing to her fear and the need to tell someone what had happened to her, but it was clear she wasn't going to stand in the middle of the street and start screaming, either.

That would have to be good enough.

Tracie spun around and hurried back into the hotel. She had to clean up her room and get the hell out, and there was very little time left to make it happen. One of two things was going to happen very soon—either the hooker's pimp would come to Room 401 looking for the woman who had kidnapped his girl, or the dead Soviet operative's body would be discovered.

In either case it was imperative she be long gone.

She sprinted up the stairs to the fourth floor, forced herself to walk at a leisurely pace the length of the hallway, and then disappeared inside her room.

It had only been rented as a staging point for her attack on the hooker, so cleanup was easy. She wiped down all the smooth surfaces, picked up her few supplies, and then, less than three minutes later, exited it for the last time. She strolled to the elevator, pressed the "Down" button, and left the hotel through the lobby, just another sexy young woman out for a night on the town.

10

November 15, 1987
1:15 a.m.
CIA safe house
Wuppertal, Federal Republic of Germany

Tracie paced inside the small safe house maintained by the CIA for Wuppertal operations. She crossed the living room and into the kitchen, circled the kitchen table and moved back into the living room, then repeated the pattern, over and over.

She squinted as she concentrated, doing her best to ignore the dull throb radiating outward from the bullet wound she had sustained in the Florida Everglades. Tried to determine whether the pain was worsening or it was just a product of exhaustion and stress.

Decided it didn't matter. What mattered was that she regroup from the fiasco this mission had become and find a way to turn things around, if it wasn't already too late.

It wouldn't be easy. She had no clue who had murdered the Russian operative, or where the killer or killers might have gone. Obviously, that meant she had no idea where to start looking for the Amber Room key.

And where was Gruber? How could her only backup have disappeared just when she needed him most? She had been about to walk unarmed straight into the clutches of a trained KGB field operative, barely dressed, counting on nothing more than the element of surprise to give her the upper hand in what would undoubtedly have been a fierce confrontation.

She felt her anger rising and breathed deeply. Forced herself to swallow her resentment, to push it aside for another time. Focusing on Gruber's untimely disappearance would do nothing to solve the problem at hand, and in fact would serve only to distract her from what was important.

So she paced.

She wondered how long it would take for the Soviet's body to be discovered and for the alarm to be raised back at the Kaminecke Hotel. The KGB would learn within hours of that happening that their man in Wuppertal was dead and the Amber Room key had slipped out of their grasp.

And once *that* happened, what came next would be inevitable. A team of KGB operatives would descend on Wuppertal in a matter of days, further muddying the already murky waters and making Tracie's mission even more difficult.

More like impossible, she thought.

Then she shook her head. There was always a way.

She whirled at the sound of a key scraping in the front door lock. The noise was soft, stealthy, but against the backdrop of utter silence inside the safe house it sounded to Tracie as loud and clear as a thunderclap.

The first thing she had done upon entering the house was to retrieve her backup Glock from the gun safe built into the living room wall, and now she stopped in her tracks and dropped into a shooter's crouch. Remained perfectly still and kept her gun trained on the widening space between the edge of the door and the frame.

For a moment nothing happened; it was as if the door had magically opened on its own. Then Matthias Gruber stepped through the space and into the safe house. His gun was holstered under his jacket and his hands were empty.

He froze when he saw Tracie.

Raised his hands slowly.

"Whoa, there," he said softly. "Easy now."

Tracie's initial stab of relief at seeing her fellow operative faded away almost instantly, and she kept her weapon aimed center-mass on his body.

Narrowed her eyes.

Said, "You disappeared from the Kaminecke at the absolute worst possible moment. Quite a coincidence that the man holding my gun and supposedly providing backup to me would make himself scarce at the exact time the KGB officer we were about to run an op on was being murdered."

"Hold on," he said. He started to lower his hands. Tracie gestured with her gun and he immediately raised them again to shoulder height.

"No, *you* hold on," she said, her voice cold and hard. "The timing is almost enough to make me believe you might have had something to do with the attack on the Russian. Almost enough to make me think maybe *you* took the man out and helped yourself to the key."

"It's not like that. We're on the same side here." He spoke quietly but his voice carried an intensity Tracie had not before seen out of the wannabe playboy operative.

"Is that so? Then what happened back there? Where the hell did you go when you were supposed to be backing me up?"

Gruber gazed at Tracie, his eyes hidden in the shadows. "Can we sit down and talk about this like civilized human beings?"

"No. Answer the question."

He sighed deeply, his nervousness evident. Good. Until Tracie figured out what was happening, she didn't want him getting too comfortable.

Or at all comfortable.

"Okay, here's the deal," he said. "I had to make a split-second decision: follow the guys who took out the Russian or stay in the stairwell backing you up. I knew the Russian was dead—or felt it was a reasonable enough assumption given what I had seen—and therefore knew you were in little or no danger. So I followed the killers."

Tracie lowered her gun slightly. "You tailed the guys who offed the Russian?"

"Yes. After we split up outside the Kaminecke and you went upstairs to run the op, I circled around to the side entrance. Guess what I saw when I got to the door?"

"It's your story, you tell me."

"There were two men, dressed in long black overcoats and fedoras pulled low over their eyes. I waited a second after they entered the hotel and then slipped through the door behind them. I got a bad vibe from them immediately, and it worsened when they reached the fourth floor and disappeared through the fire door. I hustled up the stairs and looked through the window just as they were forcing their way inside the Russian's room."

"How many attackers were there?"

"Two."

"Why would the Russian have opened his door to two men dressed like assassins out of a black-and-white noir movie when he was expecting a hooker in a skin-tight dress?"

Gruber shrugged. "They probably flanked the door and pressed themselves against the wall so he couldn't see them through the peephole. It's what I would have done. And don't forget, the Soviet was drunk and horny." He shrugged again. "That's a bad combination if people are out to kill you."

"So they forced their way into the room, and then what?"

"They weren't inside for long. The intruders must have been *extremely* persuasive. But you know all this already. You would have seen it when you went inside."

Tracie had started to relax, just a little, but now she tensed again. "What makes you think I entered the Russian's room?"

"Jesus, Fiona, take it down a notch, would you? I was watching through the fire door, remember? I saw the killers leave his room, saw that the door wasn't secured properly. The second man pulled it closed, but it struck the jamb and bounced back without latching. They were in such a hurry to get out of there, they didn't notice. Obviously, if you went to the room afterward, you entered. Or am I wrong about that?"

"You're not wrong," she mumbled, envisioning Gruber's story in her head and trying to decide if it made sense. "Go on."

"When I saw the men leave the Russian's room and turn toward the fire door, I climbed to the landing above and waited for them to start down the stairs. Then I followed, and that's why I was gone when you came to retrieve your gun."

"And?"

"And what? You asked me what happened. That's what happened."

"Come on, Gruber, don't make me pull it out of you like a dentist yanking teeth. If you followed them, where did they go?"

"They drove to a place I assume is their own safe house. They parked their car and went inside. I watched for a few minutes, just enough time to conclude they were in for the night, and then I came back here."

"Is that right?"

"That's right. And if we leave now, maybe we can take them by surprise and get the goddamn key back."

11

November 15, 1987
1:30 a.m.
Wuppertal, Federal Republic of Germany

Tracie stood silently, mentally reviewing Gruber's story and examining it for holes. He was supposed to be her partner, if only temporarily, a man the agency had at one time trusted enough to send to West Germany to work alone. A solo assignment was a major responsibility and, Tracie knew, something the CIA did not take lightly.

That the agency had deemed him worthy of working by himself halfway around the world was a point in his favor. He had then screwed the pooch in allowing the Soviets to get to Newmann and steal the Amber Room key, a development that immediately placed a giant question mark over his abilities as an operative. And he had come across as smug and smarmy during the two-hour ride from Hahn to Wuppertal yesterday.

But none of those things made him a traitor.

Necessarily.

She had a decision to make, and every second that passed increased its importance. Did she believe "Matthias Gruber" or not?

If he was telling the truth, and if his story regarding the events that had taken place inside the Kaminecke Hotel was accurate, a rare window of opportunity was open right in front of them. It represented the chance to reverse the damage that had been done, and to do so almost immediately.

On the other hand, if his story was nothing more than a fiction made up to regain her trust, and he had either murdered the Soviet operative and taken the key or was in league whoever had, trusting him would almost certainly be a lethal mistake. He would lure her into a trap, get her alone in a scenario where the fact that she was armed would become irrelevant.

She would disappear without a trace in West Germany and no one would ever know what had happened to her.

But if Gruber really was a traitor and in league with whoever had killed the Soviet operative, what would he have had to gain by returning to the safe house? He had already vanished without a trace, and by the time Tracie could have mobilized CIA resources and begun any significant search, he would have been long gone, out of West Germany and well on his way to…wherever.

He had come back. That factor was what convinced her.

She dropped her hands and holstered her weapon. "I want my gun back," she said.

"Of course," Gruber answered, the relief plain in his voice.

"And get ready," she said. "We leave in ten minutes."

* * *

Tracie had made her decision and would have to live—or die— with believing her partner. But that didn't mean she was entirely at peace with her choice. Her nerves were as tight as guitar strings and adrenaline hammered through her body as the little Opel Kadett weaved through the nearly deserted streets.

"How long will it take us to get to the safe house?" she said.

Gruber thought for a moment. "Fifteen minutes, give or take. I was focused more on maintaining a visual on the killers' car and on not being made than watching the time, so that's just a rough estimate. Plus, the driver didn't go straight to the house. He made some maneuvers designed to shake a tail."

Tracie's concern spiked. "Do you think they made you?"

"No, I don't. The maneuvers were standard stuff, nothing fancy, and there was still a fair amount of traffic on the roads at the time. I kept my distance. I'm as confident as I can reasonably be that they didn't know I was behind them."

Tracie had told Gruber to drive, not just because he knew the directions, but also because she wanted both hands—and her attention—free in case things started going sideways. Experience had taught her that scenarios had a way of changing dramatically in a matter of seconds. Her primary weapon was once again holstered in a shoulder rig, but she kept her windbreaker unzipped and open, and her right hand lingered near the gun.

"Describe the area adjacent to the safe house. Will we be able to get in undetected?"

"It's suburban, just outside the city. The house is located in a small development, but it's surrounded by trees, quite private. We should be able to access it without too much trouble, especially at this time of night."

Tracie thought hard. Looked at her watch. It was just approaching two a.m. "Okay, here's what we're going to do. We'll park on a side street, out of sight of the safe house but inside the development, close enough so we can access the car quickly. If we're successful in retrieving the key, we're probably going to have to get out in a hurry."

"Agreed," Gruber said. Tracie's first thought was that she hadn't been asking for his approval or concurrence, but rather telling him the way things were going to be. She bit back the reply she wanted to make, though. If she were in Gruber's shoes, she would probably have said the same thing.

"You told me there were two men operating as a team back at the Kaminecke, correct?"

"That's right."

"And how long did you keep their safe house under surveillance before returning to ours?"

"Not long. Twenty minutes. Maybe less. I basically noted their location and then beat feet back to Wuppertal. I knew we would have to move fast."

"So we don't know whether anyone else is inside the house or if it's just the two from the Kaminecke."

"No," he said. "I had to fall pretty far back once we left the city because the traffic lightened up considerably and I was concerned about being made. By the time I felt comfortable driving past the safe house, the men I had been following were already inside and lights were on. Shades were drawn, as you might imagine, and I couldn't see the interior at all."

"Alright, then. Park as close as you can to the safe house without raising suspicion or making us visible from inside the home. When we arrive, we're going to split up. You're going to stay in the shadows and cover the front door. Stop anybody who leaves the house via that exit."

"And you?"

"I'm going to go in through the back and hopefully take them by surprise. If we're lucky, the two you followed will be the only ones inside and they'll be fast asleep by now. If we're *really* lucky, this whole thing will be over in a matter of minutes. We secure the bad guys—whoever they are—take the Amber Room key and disappear. In and out."

"What if there's no back entrance?"

"A safe house with only one escape route? Not likely. I'm more concerned that there will be a third exit, one we don't know about and can't cover." Tracie's adrenaline continued to pound, but she was feeling a little better about Gruber. He wasn't acting like a man with anything to hide, although it was always possible he was just a good actor.

"How much farther?" she said.

"We're almost there."

They sat in silence inside the Opel and moments later, Gruber pulled off the main road and onto a side street. He took a right and then a left, then he killed the headlights and cruised to a stop on the side of the road. They were in a cluster of small, working-class houses carved into the thick German forest.

The homes were located relatively far apart, with groves of ancient trees between each, offering owners the illusion of isolation. Tracie could see why the killers had chosen this neighborhood as the location for their safe house. It was close to Wuppertal, convenient by car, and there was little likelihood of interference from nosy neighbors.

Gruber had parked as far from any homes as he could manage, and now they climbed out of the Opel and closed their doors quietly. The houses she could see were darkened and the neighborhood was still and quiet.

"Follow me," Gruber said, and set off through the trees. They skirted one small back yard and then found themselves crossing a road that looked remarkably similar to the one they had parked on.

"That's it," he whispered, gesturing toward what looked like a two-bedroom bungalow set back from the road. The front yard was weedy and the lawn sparse but overgrown, badly in need of a mowing. The blinds were all drawn, exactly as Gruber had said, but it was easy to see no lights were burning behind the shades.

A vehicle was parked in the gravel driveway and Tracie whispered, "Is that the car you followed?"

Gruber nodded, and Tracie said, "Okay, remember the plan. Stay here and cover the front. Give me time to break in through the rear entrance and secure the occupants. I'll come get you when we're ready to start searching or interrogating. Got it?"

"I got it," he said.

Tracie looked him up and down and prayed she hadn't been wrong about him.

Then she said, "Good luck, Gruber," and began circling the house before he could answer.

12

The yard that had been hacked out of the forest behind the house was tiny and badly in need of care: overgrown, choked with weeds and obviously neglected. Its poor condition was further verification to Tracie that this home was being utilized solely as a safe house. It would be hard to imagine even the laziest of homeowners neglecting his yard this badly.

A three-quarter moon provided just enough light to allow Tracie to navigate the unfamiliar terrain with a reasonable degree of confidence. She hugged the rear wall of the building, ducking under a window—blinds drawn, exactly as they had been in the front of the house—before reaching the rear entrance. Three steps up and she found herself atop the concrete-block landing.

From her jacket pocket Tracie removed her lock picking tools and a pair of surgical gloves. Pulled on the gloves and got down to work, squinting in the moonlight.

The rear door was secured with nothing more than a basic lock built into the tarnished brass knob, a fact that surprised Tracie. She had expected a safe house run by any self-respecting intelligence organization to be more difficult to access.

It shouldn't be this easy, she thought. *I'm missing something.*

She inserted her pick into the lock and felt gingerly for the tumblers. Lock picking had never been her greatest talent, and her skills were more than a little rusty—she tried to recall the last time she had picked a lock and couldn't—but even under these circumstances, this common hardware store door lock should provide little challenge.

What concerned her more than picking the lock was the possibility of tripping an alarm. It wouldn't be an aural alarm like the typical house might have, designed to make a lot of noise and frighten away the prospective burglar. Rather, it would be silent, alerting the occupants to their intruder's presence without disturbing the quiet of the neighborhood and drawing unnecessary attention to the home.

And instead of triggering a phone call to the local police, the alarm would dial the operatives' home base. Depending on how close to Wuppertal their handlers were located, reinforcements might arrive quickly once the alarm was activated.

It was an element of uncertainty that made Tracie uncomfortable. She was used to working alone in a foreign country, had been doing it for more than seven years. But in virtually every previous instance, her ops were based on solid intel and had taken place only after extensive planning and reconnaissance.

Wuppertal was very different. Intel was sketchy, planning had been minimal, and reconnaissance nonexistent. Adding into the mix a potential showdown with the killers' organization—whoever they were—was an uncertainty she wanted very much to avoid.

Which meant they would have to work fast.

She concentrated hard on picking the lock, aware of the time ticking away, aware that by all rights she should already be inside the safe house. This was the most basic of locks, and she was fumbling around with it like a high school kid in the back seat of his parents' car on prom night.

She knew why she was struggling to pick the lock. Her personality was straightforward. No bullshit. Damn the torpedoes, full speed ahead. Lock picking required subtlety, feel, the kind of laid-back approach she could never quite master, no matter how hard she tried.

The very traits that made her such an effective asset in the field—her instructors at The Farm had nicknamed her "Bulldog" years before, a moniker she wore with pride even after graduating to field work—worked against her in any scenario that involved a more nuanced approach.

Still, she had managed to master the basics of lock picking, and there was no reason for her to fail here, despite the darkness and the stress. She stepped back and took her fingers off the tool. It stuck out of the lock, taunting her.

Deep breath. In and out.

After taking a moment to clear her mind, Tracie leaned back down over the knob. She rested her fingers lightly on the lock picking tools and visualized The Farm, the humid summer afternoon she had demonstrated her proficiency to a hard-ass instructor who struck her as more drill sergeant than civilian teacher. The man had fired round after round of live 9mm ammunition over her head while she worked, ears ringing, clock counting down.

She had done it then, she could do it now.

Her fingers began moving slowly, almost imperceptibly, easing the tiny tumblers around the inside of the lock. Seconds later they fell into place.

Tracie breathed a sigh of relief and only now realized she had begun to sweat even in the cool November nighttime air. A sheen of perspiration coated her face, a drip rolling down her forehead. It fell into her eye, blurring her vision, and she blinked.

She packed her lock picking tools away in their pouch and secured the pouch in her pocket.

Then she reached down and turned the knob.

She opened the door, moving slowly, worried about a squeaky hinge alerting the sleeping occupants to her presence. The general condition of the home's exterior was poor, and there was no reason to believe the door would be any better maintained.

To her surprise, though, it swung open quietly.

Tracie stepped into the darkened house, wishing she had access to night vision equipment. With every one of the shades drawn and all the lights off, an inky blackness blanketed the home's interior, turning even a single step forward into a dangerous proposition.

She held her ground, unmoving, waiting for her eyes to adjust to the murk, unsure if they would. She didn't want to use her flashlight yet if she could avoid it, preferring to wait until she had located the sleeping occupants. She would then use it to disorient them.

A minute went by, and then two, and she began to wonder how long it had been since she left Gruber alone in front of the house. Probably no more than seven or eight minutes. Not much time at all. A seasoned operative would hold his ground as instructed.

But Matthias Gruber was an unknown, an X-factor. Depending on his level of experience, it would be a simple thing to become spooked by the dead silence and the uncertainty about what may or may not be happening inside the safe house. A rash move by the man outside was not out of the question.

For that matter, it had been less than an hour since she held him at gunpoint, unsure as to where his real loyalties lay. He had shown decent instincts in following the Soviet operative's killers, but what did she really know about him?

More things to worry about, and now was not the time. She felt her anxiety creeping upward and forced her tightening muscles to relax. *Worry about the things you can control.*

Closing her eyes would have been the best and fastest way to acclimate them to the near-total darkness inside the safe house, but she hadn't dared do that. Two killers were somewhere inside this small dwelling, and they were probably sleeping, but Tracie Tanner was not about to take *that* leap of faith and potentially offer herself up as an easy target.

Finally the bare-bones furnishings of a small kitchen began to resolve themselves—more or less—in front of her. A kitchen table stood off to her right, its outline slightly lighter than the surrounding darkness. A pair of chairs had been snugged up against the table, and across the kitchen Tracie could see what she guessed to be a stove and maybe a dishwasher.

Two doorways stood on the far side of the kitchen. One was off to her left, adjacent to the appliances, the other ahead and to her right, on the far side of the table. It was time to choose one and start clearing the house, locating the room in which the killers were holed up.

She took a hesitant step in the direction of the door next to the appliances, making an educated guess. She thought, based on the appearance of the front of the house, that the door on the left would lead to a living area, and the one on the right would perhaps lead to a hallway, with a bathroom and a couple of bedrooms opening off it.

Her goal was to establish that the front room was empty before exposing her back to it and moving down the hallway where, presumably, her targets lay sleeping.

She took a second step and then flinched at the sound of a shouted challenge coming from the front yard.

Then a gunshot.

And then two more in quick succession.

Then silence.

13

Matthias Gruber's real name was Josh Macklin, and he was no more German than was Tracie Tanner, having grown up outside Columbus, Ohio. For all his faults—and he knew he had plenty—stupidity was not among them. He was well aware he had fucked up in allowing the goddamned Russian operative to murder Klaus Newmann right under his nose and make off with the Amber Room key, and he knew also that it was only a matter of time before he faced a return to Langley in disgrace.

All of which was why he had tried to be on his best behavior with the beautiful redheaded chick, his clumsy come-on back at Hahn Air Base notwithstanding. Even that, he felt, was understandable. She was beautiful and sexy and what guy wouldn't take a shot at getting in her pants?

But she had made it clear she was all business, and Josh felt he had done a damned good job since then of focusing on work. Under the circumstances, he thought, that was probably for the best. The key was worth hundreds of millions of dollars, after all, and this sexy redhead represented his best chance—probably his *only* chance—at getting it back and maybe salvaging his career.

So when she told him to cover the front of the house while she went inside and did the heavy lifting—that wasn't how she had phrased it, but they had both known that was what she meant—he didn't even hesitate. He swallowed his pride and nodded firmly and resolved to be the best goddamned second-fiddle-slash-use-less-appendage in history.

He eased behind a tree and waited, certain "Fiona Quinn" would break into the house successfully, and equally   certain she would then disarm the occupants and call him inside to initiate a search for the key. She exuded competence and seemed like the type of person who was accustomed to getting what she wanted.

The only question in his mind was how long it would take. He left his weapon holstered but accessible and concentrated his attention on the closed front door. The near-total silence of the sleeping neighborhood gave him the willies, and he almost wished a car would drive by, just to break the monotony.

He chewed on a fingernail. It was a nasty habit, and one he knew he should break, but was something he had been doing under stress since he was a boy. He would have to learn to—

The front door swung open, slowly and silently.

The motion caught him by surprise even though it was exactly what he had been watching for. He squinted, wishing for stronger moonlight, waiting to see who was going to exit the house.

It seemed too soon for Fiona to have broken in and secured the occupants, no matter how competent she was.

He nearly stepped out from behind the tree to meet her but held his position.

And it was a good thing he did. Because it wasn't Fiona who stepped outside.

It was a man. It was almost certainly one of the assassins Josh had followed here from the Kaminecke Hotel. Both of those men had been tall, wearing overcoats and hats pulled low over their faces, so it was impossible to be sure in the darkness.

The man stepped onto the front landing and Josh slipped his weapon from its holster. The man took one step forward, still holding the door open with his left hand, and Josh eased out from behind the tree.

Raised his gun.

Said, "Stop right there," in German. "Don't move!"

The man moved. He released the door with his left hand.

Raised his right and squeezed off a shot. The gun barked and fire belched from the end of the barrel and a slug thudded into the tree next to Josh, chipping off bark and scattering slivers and wood fragments into his face.

Josh reacted instinctively, dropping into a crouch and returning fire. He squeezed the trigger once and the man staggered backward. Twice, and the man went down, crumpling to the landing as the front door swayed in the light nighttime breeze.

Josh's grip on his weapon had been steady and solid, but now his hands began to shake as the adrenaline—and shock—slammed through his body. He remained in his stance, waiting for the second man to come through the door, waiting for the sound of gunshots from inside the house, waiting for...whatever came next.

But nothing came next.

Silence dropped back over the West German countryside like a blanket fluttering to the ground. Josh counted to twenty and when nothing happened, he counted again to twenty. Then he began to edge forward.

He had to ensure the man on the landing was no longer a threat.

Had to check on his partner.

Had to avoid getting shot.

He angled toward the landing from the side, trying to prevent the man from getting a clear shot at him in the unlikely event he was playing possum. Josh's gut told him it wasn't the case, though. The guy wasn't playing possum, probably wasn't even breathing. The way he had dropped after being struck by the slug—silent and immediate and final—told Josh the man was already dead and would never again be a threat to anyone.

Still, he wasn't taking any chances. He eased up the steps, keeping his weapon trained on the motionless man. The man had dropped his weapon when he fell and it lay just inches from his hand, and Josh kicked it out of reach. It skittered across the landing and fell into the damp grass with a thud.

He leaned over the downed man and froze in sudden surprise. He didn't know what he had been expecting to see, but this was not it. Covert operatives on these types of missions tended to be young, in their twenties and, occasionally, thirties. This man was not even close to the same age as Josh.

He was older. Much older. Maybe in his sixties.

Josh swallowed his surprise and knelt. Checked for a pulse with his left hand while keeping his weapon trained on the man with his right.

By now he knew it wasn't necessary. The man was still and motionless as a stone.

And he was right. There was no pulse.

The man was dead.

14

November 15, 1987
2:05 a.m.
Wuppertal, Federal Republic of Germany

The shots rang out and Tracie froze, processing the information. The first one was loud, reverberating through the house like a thunderclap. The two answering shots were less so, and clearly came from the front yard, where she had left Gruber stationed.

Then she moved, hustling through the door on the left and into the small safe house's living area. It was clear what must have happened: the assassins had not been asleep after all. Or maybe they had been sleeping but were awakened by exactly the kind of security system Tracie had feared might be present.

Either way, one or both of the men had moved silently and without benefit of lighting, up the hallway and to the front door even as Tracie was breaking into the house via the rear entrance. They had opened the door and been immediately challenged by Gruber, and a gun battle had broken out.

This changed everything.

Tracie had to back up Gruber, assuming he was even still alive. The silence following the first flurry of gunshots meant that in all likelihood the confrontation was over.

The only question was who had won?

The living room was just as dark as the kitchen had been, but with her eyes now adjusted—relatively speaking—to the lack of light she had no trouble skirting a small coffee table and couch on her way to the picture window. The front door hung open but for now she ignored it. If Gruber was lying dead in the yard, the door may well have been left ajar by his killer intentionally, as a means to lure the dead man's partner into a trap.

She eased the blinds back a couple of inches and peered out the window.

For a moment she could see nothing. No Gruber, no nameless operatives. The yard appeared empty, the operatives' car still parked in the driveway. Then a slight movement in her peripheral vision caught her attention and Tracie glanced to the right, to the front landing.

And there was Gruber. His attention was directed downward as he checked another man for a pulse.

He had taken out one of the operatives, but where was the other?

She scanned the yard again, searching for any sign of the second man, but saw nothing. If both men had exited the front door, one of them was now gone.

She slipped across the room, her attention focused on the darkened hallway. If the second operative hadn't gone out the front door with the first, he might appear in that entry at any moment, armed and out for blood.

Tracie reached the front door and flattened herself against the interior wall, concerned about getting shot by a jumpy Matthias Gruber. She whispered, "Gruber, it's Quinn. Status?"

To his credit, the CIA man only hesitated for a second, then he responded. "I'm unharmed. This one is dead."

"What about the second man?"

"I don't know. I never saw the second man. He didn't come out this door."

"Okay," she whispered. "If you're certain this one's dead, remove his weapons and then fall back to the tree line. Watch for the second guy, but remember: if at all possible, we need him alive. I'm going to flush him out if he's still here, so be ready."

"Are you sure that's a good idea? If the gunfire woke up any of the neighbors, the police will be here within minutes."

"We need that key," she said. "And if there's any chance the second operative is here, he's our only living connection to the key, so we're not leaving without him."

She hadn't really answered the question because she wasn't at all sure it *was* a good idea. But it had to be done, so she would do it.

She crossed in front of the door, easing it closed as she passed. If the second operative was still inside this house, there was nothing to be gained by making things easy for him.

Then she hugged the wall until reaching the hallway entrance. Dropped to her knees. Eased her head around the corner, her weapon clutched in two hands and ready to fire.

Empty.

Three doors lined the hallway, all of them closed. One was on the right side, past the kitchen, and two were on the left. She thought carefully about the size of the kitchen relative to the home's layout. Took an educated guess that the door on that side probably opened onto a bedroom.

That would mean one of the doors on the left side would be to a bathroom and the other probably a second bedroom. The bathroom would likely be centrally located, which meant it would be the first door to the left.

It would have to be cleared first. There was no way in the world Tracie was going to expose her back to that door without ensuring nobody with a gun was standing behind it, ready to put two slugs into her after she passed by.

She rose to a crouch and double-timed to the door. Said something resembling a quick prayer—*Watch my back, please*—and then turned the knob and pushed through the door, doing her best to remain silent but knowing speed was essential. The element of surprise would be on her side, but would evaporate quickly.

Her guess had been right. It was a bathroom. She scanned it quickly, eyes moving left to right, Glock following her eyes. Nobody here.

A narrow door on the left indicated a linen closet. It didn't look big enough to hide a person but she checked it anyway.

Empty.

She checked behind a partially drawn shower curtain.

Empty.

She slipped out of the bathroom and closed the door quietly behind her. Only two doors remained, and if the second operative was still here, whether she lived or died might well depend upon which door she chose next. The man could be standing behind either.

She chose the door on the left for no particular reason and repeated the entry she had just made into the bathroom—quick and silent, gun up and ready.

The room was empty. Not just of people, but of anything. Not a single stick of furniture had been placed inside it. Two closets, the doors located side by side along the left wall, were the only potential hiding places. She cleared them in a matter of seconds and then moved quickly back to the hallway to face the final closed door.

The second operative had to be inside this room. If Gruber was right—and it was hard to imagine even the most inept of field operatives missing one of two men walking out a door just before shooting one of them—the only other way out of the house would have been through the kitchen door, and Tracie had maintained a direct line of sight to the kitchen from the time the gunfire broke out.

She breathed deeply.

Grasped the knob and turned.

Shoved the door open and flattened herself against the wall, waiting for a barrage of gunfire that never came.

A second passed, and then two, and the heavy silence lingered, unbroken.

She turned the corner and entered the room, leading with her gun, ready to shoot at the first sign of a threat.

Then she relaxed. There *was* no threat.

The second man was gone.

A flashing beacon, similar to the bubble light atop a 1960s police car, splashed the room in migraine-inducing bursts of red light. *Dammit,* Tracie thought. *This is what I was afraid of. They were onto us the minute I broke into the house, maybe the minute we walked onto the property.*

In the rear corner of the room, adjacent to the exterior wall, stood an open trap door. It had been built into the floor, and a ladder with iron rungs descended from the door straight down into a tunnel.

She moved cautiously across the room and covered the trap door with her weapon but there was no reason to do so. The second man—undoubtedly with the Amber Room key securely in his possession—had utilized the tunnel to exit the house, probably straight to a waiting vehicle somewhere else in the neighborhood.

The first guy distracted us so the second guy could escape, Tracie thought wonderingly. *He gave up his life to ensure we didn't get the key. That's taking fanaticism to a whole new level. What in the holy hell is going on here?*

15

November 15, 1987
7:10 a.m.
CIA safe house
Wuppertal, Federal Republic of Germany

The television set in the corner was tuned, volume lowered, to one of the local Wuppertal stations. The morning news had just started, and Tracie and Gruber sat side-by-side, sipping coffee and waiting to see how the shooting death of an elderly man just outside city limits in the wee hours of the morning would be reported.

After discovering the trap door, Tracie had considered descending the iron ladder and following the tunnel, but after a brief internal debate, had decided against it. It was highly unlikely the tunnel would be longer than a couple hundred feet. If a second vehicle had been parked at its exit point—and Tracie had no doubt that was the case—the second assassin would be long gone by the time she made her way to the end.

So she had shaken her head angrily and reversed course, backtracking through the house and stepping through the front door to the faraway sound of screaming sirens. They were still a fair distance away but were getting noticeably louder by the second, and Tracie had no doubt where they were headed.

To his credit, Gruber had held his ground despite the imminent arrival of the police, holding his weapon at the ready and scanning the area in front of the safe house for threats. Protecting her back.

Tracie began to think maybe the man's incompetence had been overstated a bit by Stallings.

"Did you relieve the dead guy of his weapons?" she asked, stepping over the corpse and pausing at the edge of the landing.

"Yes," Gruber said. "All he had on him was the one pistol."

"Then it's time to go. Come on." Tracie bounded down the steps and sprinted across the overgrown front lawn, wishing she had time to search the safe house, or at least the car sitting in the driveway, but knowing that to stick around even one minute longer would be inviting disaster.

They leapt into the Opel, Gruber once again behind the wheel. This time, it was not because Tracie didn't trust him, but because he knew the area much better than she. He hit the gas hard, wisely avoiding screeching his tires but driving aggressively and wasting little time. They exited the neighborhood and turned left, circling west of Wuppertal to avoid encountering any police vehicles before returning to the CIA safe house.

They arrived inside of twenty minutes, Gruber driving slowly and cautiously once they were safely outside the dead man's neighborhood. The exhausted pair held an abbreviated debriefing session at the tiny kitchen table, Tracie not wanting to wait until after they slept. The more time passed, the greater the chance for a critical detail to be forgotten.

Following a few hours of sleep, Tracie rose at seven a.m. to find Gruber already up and brewing coffee. She poured a cup and offered a bleary-eyed nod to her temporary partner, taking a seat in front of the television.

The "murder" was the lead story.

The anchor, a middle-aged blond man with a cowlick and a no-nonsense demeanor, stared into the camera and waited a moment before speaking. Drawing out the moment, Tracie assumed.

Then he said, *"A Wuppertal man was killed in the overnight hours in a quiet neighborhood located on the western edge of the city. Helmut Wengler, sixty-six, was shot to death in what local police are calling a burglary gone wrong. The victim died on his front steps after confronting at least one intruder shortly after two a.m."*

A photo of the shooting victim appeared in the upper right

corner of the screen. The image seemed barely larger than a postage stamp on the twelve-inch black-and-white television, and Tracie asked, "Is that the guy?"

Gruber shrugged. "I guess. Kind of hard to tell."

"That's what I thought," she said, and then returned her attention to the report.

"Wengler, a widower who lived alone, was described by neighbors as friendly but quiet, a nice man who kept to himself but was quick to offer a smile and a wave. With little evidence left at the scene, authorities are asking anyone living in the neighborhood who might have seen or heard anything to please come forward. Contact the Wuppertal Police Department at…"

Tracie tuned out the anchorman as he moved on to another story. She looked quizzically at Gruber. "Anything strike you as odd about that story?"

"Do I have to pick one item? The whole thing was odd."

"Yes it was," Tracie said.

"The neighbors calling Wengler friendly? What was that about? We know the place was being used as a safe house, which means even if the guy spent some time there, he wasn't standing on his front step waving at people on their way home from work and handing out candy to the neighborhood kids."

She chuckled. "That's human nature," she said. "People get the opportunity to become part of a big news story, and they can't pass it up. They know the reporter doesn't want to hear that they've never seen the guy before, so they give him what he wants. They tell him the same thing they've seen on news reports dozens of times: 'the victim was friendly but quiet.'"

"But beyond that, there's plenty the locals aren't saying. Even the dimmest of dim-bulb investigators would have known thirty seconds after entering the house that the killing wasn't a burglary gone wrong. How many people have a trap door in their bedroom leading to an underground escape tunnel?"

"It's pretty common in the states for the police to keep certain details of a crime to themselves, and to avoid giving anything too interesting to the reporters. I'm sure they do the same thing in West Germany." Gruber sipped his coffee and shrugged.

"Undoubtedly," Tracie said. "And that may very well be the case here. But something else the anchor said causes me concern. Any idea what it might be?"

Gruber shrugged again. It was obvious he hated admitting he might have missed something. Finally he sighed deeply and said, "What?"

"If the story is being reported accurately—admittedly a questionable premise, especially where television news is concerned—the cops are practically coming out and telling the locals to forget about the case ever being solved."

"I don't follow."

"The police spokesman told the reporters there was 'little evidence found at the scene.'"

"So? I would think that's good news for us, since we were there just ahead of them."

"It is good for us. But it also strikes me as incongruous."

"How so?"

"Think about it. The killing is only a few hours old. The body is practically still warm, and the investigation is in its earliest stages. It should be hours yet, maybe even days, before the police know what sort of evidence they may or may not have. Short of finding a signed confession at the scene that included the killer's name and address, the investigators would never expect to have anything significant this soon."

Tracie sipped her coffee and gazed over the top of the mug at Gruber. "You didn't leave a signed confession at the scene, did you?"

He laughed and said, "I most certainly did not."

She was starting to like him. "Just making sure. But you see my point? The official line should be that the investigation is continuing, and the authorities will vigorously pursue every lead, and blah, blah, blah. But here, the cops are throwing in the towel, telling people to forget it. There's no evidence."

"I see what you mean," Gruber said. "It's like they're setting people up to accept that this crime will never be solved."

"That's how it struck me."

"But why would they do that? You said yourself it's very early in the investigation. How would they know already that the murder will go unsolved, and even if they do, why tell the community that?"

"All good questions."

"Thank you. Why do I feel you have a theory?"

She smiled. "Well, it's always possible the spokesperson misspoke or was misquoted. But I didn't get the impression that was the case. I got the impression the comment was intentional, purposeful. That there was meaning behind it."

"So does that mean you *do* have a theory?"

Tracie nodded as her smile faded away. "I do."

"Well?" He spread his hands in anticipation. "Are you going to enlighten me?"

She stared in his direction, not seeing him.

Thinking.

Picturing a dead man at least double the age of a typical field operative.

Picturing a team of assassins that had appeared virtually out of thin air to kill the Soviet operative and recover the Amber Room key.

Picturing that team showing up in Wuppertal almost immediately after Klaus Newmann's disappearance, beating even Tracie—who had been dispatched by the CIA director himself, with access to a private Gulfstream G4—to the punch.

Picturing a safe house that was being described to the local media as just another suburban West German home in a quiet neighborhood.

Adding it all up.

"No," she said, shaking her head and taking another sip of coffee. She met his eyes and then looked away. "Not at the moment. I need to think this through."

16

November 15, 1987
10:30 a.m.
CIA safe house
Wuppertal, Federal Republic of Germany

"Somebody beat us to the Soviet operative. He's dead and the key is gone." Tracie held the secure satellite phone to her ear and winced, waiting for the inevitable angry explosion from CIA Director Aaron Stallings.

But to her surprise, there was no explosion. No anger. Nothing. Only a long silence through the earpiece as the old spymaster digested her statement.

"Explain," Stallings finally said.

Tracie filled the director in on the timeline of events, starting with her arrival in Wuppertal and ending with the shootout at the suburban safe house that had resulted in one man dead and the Amber Room key disappearing through an underground tunnel.

"Theories?" Stallings said after she had finished. "You're on the ground there. Who do you think has the Amber Room key now?"

"Let's start with Newmann's disappearance," she said. "Gruber claims to have kept both the old Nazi, *and* the Soviet operative, under pretty tight surveillance. He says there's no way he would have missed another operative hanging around."

"In case you hadn't noticed," Stallings said drily, "Gruber's an idiot. His track record is poor and he's going to be out of a job the minute I can get him back to Langley."

"I'm not sure he's as incompetent as you think," she said. "He's handled himself pretty well since I arrived in West Germany."

"Is that so? And that opinion's based on your lengthy track record of handling field operatives?"

"That opinion is based on working with the man and seeing his decision-making skills up close, under pressure." Tracie felt her anger rising and tamped down on her emotions. It wasn't easy. Dealing with Aaron Stallings was always problematic, but doing so under the current circumstances, with not one but two botched operations under her belt in the last twelve hours, felt nearly impossible.

"Anyway," she said, breathing deeply and continuing, "my point is that unless another country's intelligence service already had operatives here well before Newmann's disappearance, it would have been impossible to transport them to Wuppertal, plan and execute the operation against the Soviet, find a safe house and dig an escape tunnel. There just would not have been time."

Stallings was silent and Tracie said, "Sir, how confident are you that no other intelligence services besides the KGB are aware of Newmann and the existence of the key and the treasure?

"I *was* extremely confident, right up until the last few days. But I didn't realize the Soviets knew about it, either. And if the Soviets knew, or found out somehow, it's entirely possible other countries have become aware as well."

Stallings fell silent, and it was clear to Tracie this intelligence lapse was wearing on him.

"Let's face it," he finally continued. "My confidence that we were the only ones with knowledge of the Amber Room key was based on nothing more than the knowledge that Klaus Newmann had had access to this trove of riches for four decades and no one had ever attempted to relieve him of it. Even I wasn't around when Phoenix was formed, and when all this intel was gathered and archived."

"Sir, what if your assumption was correct? What if the Soviets learned about Phoenix through a security leak within the organization itself, and nobody else knows? What if it wasn't some mysterious third country's intelligence service running the op against the Soviet?"

"What are you saying?"

"I think you know what I'm saying. I think you've already thought of it."

"Don't play games with me, Tanner. Time is ticking. Spill it. I want to hear your thoughts. Now."

"Sir, I think the most likely possibility is that Newmann's own organization is once again in possession of the key."

"You think this was Phoenix?"

"I think it's the only realistic possibility."

"And why do you believe that, Tanner?"

"Think about it, sir. This Phoenix group has been preparing for the last forty years for the return to power of their precious Nazi party. No matter how much they may have trusted Newmann, it's hard to imagine they would have left *everything* in his hands, with no control and no backup. What if he got cold feet? What if he was killed in an accident? Most importantly, what if he wasn't quite the dedicated Nazi that Hitler thought he was and he got the bright idea to take the key and disappear, wait until the time was right and then access the three hundred million dollars for himself?"

Stallings considered Tracie's words. "Let me see if I have this straight. You're saying that even though Phoenix would have had plans in place for an order of succession in the event of Newmann's death, the group would also have taken steps to ensure Newmann stayed loyal to the cause, especially in the face of hundreds of millions of dollars in temptation."

"Well, not necessarily so much to ensure he stayed loyal, but to learn if he was becoming *dis*loyal, and to learn it in enough time to do something about it. And over the last few weeks—with Hitler's return finally on the horizon—it would only have made sense for Phoenix to keep a close eye on their keymaster."

"Newmann would have been under surveillance not just by us and the Soviets, but by his own organization as well," Stallings muttered, thinking out loud. "Christ, how many people were following this guy?"

Tracie ignored the last comment and pushed her point. "It makes sense, don't you think?"

"Based on what we know, it does," Stallings conceded.

"And if it *was* a member of Phoenix keeping tabs on their own man, it would most likely have seemed like business as usual, both to Gruber and to the Soviets. That would explain it escaping Gruber's attention."

"So would incompetence."

Again Tracie ignored her boss's caustic criticism and said, "It would explain their ability to get a team in place in Wuppertal in enough time to run an op against the Soviet. They didn't have to fly anyone here and set up shop because they were *already here*. And it would also explain the existence of a safe house close by, complete with underground escape tunnel. It all fits," she said. "And there are other factors that point to this being a Phoenix operation."

"Such as?"

"The guy Gruber shot was old, sir. He was much older than the typical field operative. He was easily in his sixties, roughly the same age as Klaus Newmann."

"Another old Nazi."

"Exactly. And there were a number of mistakes made that seasoned operatives simply would not make."

"Give me an example."

"The most obvious example would be the fact that the door to the Soviet's room in the Kaminecke Hotel was left ajar after they killed him. The latch was sticky, and it didn't catch properly. But the killers were in such a hurry to get out of the hotel with their prize that they didn't take the time to ensure they covered their tracks in even that most basic manner."

"Mistakes always happen, Tanner, you know that."

"Agreed. But it stretches credulity to the breaking point to think an experienced operative would make that kind of mistake. Picture an old Nazi soldier, though, someone committed to a cause but untrained in covert ops, and it becomes much easier to imagine that sort of occurrence happening."

"Hmph." Even through the less-than-ideal satellite connection, Stallings's reluctance to accept Tracie's theory came through loud and clear. But the fact that the CIA chief hadn't dismissed it out of hand by now meant that at the very least, he considered it a possibility.

He cleared his throat and said, "I don't know, Tanner. One

geezer tailing another geezer? And killing a trained Soviet field operative?"

"You know as well as I do, sir, how critical the element of surprise is in an operation like the one that went down at the Kaminecke Hotel. Think about it. The Soviet was drunk and he was expecting a hooker to knock on his door, not two men with guns. In that circumstance, it's not difficult to picture Phoenix successfully retrieving the key."

"Hmph." This time Stallings seemed less critical and more considering.

"And as I said before, sir, this also explains everything else. There's something that's bothering me, though."

"Go on."

"The way the media is reporting the shooting at the Phoenix safe house—"

"Assuming it even *is* Phoenix."

"Granted. Assuming it is Phoenix's safe house. But the way it's being covered suggests a certain…lack of motivation…of local law enforcement in investigating the murder of one of their citizens."

"What are you getting at?"

"It's almost as though someone in the Wuppertal Police Department is trying to divert attention away from all of the oddities surrounding what happened last night. And there were plenty of them."

"Meaning?"

"Meaning it looks to me like someone in a position of authority in the Wuppertal PD is involved."

"A Phoenix member, covering it up."

"That's my suspicion, but I'll admit, I don't have a lot to base that opinion on. Mostly it's just a gut feeling. I get the impression this Phoenix group might be bigger than we realize."

"It would only make sense. If Phoenix is serious about returning the Nazi Party to prominence in Germany and the world, they're going to need a lot more than just a handful of aging fanatics. They need younger people ready to step up and do the dirty work. And what better place to have contacts than in the police force?"

Tracie felt a chill as she considered the implications of her theory. If Phoenix could establish a foothold in the Wuppertal

Police Department, had they done the same thing in other depart-
ments as well? If so, how many?

Just how big was this plot?

Tracie cleared her throat. "Given what we've learned so far, sir,
I have a question for you."

"Go ahead."

"Why don't we just stake out the hiding place and wait for
whoever has the key—whether Phoenix or someone else—to try
to extract the Amber Room panels? After all, the key is worthless
without the treasure."

"Because it's been nearly a half-century since anyone knew for
certain the Amber Room's location, Tanner. I told you before, this
Nazi conspiracy began long before even I was doing fieldwork, and
I've been around a long time. We're basing everything on the very
occasional surveillance of an old Nazi soldier-turned-industrialist.
If we stake out the wrong location, we'll be stuck with our thumbs
up our asses while the Amber Room panels are loaded up on trucks
in some other location and driven away into the night."

Tracie considered the point. "Then why not keep the remaining
members of Phoenix under surveillance? If my theory is right, and
they've regained possession of the key, one of them will lead us
right to the Amber Room, and soon."

"For the very reason we just discussed, Tanner. I'm not convinced
we've identified all the players. If Phoenix is as big as you seem to
think it is—and I don't necessarily disagree with your assessment,
by the way—it's entirely possible that while we were watching the
members we know about, someone else would unlock the storage
facility and remove the treasure right out from under our noses,
whether it's where we believe it is or somewhere else."

Tracie nodded. She had never even heard of Phoenix until
forty-eight hours ago, but now the potential size and scope of the
group worried her.

"What do you want me to do, sir? Where do we go from here?"

"We can't take any chances. If there's any possibility at all that
Phoenix will be able to smuggle that treasure out of Wuppertal and
use it to fund a Nazi resurgence in Europe or South America, we
have no choice. We have to eliminate the organization's viability,
cut the head off the monster so that all the funding in the world
won't make a damn bit of difference."

"Meaning?" She thought she knew where this conversation was headed and she didn't like it.

"Remember before you left D.C., I told you the only way a Nazi party could gain traction in today's world would be through the leadership—even if it was largely symbolic—of Der Führer himself?"

"Of course." Tracie's stomach was doing flip-flops and she felt suddenly queasy.

"We have to ensure that can't happen."

"And how will we do that?"

"We need to cut off the head of the snake, even if it's a figurehead."

Tracie closed her eyes. "And by 'we' you mean…"

"That's right. You're going to eliminate Adolph Hitler."

17

Tracie realized she had been holding her breath, and now she exhaled slowly. "*I'm* going to assassinate Adolph Hitler, forty-some-odd years after the rest of the world thinks he committed suicide in a Berlin bunker?"

"That's right. Don't sound so skeptical, Tanner. The man is in his nineties by now. It should be a piece of cake."

She surprised herself by chuckling. "A piece of cake. Apparently my definition of that expression differs a little from yours."

"Give me a break, Tanner," Stallings said. She pictured him shrugging nonchalantly. "You get into his compound, you put a couple of slugs in his skull, you fly home. Simple."

"If it's so simple, why wasn't that the original plan? Why bother with the Amber Room key if you don't think the Nazis can mount a successful return without their Dear Führer?"

"Do you seriously need to ask that question, Tanner? Jesus, for such a sharp operative, you really can be dense at times."

"Enlighten me."

"What part of 'three hundred million dollars' do you not understand? Sure, we want to cut this Nazi resurgence off before it can get started, and that is the primary goal of this mission. But if you don't recognize the significance of nearly a third of a billion dollars making its way into the pockets of a potentially dangerous faction, I'm not sure there's any way I can explain it to you."

"In other words, you want to recover the Amber Room so you can keep the treasure—and thus the money—for the United States."

"In a way. I've already explained the danger of allowing that sort of influx of liquidity to replenish the Soviets' treasury. And none of this is your concern, anyway. I've only gotten into it with you so you understand exactly what's at stake. But your focus must now be on ridding the world of Adolph Hitler, once and for all."

"When do I leave for Argentina?" Further discussion would be pointless. Aaron Stallings had made up his mind and there would be no changing it, and there would certainly be no declining the mission.

"You're not going to Argentina."

"Isn't that where you said Hitler's compound was located?"

"Yes. That's where it *was* located. But we have received credible intel that says he's been moved."

"Credible intel."

"That's right."

"And where is he?"

"West Germany. Not far from your current location."

"And you're just telling me this now?"

"It's only become relevant to your assignment now."

"You didn't think it was relevant to my assignment before to know that the once and future leader of the Nazi Party had been relocated here? You didn't consider it an indication of how close Phoenix feels they are to setting their plans in motion? You didn't think—"

"That's enough, Tanner. You're getting dangerously close to insubordination. Again. You've been down this road before and I think we both know how it will turn out if you continue."

"Excuse me, Sir, but how was I supposed to do my job without having access to all of the intel?"

"The proximity of Hitler to Wuppertal was irrelevant to your assignment, which was to retrieve the Amber Room key from the Soviet operative. It is only due to your failure at completing that assignment that this new mission has become necessary."

"But, Sir, the fact that Adolph Hitler has been moved here has all kinds of ramifications. It lends real credence to the notion that Phoenix itself was behind the assassination of the Soviet operative and the retrieval of the key. It lends credence also to the theory that someone in the Wuppertal Police Department—maybe more than just one member, maybe a *lot* more—is in league with the group and is actively working toward fulfilling their goals. Hell, it makes me think Phoenix may not just consist of a handful of aging Nazi soldiers. It makes me believe those elderly zealots might be just the tip of the iceberg. Who knows how big this group might actually be, or how many members they might have?"

"Are you done, Tanner? Finished ranting yet?"

She opened her mouth to tell him…what?

She had already registered her outrage and it had gotten her nowhere. The truth was, she couldn't even really claim to be surprised by Aaron Stallings's lack of transparency regarding her mission. This wasn't the first time she had been misled by the CIA chief and, she had to admit to herself, it would likely not be the last. He was a master manipulator, a man with decades of experience moving pieces around his own personal international intelligence chessboard, and nothing she could say at this moment, over a secure satellite connection, would change the current situation.

So she closed her mouth, forced herself to step back from the edge and cool down. The silence on the line told her Stallings knew exactly what she was working through and was only too happy to wait while she did so.

"Yes, I'm finished," she finally said. "For now."

"Good. Because the clock is ticking, and as lovely as our little chat has been, we're no closer to stopping Phoenix now than we were before your call. Hell, we're no closer than we were before you left Washington. You have your assignment. I suggest you get started on it."

He gave her the precise location of the Phoenix compound—it was less than ten miles from Wuppertal—and then said, "Maybe the next time we talk, you'll be able to tell me you were actually successful."

Tracie's anger returned in an instant. She started to tell the

CIA director what he could do with his little digs and insults, but it was too late.

The line was dead.

Stallings was gone.

18

November 18, 1987
2:30 p.m.
Langenberg, Federal Republic of Germany

Tracie stood just inside the tree line, waiting. The road leading to the Phoenix compound—where the elderly Adolph Hitler supposedly now resided, poised to lead a Nazi resurgence—was narrow, quiet, barely wide enough to accommodate two cars passing in opposite directions. The compound had been constructed in a remote section of wilderness, hacked out of the forest miles away from civilization in any direction.

The location made sense as a base for neo-Nazi activity, but it worked to Tracie's advantage as well. Because for her plan to have any chance of succeeding there would have to be no witnesses to what was going to happen next.

Despite Aaron Stallings's insistence she move against Hitler immediately, she had taken two full days and part of a third to accomplish at least a modicum of surveillance. Although accustomed by now to undertaking assignments with little preplanning and even less backup—it was an unfortunate function of her role as the CIA director's one-person black ops team—she knew she would need every last insight she could muster into Phoenix's operation if she expected to have any chance of completing her mission.

Any chance of surviving.

So following the frustration of her conversation with Stallings two and a half days ago, she rounded up Gruber and some supplies and they set off for the Phoenix compound, maintaining as close to round-the-clock surveillance as two operatives could reasonably muster.

Now, she checked her watch and fidgeted, trying to force herself to stay calm. The truck she was waiting for should have been here by now. Maybe it wasn't scheduled to come today. It had rolled past this very spot en route to the compound each of the last two days at exactly this time, but there was no reason to feel confident it was an everyday thing.

Maybe the delivery truck skipped every third day.

Maybe deliveries came at a different time every third day.

There was no way to know, and this was one of the many reasons Tracie was resentful of Aaron Stallings and angry he had put her in such an untenable position. He had known all along that Hitler was in West Germany, had undoubtedly known since well before he recruited her for this op. But instead of sending Gruber here—or even a full team—to conduct surveillance in anticipation of an op against the old Nazi, he had waited and withheld critical information from her for reasons known only to himself.

And then Tracie had to deal with the fallout.

It was immoral and it was wrong, and one of these days it might just cost her life.

She waited and fumed and checked her watch, trying to develop an alternative plan she could implement on the spur of the moment in case the driver didn't show. She would give it another thirty minutes, and if the delivery truck hadn't rolled through by then, would move to Plan B.

Assuming she could come up with a Plan B.

She breathed deeply, trying to control her anger. Checked her watch again. It was less than ninety seconds since the last time she looked.

Then she heard it: the rumble of a truck approaching in the distance. The driver downshifted as his vehicle climbed a relatively steep incline, the engine whining and complaining.

Hopefully this was the truck she was waiting for. Over the last three days she had discovered that very few vehicles traveled this desolate stretch of road unless they were destined for the Phoenix compound, so she liked her odds. One way or the other, though, she would know in a few seconds.

A vehicle rounded a corner in the distance and she squinted against the brightness of the midday sun. The truck was big and boxy and she felt her adrenaline ramp up. This was the it.

She had edged out of the underbrush at the sound of the engine, and now Tracie knelt behind the front of the Opel, as if inspecting a damaged tire. She waited for the delivery truck to get close enough for the driver to see that that a young woman was stranded at the side of the road, but not so close he would have the option of continuing past if chivalry was dead in his world.

She counted down, pretending not to notice the oncoming vehicle. At what she hoped was the right moment she lifted her head as if startled. Then she stood, brushing dirt and road dust off her bare legs, plainly visible to the driver under her short skirt. Then she walked out into the middle of the road, waving her hands urgently in an appeal for help.

He had no choice, really, unless he wanted to run her down and keep going. Tracie had left the car angled out into the road as far as she dared, and now she used it and her body as a barrier, leaving nowhere for the driver to go.

He had already begun slowing, easing off the gas at the approximate moment he would have been able to see that the motorist experiencing roadside difficulties was a pretty young woman. Now air brakes hissed and squealed, and the brown-and-green delivery truck ground to a stop in the middle of the road.

The driver left the diesel engine idling and stepped down from the cab. He offered his best "I'm here to help" smile, but Tracie noticed he couldn't quite resist running his eyes up and down her body.

"Car trouble?" he asked by way of introduction.

"Yes," Tracie answered. "It just died on me. I don't know what could be wrong." Later, it would be important to speak the language like a native, to fit in if at all possible, but at the moment it didn't really matter whether the man recognized her as a foreigner or not. Still, he didn't seem to, and that pleased her.

"What seems to be the problem?" He walked toward Tracie,

still paying much more attention to her body than to her vehicle. He failed to notice Matthias Gruber step out of the woods on the far side of the road.

Gruber used the bulk of the driver's truck to shield himself from view for as long as he could, and then he crossed the road behind the man, moving quickly but quietly, and the man never saw him coming. Gruber placed his weapon against the side of the driver's head and said, "Don't move. Stay completely still if you want to live."

"What is this about?" the driver said, but seemed to take his warning very seriously. He froze in place and moved nothing but his jaw, and even that, only enough to speak.

"You are going to take a ride with me," Gruber said. "Spend a little time out of sight. Think of it as a short vacation. You'll sleep, eat, maybe watch a little television. In a day or so you will go back to work and will never see either of us again."

"I don't carry much money, but you are welcome to what I have," the man said. "Please take it and go." It was as if he hadn't heard a word Gruber said. Sweat had broken out along the driver's forehead under his *Koenig Freight Company* ball cap.

"You're not listening," Gruber said. He snugged the pistol's barrel up against the man's head and said, "Take off your shirt and cap."

"What?"

"You heard me. Do it."

Tracie looked worriedly along the road in both directions. This was taking too long. If a car came along—any car, it didn't have to be a police vehicle—things could go sideways in a hurry.

The driver looked momentarily angry, then perplexed, and then finally resigned. He unbuttoned his brown work shirt and reached back to hand it to Gruber.

"No," the operative said. He gestured with his gun at Tracie. "Give it to her."

"I do not under—"

"DO IT!"

The driver cringed. He was shaking now, confused but clearly certain he was about to die. He handed the shirt to Tracie.

"Now the cap," Gruber said. This time there was no hesitation.

The driver snatched it off his head and handed it to Tracie.

"Now, walk over to the edge of the forest."

"Please, you do not need to—"

"Shut up and walk."

"I don't want to die."

"You are going to die in the next three seconds if you do not do as you are told."

The man's shoulders slumped and he trudged, head down, in front of the Opel and across the sandy verge to the underbrush looming along the side of the road.

"Very good," Gruber said, and lifted a roll of duct tape off the ground. He pulled the man's arms behind his back and fastened the tape around his wrists, then moved to the elbows and repeated the procedure. Then he beckoned the driver deeper into the forest, like a man inviting a guest into his home.

The driver looked pleadingly at Tracie and she said, "Go."

He walked fifteen feet into the woods. When Gruber indicated he had gone far enough, he stopped immediately. Gruber secured his ankles with the tape and then held his hand out to Tracie, who passed him a small washcloth. He placed it in the driver's mouth and secured it with tape. Waited for another cloth and when Tracie handed it to him, he placed it over the man's eyes and taped it as well. He took the man by the shoulders and lowered him gently to the ground.

Gruber said, "Listen carefully. We do not want to hurt you. Do what we say and you will be released soon unharmed. Do anything *other* than what we say and you will die a painful death and then be buried deep in this forest, where you will never be found. Nod if you understand."

The man nodded.

"So you know what is going to happen: we will be leaving for a little while. I will return to pick you up within a couple of hours, and then we will move you to a much more comfortable location. If all goes well you will be free soon. Nod if you understand."

The man nodded.

"However," Gruber continued, "If you try to sit up, or if you attempt to scream, or if I find you have moved so much as a centimeter from your present position when I return, I will shoot you in the head. You will never see me coming, will not know I have returned. The bullet will enter your brain and you will never know what hit you. Nod if you understand."

The man nodded vigorously.

"Good. Now remain perfectly still. I will be back soon."

Gruber backtracked out of the thick woods and trotted straight to the Opel while Tracie climbed into the cab of the delivery truck. He started the car and drove a hundred or so feet along the shoulder, moving it well away from the helpless delivery driver. The goal was to avoid anyone stumbling over the trussed-up man in the event a Good Samaritan should stop and check on the empty vehicle abandoned along the side of the road.

While Gruber was occupied with the Opel, Tracie checked the front of the truck for the bill of lading she knew they would need. The driver had thoughtfully left a clipboard containing the relevant paperwork on the passenger's side of the bench seat.

Down the road, Gruber killed the Opel's engine and leapt from the car. He locked the doors and sprinted back to Tracie as she climbed down out of the cab. They met at the back of the box truck, where he wasted no time pulling open the doors.

Tracie could feel the nervousness vibrating off Gruber like a force field, and she shared his tension. If a sufficient amount of supplies weren't packed inside the cargo box, the whole hastily devised plan would crumble like a stale cookie.

They shared a look inside the truck and Tracie felt a bit of her worry melt away. The cargo box was nearly full. Cases and wooden boxes and cardboard cartons supposedly filled with canned soup, vegetables cleaning supplies were stacked on wooden pallets half-a-dozen high. The supplies were packed nearly to the top of the cargo box, and the sheer volume of materials made Tracie wonder just how many people Phoenix was planning to recruit—or perhaps already *had* recruited—for their big Nazi comeback. The truck had shown up at the compound each day of her surveillance, meaning the amount of materials being stockpiled had to be significant.

There was no time to worry about that now. She handed Gruber the driver's Koenig shirt and ball cap and while he was slipping them on, she grabbed her backpack and climbed into the back of the truck. She boosted herself into the cargo box, shifting cartons around and slithering through the resulting gaps. She continued in this manner until she had made herself invisible from the rear door.

"That's far enough," Gruber called, his words floating to her from the roadway behind the truck. "Good luck, Quinn."

"Good luck to you too, Gruber," she replied.

He slammed one of the doors closed, and she said, "Oh, and Gruber?"

"Yes?"

"Good work today."

"Right back atya." He closed the second door and instantly the back of the delivery truck was plunged into darkness.

A moment later she heard the pitch of the engine change, and then they were moving, the truck rumbling down the narrow road.

19

November 18, 1987
Approximately 3:00 p.m.
Phoenix Compound
Langenberg, Federal Republic of Germany

The Phoenix compound was massive.

As far as Tracie could tell, based on her rushed and incomplete surveillance over the last two and a half days, the front portion of the camp consisted of a series of buildings resembling private residences set back from the front gate by maybe an eighth of a mile and accessible by a long, narrow dirt driveway.

Behind the front cluster of buildings by perhaps another eighth of a mile was a massive building being used as a warehouse, and then row after row of long, narrow structures she assumed had been constructed to serve as barracks for the training and indoctrination of recruits.

What was located behind the barracks buildings in the hundreds of acres contained within the ten-foot-high electrified barbed wire fence was a mystery. Most of it had been hidden from sight by the thick forest during surveillance, and climbing over the electric fence to get inside the compound had been out of the question.

Tracie had preferred to concentrate her time and attention on the front of the complex, anyway. The residential-type buildings represented the most likely place Phoenix would have squirreled away their prized possession—Der Führer himself, Adolph Hitler—which meant those were the buildings she would probably have to breach.

From the darkness inside the cargo bed, Tracie had no way of knowing how soon they would arrive at the compound, but based on her previous surveillance and the location where they had hijacked the truck, she knew they must be getting close. She sighed deeply and tried to control her nerves.

* * *

The truck rounded a corner and in the distance Matthias Gruber—he liked to remain in character during an assignment, even when he was by himself—could see the compound resolve into view. A wooden guard shack stood at the entrance, and as he began to slow, Gruber wondered how in the hell Phoenix explained the existence of an electrified fence and armed guards to the local authorities, when the facility was technically supposed to be a hazardous materials disposal facility.

Then he recalled Quinn's concern about the odd phrasing the Wuppertal Police spokesman had used on the TV news, about her conviction that the local cops weren't interested in finding the shooter, about her suspicion that some official high up on the food chain in the Wuppertal Police might be involved with Phoenix.

If any of that were true, the last thing that official would allow would be any kind of close inspection of this compound, which was close enough to Wuppertal to be quickly accessible, but also set off by itself, isolated and forbidding.

Gruber eased the truck to a halt at the guard shack, brakes squealing and hissing, diesel engine growling, and waited to be challenged. During surveillance, Quinn and he had observed the procedure through their binocs. It seemed straightforward: one guard would leave the shack and approach the cab, examine the bill of lading, and then wave the driver into the camp while an invisible partner inside the shack activated the electric gate.

Knowing what to expect didn't do much to ease his tension,

though, and he forced himself to adopt the bored air of nonchalance any delivery driver would likely project. He wanted to evoke the feeling in the sentry that this was just another stop in a long day of deliveries.

After a short delay, a man stalked out of the small guardhouse. On his hip was a sidearm, and while his hand hovered near it, the fact he had left it holstered Gruber took as a positive sign.

"Papers?" he said, lifting his hand toward the open window and then blinking in surprise as he caught sight of Gruber. His eyes narrowed and he said, "Where is the usual driver?"

"Sick," Gruber said gruffly. "He's home with a fever, so I have to work a double. And it's my wedding anniversary. Just my luck."

The guard didn't answer.

Gruber turned his head and frowned, staring through the dirty windshield, doing his best to project the aura of bored worker bee, someone who didn't really care whether he was allowed inside the compound to complete the delivery or not.

A second passed, and then two, and the guard shrugged. "I still need to see the paperwork," he said, and Gruber lifted the bill of lading off the seat and passed it through the window.

He examined it uncritically and then passed it back. "You know where to go?"

He hesitated and then shook his head, almost forgetting he was not supposed to be familiar with the compound's layout.

The guard pointed along the driveway, which seemed unnecessary given the fact it was the only driving option. "Follow the track, past the first cluster of buildings," he said. "Once beyond them, continue for maybe a tenth of a kilometer. You will come to a warehouse with a loading dock. Back your truck up to the dock and open the garage door. Unload your items and leave them just inside the building. Pull the door closed before you leave. Our people will redistribute the items from there. Do you understand?"

Gruber nodded, still doing his best to maintain the fiction of boredom while his heart hammered in his chest.

The guard stepped back and waited with an air of expectation.

Gruber spread his hands in confusion.

"Get out of the cab," the guard said impatiently. "I must examine the cargo before you enter."

He had known this was coming, had seen the procedure repeated twice already during surveillance. Still Gruber had hoped against hope the step would be forgotten or otherwise overlooked during this delivery.

As long as today's inspection was as perfunctory as the ones they had watched from a distance, he knew they would be fine. But if this guard suspected something might be wrong, or decided for whatever reason to be more thorough than his comrades, Gruber knew he and Quinn would be in handcuffs—or worse—within the next few minutes.

He climbed down from the cab and trudged to the rear of the truck. Twisted the iron handle and opened first one door and then the other. Held his breath as the guard climbed into the back of the truck and began reading labels on boxes, comparing them to the items listed on the bill of lading. He checked one and then another. Moved a couple of boxes and randomly checked a third and then a fourth.

The guard's progress was taking him closer and closer to Quinn. Gruber pictured her crouched, gun drawn, ready to blast the guard to hell.

He prayed it wouldn't come to that.

It didn't.

After examining two more boxes the man seemed satisfied. He climbed down from the cargo box and initialed the paperwork, then handed the clipboard back to Gruber, who made a concerted effort not to display the relief he was feeling.

The guard turned and retraced his steps to the front of the truck, waiting while Gruber closed and secured the rear doors. He stood impatiently as Gruber climbed back into the cab. Then he turned and gestured at the shack, making a circular motion with his hand. A moment later the gate began to roll open.

First hurdle down, Gruber thought as he waited for the opening to widen enough to drive through. When it had, he offered a perfunctory smile to the stone-faced young guard and then eased the truck into the Phoenix compound.

Through the rearview mirror he watched as the gate reversed course and closed behind the truck. The sight felt final and irrevocable.

* * *

The wait had seemed interminable to Tracie. She could hear the guard moving boxes and shuffling around as he performed his inspection, and she concentrated on remaining perfectly still and controlling her breathing.

By the time he climbed down from the cargo box, her muscles were sore and beginning to cramp. After the doors slammed closed, she flexed them, careful not to knock over any boxes or make any undue noise, but determined to maintain flexibility. The still-healing gunshot wound in her leg throbbed and she gritted her teeth against the pain.

The truck was moving slowly, and in her mind, Tracie tracked its progress. Deliveries were accomplished at a big wood-framed building set up as a warehouse, complete with raised loading dock. The structure was positioned behind the residential buildings but in front of the barracks, and even driving as slowly as Gruber was, they should be just about there by now.

As if confirming her suspicions, the truck turned and slowed, then came to a complete stop. After a moment, it began backing, still in a turn, and a few seconds later came to a jarring stop that threw Tracie off her feet and against the boxes. She knew immediately what had happened—Gruber misjudged the distance to the loading dock and slammed the rear of the truck into it.

She picked herself up and waited as the sound of a garage door rising on its tracks drifted through the thin steel walls of the cargo box. A moment later the rear doors opened and Gruber stepped into the rear of the truck. He hefted a box and stepped back out of the truck, carrying it to the warehouse as instructed.

A moment later he returned and repeated the process.

Tracie felt her breathing quicken and her muscles tense.

It was time to go to work.

20

November 18, 1987
3:10 p.m.
Phoenix Compound
Langenberg, Federal Republic of Germany

Gruber felt a light sweat beginning to form under his clothing, even though the day was cool and overcast.

The boxes were heavy.

Most of them were marked, but he had doubted the legitimacy of the markings from the beginning. Now, after hefting and carrying just the first few, he became convinced that rather than unloading a shipment of food and dry goods, it was much more likely these crates contained weapons and ammunition.

He moved deliberately, not wanting to finish too quickly but determined not to invite any unnecessary attention, either. He wanted nothing more than to signal Quinn to exit the truck, but didn't dare.

Not yet.

Their surveillance had revealed that each of the previous two days, the truck had been unloaded under armed guard, a grim-faced young man wearing an unmarked wool overcoat with no insignia, carrying what appeared to be an automatic or semiauto rifle slung over his shoulder.

Gruber had remarked to Quinn that it was surprising the guard wasn't outfitted in Nazi regalia. "For that matter," he had said, "I would have expected all the people working inside the compound to be in uniform."

Quinn had shaken her head, and her response had made perfect sense. "This place is supposed to be a hazardous waste facility, remember? As such, they're probably subject to government oversight. I'm sure they wouldn't want to take the chance of a surprise inspection uncovering dozens of Nazis. Even if the local authorities are paid off like I think they must be, Phoenix wouldn't be comfortable enough—yet—to advertise their mission so openly."

Gruber continued to work. Delivery truck to warehouse, back to delivery truck to begin again. After the fourth trip, when the guard still hadn't put in an appearance, Gruber's nervousness began to intensify. The ability to work without someone holding a gun on him should have made him breathe easier, but the opposite was true. Had they been found out? Was there a squad of men even now moving unseen across the compound to take Gruber—and eventually Quinn—into custody?

And what would happen then?

He considered whispering to Quinn, getting her opinion on the subject. The utter, deathly quiet inside the compound was beginning to give him the willies, and his fellow operative's silence wasn't helping. It was moments like this that made him question his career choice.

One more trip, he thought to himself. *I'm going to carry one more box into that damned warehouse and then I'll get Quinn's opinion on what the hell is going on here.*

He lifted another crate—this one was even heavier than the ones that had come before it—and turned and nearly ran right into the guard. He couldn't tell if this was the same grim-faced man he and Quinn had watched through binoculars the previous two days, but if not this one was cut from the same cloth. His lips were compressed into a thin line and his eyes were little more than slits, and he offered Gruber a look of barely concealed hostility before stepping aside to allow him to pass.

Gruber muscled the crate into the warehouse and dropped it onto the concrete floor with a grunt. He stood and ran the back of his wrist across his face and smiled. "I was starting to wonder where you were," he said.

The guard ignored the comment and said, "Where is the regular driver?"

"Like I told the gate guard, he's sick, so I'm stuck working a double shift."

"You have never been here before."

"I told you, the other driver is sick so I'm taking his place for the day." He tried to keep the exasperation out of his voice. How stupid was this man?

"That is not what I mean. If you have never been here before, how did you know to expect a guard?"

Gruber paused, willing back the panic that tried to take over his brain and shut it down. The silence lengthened as he searched for an appropriate response. "Well, it's not the sort of thing that we tend to run across every day, so the company warned me what to expect before sending me out here."

"Your company is being paid very handsomely to keep quiet about these deliveries," the guard said. "That means no one should be talking about this facility at all, is that understood? Or will a follow-up telephone call to the home office be necessary?"

"No, of course not. That won't be necessary. My buddy was just trying to keep me from falling over dead with a heart attack when I saw guys with guns, that's all. And I'm already on thin ice with the boss, I really don't need a complaint from such a valuable client."

Matthias Gruber had been blessed with good looks and a ready smile, two traits that he had used since adolescence to ring up a remarkable string of successes with the opposite sex, at least until running headlong into the brick wall put up by Fiona Quinn. Now he prayed he hadn't gone too far as he flashed what he hoped was a disarming smile at the guard.

With any luck, the man would accept his words at face value.

The guard returned his gaze impassively. Then he turned and moved to the edge of the loading dock and gestured with his rifle at the truck. "Get moving," he said.

Gruber nodded and ducked back into the cargo box. He began working in earnest, transferring boxes with a speed he had avoided while waiting for the guard to show up. He began sweating more, breathing heavily, pushing himself intentionally.

A few minutes later he estimated he had moved close to half the cargo. He was panting now and before long would be getting close to the tiny space Quinn had burrowed into after they had disabled the real truck driver. He lifted another crate and whispered, "Now."

He waited for the response and after less than a second, received it. "Check," was all Quinn said. Then he turned back toward the warehouse. The next few seconds would determine their fate.

He dropped the crate onto a rapidly growing pile of boxes inside the warehouse and then trudged back onto the loading dock. This time, though, instead of climbing into the delivery truck, Gruber crouched down and dropped off the edge of the dock to the dusty ground.

The guard eyed him suspiciously and said, "What are you doing? I know the truck is not empty yet. Get back to work." He didn't make a move for his gun, but he didn't have to. It wasn't like Gruber could ignore its presence.

Breathing heavily, he said, "Need water. I've got some in the cab."

"Just finish the job," the guard said, but before he could react Gruber had brushed past him on the way to the front of the truck.

"I said get back there and finish, or—"

Gruber stumbled on the uneven surface, pitching forward to the ground. The guard rushed up behind him. "Get up," the man barked, utterly unsympathetic to his plight.

"Okay, okay," Gruber answered, pushing himself up onto all fours before rising tiredly to his feet. "Can I please just get my water first?"

"Hurry up about it," the guard said. He fixed Gruber with a glare and then marched back to the edge of the loading dock. "Well? What are you waiting for?"

Gruber nodded and opened the driver's side door. He reached into the cab for his thermos of water and opened it, drinking greedily. *I hope that worked*, he thought. *Or we're both in big trouble.*

* * *

The walls of the cargo bed were thin, and Tracie was up and moving the moment she heard Gruber drop to the ground on the other side of the sheet metal. She had listened to the exchanges between her partner and the hard-ass guard, and she knew she would likely have an opening of no more than a couple of seconds.

She moved silently to the rear door, backpack slung over one shoulder like the college student she used to be. She felt as exposed and vulnerable as she ever had, knowing that if another guard happened to appear in the warehouse door right now she wouldn't even have time to go for her weapon.

"Get up!" the guard barked from next to the truck, and Tracie knew this was the best chance she was going to get. Probably the only chance. His words were muffled slightly by the cargo bed wall and she knew Gruber had been successful in drawing him away from the edge of the loading dock.

She made her move. She stepped lightly off the back of the truck and onto the dock, moving quickly but not so fast she would risk tripping or making any noise, the slightest of which would give her away.

She didn't look back, didn't dare check to see if the guard's attention had drifted away from Gruber yet. If it had, she would find out soon enough.

She crossed the loading dock in less than a second and entered the warehouse through the big garage door. The air felt chilly and damp, and she shivered, mostly—but not entirely—from the temperature. From behind she could hear the frustrated guard prodding Gruber more insistently now about getting back to work.

Then she disappeared deeper into the warehouse and the sounds faded away.

21

Finding a secure place in which to hole up and observe the cluster of residence buildings near the front of the Phoenix compound was relatively easy. Tracie worked her way through row after row of supplies already packed away inside the warehouse, moving steadily deeper into the building. Two-thirds of the way toward the rear wall, she selected a location next to a window and then quietly moved crates and boxes aside until she had made a small hideaway for herself. It was similar to what she had done back in the delivery truck.

Within ten minutes she had made herself as comfortable as possible while still being able to observe what she needed to outside. The only way she could be discovered, short of a guard weaving through the stacks of supplies and stumbling upon her exact location, would be for someone to see her through the warehouse window as she was monitoring the camp.

Tracie had performed innumerable stakeouts over her years as a field operative and had long ago learned to deal with the somewhat illogical combination of extreme boredom and unrelenting tension. She expected no less out of this mission, and settled in for the long haul: hour after hour of observation, trying to stay sharp when the majority of her time would be spent observing nothing of interest.

The first thing she discovered, after less than an hour with her eyes glued to the compound, was that Phoenix had not yet begun to ramp up their operation. The camp was massive but understaffed. Rather than wannabe Nazis marching around and preparing to take over the world, she saw the occasional patrolling guard walk by, or a bit of similar activity, someone moving from one building to another.

Nothing earthshaking.

So far.

But the everyday pace of deliveries, and the amount of armaments and ammunition already cached inside the warehouse, suggested strongly that at some point, and soon, the situation would change. To Tracie it appeared preparations were being made to stock the camp in advance of a massive influx of recruits who would be arriving subsequent to the Amber Room treasure being liquidated on the black market.

Most of the camp's activity seemed to be concentrated in the vicinity of a large wood-frame structure adjacent to the dirt-packed driveway near the front gate. After watching a number of soldiers enter and then exit in a trickle of steady activity, Tracie felt confident she had identified the camp's administration building or headquarters.

All the men she observed entering and exiting the building were dressed exactly like the guard who had supervised Gruber's offloading of crates: wool overcoat to protect against the November chill, automatic or semiauto rifle slung over one shoulder, pistol holstered at the hip. The lack of Nazi identification, and especially the lack of any insignia indicating rank, convinced Tracie that the compound was at this point still manned only by true believers, those fanatical Nazi followers who would be critical in rebuilding the party from scratch.

Once the process of trucking foot soldiers and other recruits into the facility for training and indoctrination began, that situation would change, as a command structure would have to be identified.

Tracie aimed to ensure this insane Nazi training facility would never reach that point.

She made herself comfortable on a crate she had dragged in front of the window. Thought about a movie she had gone to see early in her CIA career. It was called Raiders of the Lost Ark, and featured a hunky Harrison Ford fighting pre-World War II Nazis.

That movie had been set in the 1930s, with director Stephen Spielberg probably never realizing he could have set the film in 1987. Tracie shook her head. Who would have guessed repelling a Nazi threat would become necessary four decades after the world assumed that particular plague on humanity had been wiped out for good?

Her reverie came to an abrupt halt as a door opened in one of the residence buildings clustered behind Phoenix headquarters. A young woman stepped out, one of the very few females Tracie had observed in two and a half days of surveillance plus the couple of hours she had been holed up inside the warehouse.

The woman was dressed in scrubs. A pale blue blouse over white pants. Perched on her head was a nurse's cap.

Tracie had seen no evidence of anyone in scrubs until now; certainly no one dressed like that entering or leaving the camp during the sixteen-plus hours per day she and Gruber had observed the facility in preparation for this op. She realized watching the woman walk that the angles from which they had been forced to conduct surveillance would have hidden the nurse from view, however.

This was interesting.

Little training seemed to be taking place inside the facility to this point, thus there was no reason she could conceive of why Phoenix would need medical personnel on-site and available twenty-four hours a day.

Unless it was to provide care for someone who could not care for himself.

Someone elderly.

Someone like a Nazi leader presumed long dead, a man poised to become the rallying point for a new generation of fanatical followers bent on restoring the Thousand Year Reich to its decades-interrupted former "glory."

Tracie tracked the nurse's progress as the young woman skirted the building she had just exited, rubber-soled shoes crunching along a gravel walkway. She walked to a pair of buildings located roughly midpoint in the cluster of structures but somehow different from the rest. They looked better maintained, nicer. Homier. They were smaller, not much larger than a pair of summer cottages, but each sported a fresh coat of immaculate white paint, with royal blue shutters flanking the windows and a farmer's porch spanning the entire width of the front.

Upon reaching the cottages, the nurse turned and climbed the steps leading to the front door of the building on the right. A wicker rocking chair sat unused on the porch, red wool blanket draped over its back. A black-crested design set against a circular white background adorned the blanket, and although the design was not fully visible given the fact the blanket was half-folded, Tracie thought she had a pretty good idea what it was anyway.

A gammadion cross.

More commonly known as a swastika.

The nurse crossed the porch and knocked politely at the door. A moment later it swung open to reveal a guard. The wool overcoat Tracie had seen all the other guards wear was absent, which made sense since the man was indoors. Otherwise he was a near-identical match to all the rest, right down to the rifle slung over his shoulder.

In the back of her mind she wondered why on earth a man standing watch inside a building that small would carry an automatic rifle. Perhaps he had only picked it up at the sound of the knock, but in any event, it was potentially critical intel, and Tracie filed it away as she watched the nurse enter the building.

The stone-faced guard stood aside until she passed, then scanned the area outside the little house from left to right before easing the door closed.

This was getting more and more fascinating. Tracie reached into her pocket and removed a stick of gum. She unwrapped the gum and popped it into her mouth before smoothing the foil wrapper and placing it neatly on the concrete floor at her feet. She leaned back, never taking her eyes off the portion of the Phoenix compound she could see, and considered the implications of what she had thus far observed.

Her time spent hidden away inside this warehouse had been productive thus far. Its positioning allowed her to observe everything of importance to her mission, and while as yet she possessed no irrefutable proof Adolph Hitler was tucked away inside the cottage across the compound, she could not come up with a single credible scenario to explain what the woman would be doing inside the camp if it wasn't providing care for an elderly patient.

Night had begun to fall, and Tracie's stomach growled. She spit her gum into her hand and then placed it in the center of the foil wrapper. She crumpled the wrapper around the gum and dropped it into her pocket, then fished an energy bar out of her backpack. She began munching, still focusing her attention on the cute little cottage that looked so out of place inside this grim Nazi training camp.

A little while later, the nurse exited the building. She pulled the door closed and then retraced her steps along the gravel path, entering the much bigger building from which she had made her first appearance perhaps twenty minutes prior.

Tracie chewed her energy bar slowly as she watched the nurse disappear from view. She felt the seeds of a plan beginning to develop, but could not begin firming up the plan until full darkness had fallen.

Across the camp, sporadic activity continued at the administration building. Upon exiting, all the soldiers turned left and marched directly past Tracie's viewing position and into just one of the five barracks buildings. Apparently the other four were as-yet unused. The structures were located to Tracie's right, almost but not quite out of her sight.

All five barracks were identical: long, narrow wood-frame structures that had been built side by side and, for the time being at least, made up the southernmost useable portion of the camp. Beyond the barracks buildings were a mixture of forests and fields, hundreds of acres of land that lay inside the electric fence and would presumably be used for training once the camp began to be stocked with Nazi recruits.

Tracie studied the barracks, paying particular attention to the one in use. It was located directly in the middle, flanked by two still-empty structures on either side. The time would likely come—and soon—when Tracie would need to pass those buildings on foot, and it was critical to learn as much as she could about them now.

She split her time between examining the barracks and monitoring the headquarters building. The locations were on opposite sides of the camp and doing so allowed Tracie to sweep the entire compound with her eyes every few seconds.

It was on one of these visual sweeps, moving south to north, that her gaze passed the pair of blue-shuttered cottages she had seen the nurse enter and then exit earlier. The front door of the cottage on the left opened, and she stopped her sweep to focus on him. It was the first time she had seen any activity at that cottage.

A man stepped out.

Tracie's breath caught in her throat.

It was Adolph Hitler.

22

The man paused in his doorway and Tracie froze in stunned surprise. She shook her head to jumpstart her brain. Then she snatched her mini-binoculars off the floor and pressed them to her eyes.

The man was Hitler but he could not possibly *be* Hitler. The leader of the Third Reich, the bloodthirsty dictator who had been instrumental in plunging the world into war in the middle of the twentieth century and who had murdered millions of Jews, would be elderly now, more than forty years later. He would be well into his nineties.

Tracie trained her binocs on him and finally remembered to breathe. This man was not elderly. He appeared fit. He looked like a man in his late thirties or early forties.

But he looked exactly like every picture Tracie Tanner had ever seen of the German Führer: black hair, parted on the right side of his head and combed over, angular face with piercing dark eyes and, of course, the tiny mustache, shaved so that it was barely wider than his nostrils.

Adolph Hitler.

But *not* Adolph Hitler.

Tracie was adept at reading people. Their body language, expressions, attitudes. It was a skill any successful field operative needed to develop if he or she hoped to survive. But it would not take someone with her unique skill set to see that *this* man was not in his nineties. He was nowhere near his nineties.

Tracie watched, spellbound, as the man sauntered across the porch and down his front steps. He moved languidly, confidently, a man comfortable being in charge, a man who expected others to comply with instructions immediately.

Or else.

The man followed the gravel walkway out to the packed-dirt driveway and then turned right, moving toward the Phoenix headquarters building. He entered the building, and Tracie shook her head in equal parts wonder and revulsion. He even moved like she had seen Hitler move in the rare snatches of video that had survived the last four decades: posture erect, head up, backbone ramrod straight.

The door closed behind the ghost of Adolph Hitler and she leaned back against a stack of crates. Rubbed her eyes. Tried to determine what in the holy hell was going on here.

The plan she had begun to develop for dealing with elderly Adolph Hitler had instantly been rendered irrelevant. She needed to abandon the warehouse and somehow make her way past the five barracks buildings to the hundreds of acres of unused compound, where the thick forest would shield her from view of the Phoenix fanatics and allow her to speak freely.

She needed help.

23

November 18, 1987
9:50 p.m.
Phoenix Compound
Langenberg, Federal Republic of Germany

Tracie had almost not bothered to include her secure satellite phone among the supplies she brought inside the Phoenix camp. It was bulky and heavy and, she had thought, unnecessary. She had received her orders and was prepared to carry them out.

But something had told her to sacrifice the room and deal with its extra weight and include it inside her backpack. A little voice in the back of her mind that had whispered, *you're going to be alone inside a camp run by murderous fanatics, with virtually no intel to fall back on. Be smart. Be prepared.*

So she had packed it away, certain she would not need it.

Now she needed it.

After watching the Hitler clone enter the Phoenix headquarters building, Tracie wasted no time. She returned all of the boxes and crates she had previously moved in order to carve out a viewing position, dragging and hefting them back to their original locations. Then she shrugged her backpack over her shoulder and began moving carefully to the rear of the warehouse, hoping to find an exit door.

Getting caught inside the warehouse had ceased to be a major concern. Men had come hours earlier to reposition all of the supplies Gruber dropped off, but their voices remained far in the distance toward the front of the building. They packed away the supplies in a matter of minutes, and then they disappeared, pulling the big garage door closed behind them. No one had come near the warehouse since. It sat dark and quiet.

Tracie worked her way through the rows of boxes and before long found herself at the rear wall. To the right was a door, placed directly in the center of the building, just as she had hoped. It was locked, but from the inside, a series of dead bolts that she was able to unfasten in seconds.

The warehouse was positioned in such a way that the rear door was visible only to the barracks buildings. The amount of German forest that had been cleared was barely wide enough to support construction of the camp, and Tracie thought if she exited the door and moved at a right angle to the warehouse, making straight for the cover of the trees, she would be exposed for no more than ten seconds.

Activity had been dwindling.

She liked her chances of remaining undetected.

The patrolling guards represented a dangerous wild card, but their activity—at least during the daylight hours—had been sporadic and half-hearted.

She didn't have many other options.

She opened the door and slipped through it, eyes glued to the barracks. Turned right and hugged the wall until reaching the corner. Then she continued across the narrow strip of field and straight into the forest, slipping into the underbrush. Finally she took a deep breath.

She walked on, struggling through the trees and underbrush, not wanting to hike any farther than necessary but determined not to take any chance of being seen or heard by anyone from Phoenix.

* * *

November 18, 1987
10:05 p.m. local time
Phoenix Compound
Langenberg, Federal Republic of Germany

"Do you have any idea what time it is, Tanner? Whatever you're calling about, couldn't it wait until morning?" CIA Director Aaron Stallings was his usual acerbic self, and Tracie had to bite back the response she wanted to make: that she doubted the time of day would make any difference in his reaction to her call.

"Nice to talk to you too, sir. And, yes, I know exactly what time it is in D.C. It's just after two a.m., but I need to talk to you. And to answer your question, no, it couldn't wait until morning."

Stallings sighed theatrically for her benefit. "Fine. What is it, Tanner?"

"I just saw Adolph Hitler."

"Congratulations. Since your assignment involved seeing him, I assume he's no longer breathing. And I can't help but wonder why you're bothering with the call."

"No sir, the job's not done yet."

"Explain."

"Something's come up. Something involving a guy who's a dead ringer for the World War II-era Führer, a guy who can't be more than forty-five. I'm talking about a man who's an identical match to the photos taken of Hitler from the early 1940s."

There was no response from the other end of the sat phone, and Stallings's silence told Tracie the news didn't come as a surprise to the CIA chief.

When it became clear no reply would be forthcoming, Tracie said, "Hitler had a son, didn't he? A child no one knows about."

"There have been persistent rumors through the years," Stallings said. She could practically feel his shrug through the sat phone.

"Rumors? You expect me to believe the CIA was unaware of the fact that one of the most evil men of the twentieth century had an heir?"

"You seem to be under the impression that I answer to you, Tanner. It's the other way around, remember? And to your point about Hitler having a son: the Nazis were utterly defeated by the spring of 1945. There was no reason for anyone to believe they would ever be a factor in world politics again. Therefore, Adolph Hitler became a very minor persona. A historical footnote. Did we monitor the man over the years? Yes. Did we have people watching his every single move? Of course not."

"So you're telling me the CIA knew Hitler had a son but didn't care."

"Is there a question in there, Tanner?"

"Come on, sir. I think you, of all people, recognize the implications of this. Phoenix isn't going to use the ninety-something-year-old Adolph Hitler as the face of their uprising. Or, to be more accurate, they probably still will, but they're going to build the actual organization around the younger Hitler, the guy who's a spitting image of the man feared around the world back in the 1930s and 1940s. I believe a young, vital Hitler will be far more successful in rallying people to his cause than would an elderly, infirm man."

"Again, is there a question in there somewhere?"

Tracie ground her teeth in frustration. Interacting with Aaron Stallings was like dealing with a recalcitrant five-year-old, except this five-year-old had the president's ear and was one of the most powerful—and duplicitous—men in the world.

"Yes, there's a question," she growled. "What am I supposed to do about the younger Hitler?"

"His name is Adolph, also. No surprise there, I suppose."

"So you did know about him." Her temper was near the breaking point. She was alone, thousands of miles from home, putting her life on the line inside a Nazi training camp, and Stallings was playing his usual—and dangerous—games.

"I think you already know the answer to that question, Tanner."

"You expect me to take him out, too? Two Hitlers for the price of one? Is that it?"

"You said yourself a young Adolph Hitler cannot be allowed the opportunity to repeat the havoc wrought decades ago by his father. Excellent analysis, by the way. Very insightful."

"Come on, sir, how am I supposed to put down both men? The minute one of them is discovered dead Phoenix will close ranks so tightly I'll never be able to get at the other. Plus, this camp is big but not massive. Once they know they've been compromised they'll capture me within hours, maybe within minutes. It can't be done, not by one person."

"Spare me the sob story, Tanner. You're the operative and you've been given your assignment. Figure out a way to get it done, for chrissakes."

"My assignment has changed so many times it's a wonder I can even keep it straight."

"Will there be anything else, Tanner?"

She realized she was grinding her teeth again and forced herself to relax her jaw. It wasn't easy. "No sir, there's nothing else."

"Then I suggest you get moving. It sounds like you have a lot of work to do."

24

Tracie replaced the satellite phone in her backpack and began retracing her steps out of the forest, trying to control her anger as she returned to the edge of the developed portion of the Phoenix compound.

She considered remaining in the woods behind the camp—it offered the least likelihood of discovery and capture—but it also provided no access to the camp and no opportunity to observe Phoenix's activity. She had no choice but to return to her previous reconnaissance position inside the darkened warehouse. It was centrally located and once inside, would offer a relatively safe place from which to consider her next move.

She waited for the right moment and broke cover. The camp at night was illuminated by a series of sodium arc floodlights perched high atop wooden poles erected at regular intervals around the security fence, but their focus was more on the middle of the compound than the tree line. Tracie had little difficulty traversing the short distance from the edge of the woods to the side of the warehouse.

From there it was simple matter of reentering the building through the unlocked rear door. She made her way to her previous location, moving cautiously in the near-total darkness.

Finally she was situated in her familiar spot. She sat on a crate and kept watch through the window, trying to develop some semblance of plan that would allow her to complete her utterly unfair assignment. If it had been a long shot before, it was now a near-impossibility.

She sat quietly and allowed the tension to drain from her body. Tried to think, running various scenarios through her head, hoping to settle on something that would allow her to complete her mission and survive.

She couldn't come up with one.

* * *

November 19, 1987
1:15 a.m.
Phoenix Compound
Langenberg, Federal Republic of Germany

Activity inside the Phoenix compound had become virtually nonexistent. Every so often a guard would pass the warehouse, ever-present rifle slung over his shoulder. The patrols seemed to occur with no regularity that Tracie could discern. By her watch, the interval between sentry sightings was at times as short as five minutes, and at other times as long as thirty.

And the routes taken by the guards seemed random as well. Sometimes they walked the perimeter, remaining just inside the electrified fence. At other times they weaved in and out among the camp's buildings, paying particular attention to the residences clustered toward the front of the camp, but also patrolling around the long, mostly empty barracks buildings.

This was not ideal.

It was also not unexpected.

She shifted her attention toward the rear of the camp. Thanks to the near-blinding glare of the sodium arc lamps illuminating the main portion of the compound, the unlit area beyond the barracks buildings disappeared into a black void that was as complete as anything Tracie had ever seen.

She began to consider the possibilities such a scenario presented. Was there a way to use the extreme difference between light and dark to her tactical advantage? And if so, would it be possible to tie that advantage to what she now knew regarding the nurse's schedule?

Over the last few hours, Tracie watched as the same nurse she had seen previously made several more trips to the cottage on the right, each one occurring approximately an hour after the last. The duration of all the visits was the same: approximately twenty minutes. Then she would exit the cottage and return to the bigger building.

A new plan began to take shape. It wasn't a great plan. Tracie couldn't even convince herself it was a good plan. But with a little bit of luck—*okay, a lot of luck,* she thought to herself—and impeccable execution, it might work.

Maybe.

She waited one more nursing cycle, paying close attention to the exact times the young woman entered and exited the cottage, and then nodded to herself, all alone in the dark silence of the Nazi warehouse.

She would make her move on the next visit.

*   *   *

November 19, 1987
1:45 a.m.
Phoenix Compound
Langenberg, Federal Republic of Germany

Exiting the rear door of the warehouse, as she had done earlier to make her sat phone call to Aaron Stallings, would not be feasible. Last time she was heading for the cover of the forest, but now she needed to move in the opposite direction.

Toward the center of the camp.

Through the floodlights.

There had to be a better way, a more direct way, a route that would minimize her exposure to the potentially lethal glare.

Tracie had been staring out the side of the warehouse for hours, but now she focused her gaze not *through* the window, but rather *on* it, examining the hardware itself. There was more than enough ambient light to see that the window was old and cheap. Dirty. It had clearly been scavenged from a job site, or an abandoned building, maybe even a junkyard.

But the Phoenix camp was new. The lack of weathering of exposed, unpainted siding on the buildings made clear the construction had occurred within the last year or so, and the window in front of Tracie's location hadn't had the chance yet to become warped or sticky from moisture.

Her objective—the pair of blue-shuttered cottages—was situated directly across the access road from her present surveillance position. If she could move in a straight line, her exposure would be minimal.

She leaned in close to the window, squinting to see in the shadowy light. A brass locking mechanism was currently engaged, and Tracie thumbed it, releasing the lock.

Then she tested the window by pushing gently, smiling when it pivoted open. It was designed to open approximately eight inches to allow for airflow through the building, and came equipped with a rod built into the lower portion of the frame that could be swung outward and fastened to the casement to prevent the window from slamming shut.

Tracie ignored the rod. Instead, she tested the clearance by swinging the window as far as possible after first checking to ensure no guards were in the vicinity.

There was plenty of clearance for what she had in mind.

She eased the window closed again and waited.

* * *

November 19, 1987
2:15 a.m.
Phoenix Compound
Langenberg, Federal Republic of Germany

This time, when the nurse exited the larger building and crunched along the path leading to the cottages, Tracie was up and ready. She stood next to the window with one hand on the frame, waiting to push it open.

She watched closely as the nurse repeated what had by now become a familiar routine, knocking on the cottage door and entering a moment later when the guard swung it open.

As soon as the nurse disappeared inside, Tracie slipped the window open far enough to check all directions for a patrolling sentry. She cursed silently when she saw one in the distance. The man strolled slowly in front of the headquarters building, far enough away that there was little danger of him spotting the open warehouse window—and virtually no chance he would see Tracie behind it—but close enough that she could not yet risk trying what she had in mind.

And he was moving in her direction.

She eased the window closed and crouched below it, exposing just her forehead and eyes as she tracked the man's progress, tapping her foot impatiently while she waited for him to pass. He crossed in front of the building the nurse had exited just moments ago—apparently the dormitory for the nursing staff, along with untold other staff members—and then turned left, duplicating the nurse's path almost precisely.

The guard disappeared into the shadows, continuing south between the blue-shuttered cottages. He paid close attention to the exteriors of both buildings but continued walking.

Tracie waited sixty seconds for him to reverse course and reappear. When he didn't, she added another thirty, just to be sure.

Still nothing.

She eased the window open and double-checked the area.

Deserted.

Now she moved decisively, all hesitation gone. She swung the window outward once again, but instead of fastening the rod to prop it open, she forced it wider and then sat on the sash. Lifted her feet and pivoted sideways until they were dangling outside. Then, while supporting the window with her hand to prevent it from swinging closed and banging into the frame, she dropped noiselessly to the ground.

She slipped the window back into place and breathed deeply. She was still in the shadows of the warehouse at the moment, but the next few seconds would literally spell the difference between life and death. She would be completely exposed crossing the access road, bathed in the glare of the floodlights, casting shadows in all directions.

In one sense she was fortunate. There were no guard towers surrounding the camp. But still, if anyone were to glance out a window in any of the cluster of buildings she would be approaching—or worse, if a patrolling guard should happen along—she would be easy prey, blinded by the lights and armed only with her pistol.

Tracie could feel the clock ticking. The longer she remained hidden in the shadows, the more she tempted fate.

She had to move. Now.

She checked all directions for sentries, paying special attention to the alleyway between the two cottages into which the guard had disappeared ninety seconds ago.

All was quiet. The compound was hunkered down, most of its residents asleep. Tracie took a deep breath and pushed away from the safety of the shadows. She began walking briskly across the dusty driveway, head up, projecting an air of confidence, like she had every right to be where she was.

Just another Nazi fanatic re-advancing the cause of the Third Reich.

The fiction wouldn't help if she were to be spotted by someone up close. But if a sentry should happen to walk out the headquarters door, or enter the camp from the guardhouse at the front gate, perhaps she would blend in and avoid suspicion.

Although, given the time of night, she doubted it.

Heart racing, she forced herself to walk at a rapid but measured pace, expecting at any moment to hear a shouted challenge, or the sound of the gunshot that would catch her between the shoulder blades and drop her in the dirt.

The crossing seemed to take forever, but in reality it was over in a matter of seconds. Her shadow danced around her as she walked, the light striking her from multiple locations, and then it disappeared as she slipped into the shadows projected by the pair of blue-shuttered cottages.

The relief she felt from once again being mostly hidden from sight was palpable. It was also misleading. There was still the possibility that the guard she had watched walk between these two buildings would return. If he did, Tracie knew she would be almost totally helpless until she regained her night vision.

She willed herself to see, knowing it was silly but trying anyway. The thought of slinking farther back into the shadows was tempting, even if only for a couple of minutes. But Tracie knew she couldn't afford to miss the sound of the cottage's front door opening and then closing again when the nurse's hourly visit ended, a scenario that should occur any minute now.

So she waited. She stood as still as possible against the side of the cottage, moving only her head, and even then almost imperceptibly, as she scanned back and forth for the patrolling guard or for any other sign of trouble.

Still quiet in the camp.

A minute passed, and then two, and she breathed marginally easier as her eyesight began to adjust to the low light in the shadows.

And then she heard it. The muffled sound of voices from inside the cottage, one girlish and flirty, the other masculine and amused. Both were muted, like teenagers making out on a couch while trying to keep from waking the girl's sleeping parents. The voices grew marginally louder and then the door opened and the nurse stepped onto the front porch.

"Try to stay awake until my next visit," the nurse said with a smile in her voice, and Tracie could picture her trailing a teasing finger across the guard's lips.

"I'll stay awake because I'll be fantasizing about you," came the reply. The man's voice was subdued, quiet, almost a whisper.

"And what will we be doing in this fantasy?"

"You'll find out when you come back next hour."

"Ooh, sounds like fun." The nurse giggled and then descended the steps. The front door closed quietly and the only sound was the crunching of the young woman's rubber-soled shoes on the gravel pathway.

Tracie waited until the nurse rounded the corner of the much larger building ahead, then she turned and skirted the front railing of the porch.

Climbed the steps.

Moved to the side of the door and knocked quietly.

25

November 19, 1987
2:20 a.m.
Phoenix Compound
Langenberg, Federal Republic of Germany

The door opened almost immediately. The guard hadn't had time to settle back into his between-nurse-visit routine.

"What, did you miss me already?" he said, the smile on his face freezing in confusion as he saw someone other than the woman he was expecting. He opened his mouth to shout a warning while reaching for his weapon but he never had a chance.

Tracie's right fist flashed out and she punched the guard in the throat. He staggered backward and the cry he had been about to unleash died out, replaced by the strangled sound of gagging and wheezing.

He snatched at the pistol holstered at his hip even as he struggled to breathe. Tracie grabbed his wrist and twisted it behind his back, using the guard's own momentum against him. She spun him around and shoved his head against the far wall, and when it bounced off, she forced the stunned man to the floor.

Plucked his pistol from his holster.

Slammed its butt against the side of his skull, just behind the ear.

The guard's eyes rolled up into his head and he went limp. Tracie slid the weapon across the room and out of arm's reach.

She had to hurry. The man was unconscious but his brain would reboot quickly. He would awaken with a massive headache but could still be deadly to her as long as he could scream.

To her right was a plush chair, which the guard had obviously been sitting in while he passed the long duty hours. A small table stood next to the chair, upon which had been placed a reading lamp and a copy of *Mein Kampfe*, Adolph Hitler's autobiography.

"Kiss-ass," she muttered, reaching up and pulling the lamp off the table. She unplugged the power cord from the wall and wrapped it around her fist, then yanked hard. The electrical wires ripped away from their connections in the lamp's base, and Tracie was left with approximately an eight-foot length of cord.

She reached around and removed her combat knife from its sheath at the small of her back. Cut the cord into three roughly equal sections and placed them on the floor before returning her knife to its sheath. The guard's eyes had begun to flutter again and he moaned softly. She had to hurry.

Tracie pushed to her feet and crossed the room to the front window. The shade had been drawn, so no one outside the cottage could see in. *Thank God for small favors.*

A gingham valence hung over the window, giving the cottage's interior the look of a cheap Italian restaurant. *Who the hell did their decorating?* she thought, and then reached up and lifted the curtain rod off its supports. She yanked the valence from the rod and dropped the rod to the floor, then hurried back to the guard. His eyes were open but unfocused, and as she came into his field of view they widened in panic and he tried to sit up.

"Uh-uh," she said softly, leaning forward and placing her left forearm against his throat. She used her body weight as leverage, forcing his head back down to the floor and cutting off his air supply.

He began to thrash and she said, "Lie perfectly still and I'll allow you to breathe, do you understand me?"

The man's eye's narrowed but he nodded grimly, and Tracie eased off the pressure slightly. The air whistled in and out of his throat and she said, "Make one move I don't like and I'll suffocate you. You will not get another warning."

The guard nodded again. He didn't seem to trust himself to try to talk. Maybe she had damaged his windpipe and he couldn't talk. Tracie didn't know and didn't care.

One thing she *did* know was that he was biding his time, waiting for an opening, for a chance to use his superior strength to gain the upper hand.

She needed to secure him. Now.

"Roll over onto your stomach," she said. She reached back and plucked her combat knife from its sheath again. Displayed it inches from his eyes. Then she removed her forearm from his throat.

He looked from her knife to her eyes and then back again. He didn't move.

"Roll over right this second or I gut you like a fish. Your choice," she said. "One dead lunatic won't bother me a bit."

"Whatever you think you are doing, you will not get away with it," the guard muttered through clenched teeth. Apparently his windpipe was just fine.

"Not your problem," she answered. "I suggest you just worry about staying alive. Now, do as you're told, or die."

His lips compressed into a furious line and he began to turn onto his belly. Slowly. Tracie shoved him over and immobilized him with her knee as she pulled his hands behind his back. She picked one of the three lengths of electrical wire off the floor and began winding it around his wrists, forcing them tightly together.

Then she tied it off with a double knot and nodded. It wasn't pretty but she didn't need pretty. She needed effective.

With the guard now more or less immobilized, she lifted the gingham valance off the floor. It hadn't been cleaned recently and a layer of dust coated the material. "Open up," she said.

The guard's eyes narrowed and he stared, pure hatred in his eyes.

"Have it your way," Tracie said with a shrug. She picked up her pistol and lifted her arm as if to strike the guard in the skull again. Before she could begin the downward motion, his mouth popped open like a fish trying to breathe out of the water.

"Good choice," she said, and then stuffed the dusty cotton inside the man's mouth, forcing it in until it was nice and tight. She picked up the second length of wire and secured the improvised gag, then wound the ends around his head several times before tying them off as she had done with his wrists.

Finally, she repeated the procedure with the guard's boots, securing his ankles tightly together.

He was now helpless.

But the clock continued to tick. Tracie knew the guard's nurse-playmate would return within the hour, and there was a lot to do before that happened.

She stood and turned toward a closed door to her right. Her pulse quickened. This entire insane mission hinged upon her guess about what was behind this door being proven correct.

She reached for the knob and pushed the door open.

* * *

Tracie's first thought was that Adolph Hitler was already dead. The body propped in the bed across the small room was clearly the Führer. That much was obvious, even ravaged as he was by age and disease.

But just as obvious was the fact that this man would be dead soon, if he wasn't already. He was as helpless as a baby and would never be leading a revolution. Not literally, not symbolically, not in any way, shape or form. A blanket had been pulled up to his waist, and she thought she could almost see his ribs protruding through the light pajama top covering his chest and upper body. His skin looked waxy and paper-thin.

A stainless steel IV stand had been set up on the far side of the bed, and a bag of clear fluid dripped slowly through a plastic tube and into the old man's arm. Another copy of *Mein Kampf* lay on the bedside table next to Hitler—as if a man in his condition would be able to read—but otherwise the room was nearly empty of furnishings. It was sterile and antiseptic and depressing.

A bare-bones light fixture screwed into the ceiling provided dim illumination, and Tracie squinted from just inside the doorway as she took in the scene. It was surreal. Her feet felt frozen to the floor and she found herself suddenly reluctant to approach the monster responsible for so much death and misery. That it had occurred decades ago was irrelevant; the result of this man's actions was still real and horrifying.

An aura of darkness surrounded Adolph Hitler, of evil, even as he lay old and dying. A part of her feared becoming infected, not by whatever disease might be killing him, but by his moral rot. His malevolence. The sensation was illogical but very real.

She stood motionless, concentrating her gaze on his upper body. After what felt like an eternity, she watched as his chest rose imperceptibly and then fell. The room was deathly silent and she realized she had been holding her breath.

Despite the need to get this over with quickly, despite the knowledge she remained surrounded on all sides by Nazi fanatics with deadly weapons and ill intent, despite the fact that a soldier lay trussed up just outside this door and she would be discovered the moment anyone entered the cottage, Tracie found it almost impossible to move.

To do what had to be done.

The moment stretched out, time becoming elastic. Over the course of her career she had seen and done things no human being could ever forget, but she knew this moment—standing alone in a room with one of the biggest butchers of the Twentieth Century—would remain seared into her brain like a cancerous growth, that from this day forward she would see Adolph Hitler in her nightmares forever.

Assuming she survived.

"God help me," she whispered to no one, and she forced herself to cross the room.

And then she was next to the bed.

Hitler was dying. It was clear to Tracie he would be gone within days, maybe less. Maybe within hours. But she had her orders and was duty-bound to complete her mission or die trying.

And that was exactly what she would do.

The dying man's eyes remained closed but she had the unshakeable feeling that he knew she was there. She imagined him opening those eyes, cold and dead and murderous, and lifting a hand from the side of the bed. The hand would be palsied and liver-spotted, but it would be strong, and it would clamp onto her wrist, and he would hold her down, and then he would smile through a mouth filled with rotted teeth, and he would pull a German Luger from under his blankets and he would—

No.

Stop it.

He was ill, and old, and helpless.

No matter how black his soul might be, no matter how evil, he was nothing more now than wasted skin and brittle bones, no more capable of harming her than he was of popping out of his deathbed and dancing a German waltz.

She pulled one of the pillows out from behind his back. His body tilted to the left and his eyes fluttered briefly and almost opened as his body spasmed in protest against this unexpected change in the status quo. Then he fell still again.

Tracie examined the pillow. It was thick and comfortable and would serve her purposes well.

She bent over the ancient Nazi and placed the pillow over his face. Then she leaned down and, using both hands, provided steadily increasing pressure to his mouth and nose.

He barely struggled. His rail-thin arms lifted off the mattress and flailed randomly as his feet kicked under the covers.

Then he stopped and remained utterly still. It took almost no time at all.

It was as if he had recognized his fate, so long in the making, and accepted it.

Tracie maintained pressure longer than necessary, then lifted the pillow.

She checked his pulse, and then checked it again to be sure.

Adolph Hitler was dead.

26

The trussed-up guard followed Tracie's progress with his eyes as she exited Hitler's death chamber and closed the door. His head was twisted at a plainly uncomfortable angle, yet he held it steady. His eyes glittered, dark and cold in the dim light of the cottage.

"One down, one to go," she said softly, locking eyes with the guard as she knelt and checked his bindings. The clock was ticking but it would only take a few seconds to ensure he was still immobilized. It would be time well spent. Were he to work himself free before she completed her mission she would never survive.

All three electrical cords remained tightly secured. Tracie smiled. "Now don't go anywhere," she said. "Just stay here and wait for your girlfriend."

She sprang to her feet and hurried to the rear of the cottage. Besides the combination kitchen/sitting room in which she had left the trussed-up guard and Hitler's bedroom, the cottage contained only a small bathroom.

The bathroom's lone window had been left cracked for circulation, and Tracie pushed it open fully. She unlocked the screen and opened that as well. Then she boosted herself up, much as she had done exiting the warehouse, and dropped to the ground on the outside of the cottage.

The shadows were deep and full on the back side of the two identical Hitler residences, and Tracie felt much more comfortable proceeding this way than she would have using the front door again. The window was placed too high above the ground to enter through it, but for exiting the structure it was perfect.

She held herself flat against the rear cottage wall, getting her bearings and allowing her eyes to once again adjust to the low light in the shadows. The patrolling sentry was nowhere to be seen. She turned right and crept toward the rear of the Phoenix camp.

*　*　*

The sentry was on her before she ever saw him.

"Halt!"

She was partially shrouded in the shadows projected by the barracks buildings when the challenge rang out.

She pivoted toward the sound of the voice and the guard said, "Frieren! Jetzt."

Tracie lifted her hands slowly. "I will freeze," she answered in German. "Please don't shoot."

"Who are you and what are you doing out here in the middle of the night?" The guard stood about ten feet away—too far for Tracie to neutralize—and his right hand rested on the butt of his sidearm, which was still holstered. For the moment. The rifle all the guards seemed to carry remained slung over his shoulder.

"You don't recognize me?" she said innocently. "My name is Helga. I am one of the nurses. We have spoken several times."

The sentry took one step forward, then another. He radiated suspicion. His hand left his pistol and fumbled for a flashlight. This was a bad development. The second he got a good look at her clothing she would be finished. Tracie had to put him down before that happened.

"I asked you what you are doing out here," he said.

"I was looking for you. Or to be more specific, I was looking for any sentry." She stepped toward him, hands held away from her body where he could see them.

"Why do you need a sentry?" His voice was becoming more stressed as his suspicion intensified, but he was now almost within striking range.

"It is about the Führer." She took another step.

"What about the Führer?" She needed to be one...step...closer.

He took that step and stopped in his tracks. Did a double take. "You are not a nurse," he said, and his hand flashed toward his weapon.

"What are you talking about?" She raised her hands quickly, palms out, in front of her face, as she pivoted and launched a sidekick to the sentry's left knee. A sharp *crack!* told her the blow had connected solidly.

He staggered backward in a desperate attempt to maintain his balance on one remaining good leg. Tracie leapt forward as the soldier retreated. She ripped the rifle off his shoulder and drove its butt into the side of his skull before he could scream a warning. A second *crack* and the soldier dropped.

He crumpled to the ground at her feet and lay unmoving. She lifted his sidearm from its holster and tossed it into the forest. His rifle followed right behind it.

She continued on, praying the sentry's first confused warning to her had not been loud enough to wake anyone or alert another sentry. Praying also that he would remain unconscious for a few more minutes.

After that he could shout as much as he wanted, it would play right into her hands.

* * *

The barracks buildings were long and narrow, utilitarian wood-framed structures that had been thrown up hurriedly and for the moment remained unpainted. Their siding appeared relatively dry, and Tracie hoped that in this case appearances weren't deceiving.

She stood for a moment at the southwestern-most corner of the southwestern-most building. Licked her index finger and held it in the air, then smiled. A light but steady breeze was blowing from the southwest. Perfect. The wind wasn't necessary for her plan to succeed but represented an added—and unexpected—bonus.

Tracie knelt and dug a lighter out of her pocket. Flicked it and held it against the wood siding. Watched anxiously as the flames flickered and then lengthened. They devoured the siding greedily and began to work their way upward. Toward the roof. Toward the sky.

She trotted along the rear wall and stopped at a point roughly midway to the next corner. Lit the siding and waited for it to catch. Looked behind her in grim appreciation of her handiwork. The flames were now spreading not just upward, but also along the rear wall, moving toward her, and she knew they would be doing the same thing along the portion of the building she could not see.

Continuing on, Tracie repeated the procedure at the southeastern corner of the empty barracks building. Then she hesitated, torn between the need to return to the cottages before it was too late and the necessity of ensuring the barracks building be fully consumed in flames when she did.

After a moment she made her decision. She retraced her steps, past the rear of the structure, feeling the intense heat of the flames radiating off the burning building. She turned the corner and sprinted to roughly the midpoint of the long side wall. Then she stopped and took the time to light one more section before dropping the lighter into her pocket.

"For better or for worse," she muttered, taking one last look at the flames. Sparks were beginning to rise into the air, carried by the breeze toward the next barracks building in the row of five. It was only a matter of time, and likely not much of it, before that building caught fire as well, and then the one next to it and the one after that.

This would have to be good enough. If the burning buildings didn't accomplish the distraction she needed, nothing would. The success or failure of her plan from this point out would be determined largely by the discipline—or lack thereof—exhibited by Phoenix.

Tracie turned and crept toward where she had left the sentry lying face down in the dirt. She doubted he could possibly have recovered enough already to make himself a threat; he had suffered a concussion at the very least, and quite possibly a fractured skull.

But she wasn't about to take anything on faith.

At the northwest corner of the burning building she paused. Eased her head around the corner. The sentry was still down, but he had rolled onto his side and was struggling to stand while moaning softly.

She re-holstered her weapon and padded to his side. Prodded him in the chest with the toe of her boot, not kicking hard enough to injure him, just ensuring she had his full attention.

Speaking quietly, she said, "Get up. Get your act together. You have work to do."

The man shook his head groggily and held a hand to his skull where Tracie had rapped him with the butt of his own rifle. Blood was leaking down the side of his face, thick and black in the shadows. He looked up and his eyes widened.

He reached for his pistol and she shook her head. Wagged her right index finger at him. "Come on. You don't think I'm that stupid, do you? Your pistol is long gone. And stop worrying about me," she added. "You've got bigger issues at the moment. You need to sound the alarm."

"A-alarm?" He shook his head again. "What in the hell are you talking about?" Between the massive headache she knew was pounding through his skull and the utterly unexpected statement she had just made, his confusion was complete.

He would know what to do soon enough, though. All he would have to do would be to follow her lead.

"FIRE!" she screamed, turning toward the residence buildings near the front of the camp and then pivoting and facing the barracks, three of which had now begun to burn. She cupped her hands around her mouth to fashion a makeshift bullhorn. "FIRE!"

She leaned down over the prone sentry. "I suggest you continue to raise the alarm and get as many of your fellow lunatics as possible back there to fight the blaze. Because if you don't, before you can say 'Heil Hitler' this camp is going to be nothing more than a smoking hole in the ground."

At least, that's the plan, she thought. *Part of it, anyway.*

She turned and sprinted toward the twin cottages with the blue shutters, leaving the confused and injured sentry in her wake. From behind her came muttered curses, and then shouts of alarm as the man finally caught sight of the still-spreading fire. Out beyond the front gate she could hear the confused shouts of the guards manning the entry checkpoint.

Maybe she would get lucky. This suicidal plan just might work.

27

November 19, 1987
2:45 a.m.
Phoenix Compound
Langenberg, Federal Republic of Germany

In the short distance between the downed sentry and the two Hitler cottages, Tracie encountered two more soldiers, both partially dressed and both stumbling toward the flickering glow in the distance. Each man had clearly been roused from a deep sleep, and they rubbed their eyes and yawned as they moved. The barracks were behind her, so she decided these guys must be officers and had been awakened inside the residence buildings north of the Hitler cottages.

The first man stiffened and froze when he caught sight of her. *He probably thinks he's still dreaming,* Tracie thought with a hint of amusement.

She took advantage of his exhaustion and confusion and began haranguing him. "What are you stopping for? Get moving! Every second you hesitate is a second bigger that fire becomes! Move, move, move!"

The man began sprinting toward the fire. He hadn't thought to grab a weapon as he rolled out of his bunk and never even questioned her.

She was almost back to the cottages, sprinting at full speed, when the second soldier spotted her and moved to cut her off. This man seemed much less confused than the first, and much more suspicious. "Halt," he said authoritatively. "Stop right there."

Tracie didn't halt.

She didn't stop right there. She never even slowed.

She veered left, running straight into the man, and raised her knee at contact, ramming it directly into his groin.

"Uhhh," he gasped, and they went down in a tangled heap, tumbling backward and then rolling in the dirt. They came to a stop with Tracie atop the soldier as he writhed in pain. She reached back with her right fist and rabbit-punched him below the ear.

She was up and running again almost before his head hit the ground. She skirted the rear wall of the now-dead Adolph Hitler's cottage, and then did the same with the younger Hitler's residence. She prayed he was still inside and tried to determine how long it had been since her first cries of "Fire!"

Thirty seconds? Forty-five?

It had certainly been no more than a minute. She reasoned it was highly unlikely the new Nazi leader had had time to awaken from a deep sleep, throw on his clothes and then exit his residence to take charge of the firefighting effort.

Still, the two men she had already encountered were all the proof she needed that it *was* possible. And if she arrived at Hitler Junior's cottage to find it empty, she didn't know what she was going to do.

There was no Plan B.

Tracie rounded the second cottage's rear wall and then flattened herself against the siding as she crept toward the farmer's porch. She listened for any sounds that might indicate the younger Hitler was inside the residence, but heard nothing.

Her tension began to rise. This was a dangerous spot to be loitering, and she was far too exposed for her liking as the compound began to come to life. Men were pouring out of virtually all the residence buildings in the cluster surrounding the Hitler cottages, rushing toward the rear of the camp and the burning barracks buildings.

So far, none of the men had spotted her, but it would only be a matter of time before someone did. And she couldn't hope to continue immobilizing soldiers without eventually being caught.

Or worse.

A man trotted past, directly in front of Hitler's cottage, not six feet from Tracie's position.

He didn't see her.

A pair of nurses wandered out of the building from which Tracie had seen them come and go all afternoon and evening. They stood in the middle of the access road, using their hands to shield their eyes from the spotlights as they gazed southward.

They didn't see her either.

Tracie perked up at the sound and vibration of footfalls inside the cottage. Someone was still inside the building, although there was no way to know—yet—whether that someone might be Hitler.

The footsteps approached the front door. Tracie edged closer to the side of the porch, balancing the need to remain unseen with the equally important requirement to be as close to the door as possible when it came time to make her move.

A moment later the door opened, and a voice from deeper inside the cottage barked, "What is happening? I want to know *now!*"

The footsteps clomped onto the porch, and Tracie watched from just around the corner as a sentry—fully dressed, wool overcoat on, rifle slung over his shoulder—stared for a moment toward the burning buildings.

"Fire," he said, an edge to his voice. "The barracks, they are on fire!"

"How bad is it?" Although Tracie had yet to see the man this voice belonged to, she knew it had to be the younger Hitler. His tone was crisp and authoritative, like a man who was accustomed to being obeyed immediately and fully.

"It looks bad," the sentry said. "It looks very bad."

"Go. Take command of the firefighting efforts until I arrive. I'll dress and be there in two or three minutes."

"But, Mein Führer, I am not to leave your side. Ever. Those were your father's orders, sir. He was very explicit."

"Who is your commanding officer, Hans?"

"Well, you, sir."

"Then you will do as you are told. Begin organizing the men into a fire brigade and I will be there in minutes."

"Yes, Mein Führer." The sentry's reluctance was plain, but he had no alternative than to obey a direct order. He descended the steps and began double-timing in the direction of the barracks, shouting orders toward the rear of the camp almost as soon as his feet hit the dusty ground.

Tracie was moving, grabbing the railing with both hands and vaulting it, landing as quietly as she could on the pine plank floor. She was sure she knew what Hitler would do next. It was human nature. He would walk through the front door and onto the porch to see the blaze and try to assess the damage with his own two eyes before returning to his bedroom to dress.

And she was determined to meet him when he did.

The porch was engulfed in shadow, minimizing the risk of being seen by a soldier passing in the glare of the floodlights. At this point, though, any risk of being seen was secondary to the necessity of an up-close-and-personal meeting with Adolph Hitler Junior. Tracie had worked hard to set up the best distraction she could, and if she failed now that she had done so, she would likely never get a second chance.

She padded across the porch and reached the doorway at virtually the same moment as Hitler. She stopped short, pressing herself against the front wall of the cottage as the door flew open and the Nazi leader barreled onto the porch.

He never saw her.

He stood at the top of the stairs, shielding his eyes in unconscious imitation of the nurses still standing in the middle of the access road. He stared for a moment into the distance, shaking his head and muttering to himself, before turning on his heel.

And running directly into Tracie Tanner.

He stopped and glared at her in obvious surprise but absolutely no fear. It didn't seem to have occurred to him that he might be in danger inside his own training camp, surrounded by dozens of fellow fanatics.

"Who are you, and what do you want?" the Nazi demanded.

"I'm your worst nightmare, and I want you."

He furrowed his forehead. His confusion was evident but he still showed no sign of concern.

"Whatever this is about," he said, "I will deal with it later. Right now I have more pressing priorities, as you can see." He gestured toward the rear of the camp and the burning buildings, as if perhaps Tracie had not yet caught sight of them.

"I don't think so." She shook her head and drew her weapon. It wasn't technically necessary, Hitler Junior wasn't armed and she had no doubt she could maneuver him physically if it came to that. But physical action would be much more likely to draw the unwanted attention of passing soldiers than would holding a pistol and shielding it from view with her body.

So that was what she did.

"Right now," she continued, "your priorities are whatever I say they are. And I say you're going to turn around and march right back inside your lovely little cottage."

He glanced from the pistol to Tracie's face, his features arranged in an expression of sheer disbelief. "I will do no such thing."

"Walk or die. It's your choice. But make it now, because time is at a premium."

Hitler Junior's entire body began shaking. His head, his hands and arms, every exposed body part trembled. At first, Tracie thought it was out of fear, but then she realized he still wasn't afraid. He was shaking from fury. This was not a man accustomed to being crossed.

He glared at her, his eyes dark and angry. And then he stalked past her and into the cottage. He didn't go for her gun, didn't try to slam the door before she could react. He simply walked inside and waited for her to join him.

28

"What is it you want? Why do you come here and threaten me?" The younger—and now only living—Hitler spoke quietly, his voice cold and hostile, and he stared at Tracie with undisguised loathing.

"What do I want? At the moment, I want my curiosity satisfied. I want to know just what the hell you hope to accomplish with… all of this."

They faced each other in the tiny living area of what appeared to be an exact duplicate of the Hitler Senior's cottage, right down to the minimalist furnishings. Tracie wondered whether the bedroom would feature just a single bed and small end table, as it had for the frail, obviously dying Hitler. She doubted it.

"What do I hope to accomplish? Are you serious? I hope to—I *will*—accomplish what was so unfairly denied my father. I will accomplish a world where the Thousand Year Reich reigns supreme once again, a world where the superior, both mentally and physically, shall rule. I will accomplish a world as it should have been so long ago."

"The 'superior' being you, and those who look and think like you."

Hitler was silent. He gazed impassively at Tracie. He silence was answer enough. She was aware of the time passing, understood implicitly that the bodyguard who had so reluctantly gone off to take charge of the firefighting efforts would return soon, once it became clear his boss wasn't following as he had promised to do. She understood also that the bodyguard's return would occur sooner rather than later, and that if she were still here when it happened she would likely never leave the camp alive.

And yet she stood rooted to the spot, frozen by the sheer audacity—and apparently limitless evil—of the man standing before her. He hadn't even been alive when his father murdered millions of men, women and children solely due to their heritage, and yet he seemed to be cut from exactly the same cloth, seemed to suffer exactly the same delusions.

Was it DNA? A strand of insanity that had imbedded itself in Adolph Hitler and then been passed along to his heir, born when the elder had already been eliminated as a threat to world security?

Or was this evil learned? The product of an upbringing where the son had been subjected day after day to the twisted philosophies and moral rot of a father who had come far too close to fulfilling his dream the first time and been hell-bent on accomplishing those same goals decades later through his proxy. His son.

It was a question Tracie knew she would ponder over the course of dozens—hundreds—of sleepless nights, and also one that would be the source of endless nightmares to be suffered through when she *did* sleep.

But at this moment, the question was irrelevant.

At this moment, she had an assignment to be executed.

So to speak.

Hitler had backed away from Tracie as they faced each other, eventually running out of room in front of a small fireplace with a plain mantel, adorned only with a pair of potted plants.

He raised his hands in what was apparently supposed to be interpreted as a gesture of reason, or perhaps of compromise. "Now I will ask you the same question. What do you hope to accomplish? It is obvious you are the one who set fire to my barracks."

"That's right."

"But all of them are empty except one. And even if every last building is destroyed, even if this entire camp burns to the ground and is leveled, we will simply rebuild." Hitler's eyes glittered in the low light with manic intensity, his face burning with a passion that had to equal—and maybe surpass—anything his father might have displayed as he was building his empire of evil back in the 1930s and 1940s.

It was awe-inspiring and terrifying.

"We will come back bigger and stronger and better," he continued, "because *we* are the men of destiny. *We* are the ones who will craft a new world, a world that will come as close to perfection as humanly possible. *We* are the ones, don't you understand? The world has been waiting four long decades for the return of Nazi Germany, and when we *do* return, we will be bigger and stronger and better armed than before. And we will be unstoppable."

Tracie watched and listened, spellbound. Adolph Hitler Junior was every bit the charismatic presence his father must have been. Evil and black-hearted, clearly, but charismatic nevertheless.

His hands remained spread as he continued speaking with messianic fervor. His right hand hovered directly in front of one of the plants atop the fireplace mantel. "We are on the verge of receiving an influx of financial support the likes of which even the richest nations on earth have never seen. This windfall will constitute the final piece of the puzzle. The New Third Reich will have the ability to recruit and train warriors far superior to those available to any misguided nations who might seek to oppose us. It will take time, that is true, but we are far closer to realizing our goals than you or any others on the outside realize."

Too late, Tracie realized she had allowed the Nazi fanatic to take control of the conversation, to dictate the terms of engagement. She had unconsciously lowered her weapon during Hitler's soliloquy, and now she began to raise it, internal alarm bells jangling.

Hitler continued speaking as he reached behind the potted plant atop the fireplace mantel and swept it to the floor. Its ceramic base shattered, exploding in a hail of shards and dirt. In one smooth motion, he grasped a handgun that had been hidden behind the plant.

He fired even before aiming, even as he was still pulling the gun off the mantel. Tracie squeezed her trigger at the same time, the pair of percussive blasts melding into one single awful explosion.

Her shot missed its target.

Hitler's shot missed its target.

Tracie cursed her carelessness even as she dropped to the floor and rolled. Hitler's gun roared again, the slug thudding into the wood plank floor inches from her head. Her ears were ringing and the sharp smell of gunpowder filled the room and she rolled again before her shoulder banged against Hitler's closed bedroom door.

The Führer fired a third time, but he had expected Tracie to stop, not to roll a second time, and his bullet hit the floor again, this time in the space her body had occupied until a half-second ago.

Tracie was on her side, unable to roll further. She sighted up the barrel and squeezed the trigger before Hitler could manage a third shot, and the slug hit home, square in the man's chest. He had taken one step forward as he fired, and now he staggered back, slamming into the fireplace mantel as a crimson circle bloomed on the front of his white nightshirt

He glanced down incredulously, as if unable to comprehend what had just happened, and then he raised his weapon again.

Tracie squeezed off another shot, and this one hit home less than an inch from the first, and now more blood flowed, and Adolph Hitler Junior pulled his own trigger, but his body had spasmed when the second bullet struck home, and his gun belched fire and roared for the last time as the bullet blasted harmlessly into the ceiling.

Then he sank to the floor, coming to rest on his knees.

His mouth opened.

Closed.

Opened again.

He tried to speak, but any words he might have managed were lost in the ringing in Tracie's ears. She was at the moment totally deaf.

He didn't fire his gun. He seemed to have forgotten he was holding it. The fanatical glitter in his eyes was replaced by a look of stunned incomprehension, and as Tracie watched, they glazed over completely.

He was no longer looking at Tracie.

He was no longer looking at anything.

He stared straight ahead as he tumbled forward onto his face.

29

Tracie pushed herself to her feet, never letting her weapon stray from the motionless body of Adolph Hitler II. He was dead, she was sure of it, and yet a career's worth of training and experience had taught her to take nothing for granted.

She edged across the room and stopped next to the prone man. Hitler's gun had dropped to the floor next to his hand, and Tracie reached forward with one foot and kicked it across the floor.

She reached down with her left hand. Kept her Glock trained on Hitler with her right. Pressed two fingers to his neck below his ear. Felt for a pulse.

Didn't get one.

Checked again.

Still nothing.

Finally satisfied he was no longer a threat, Tracie rolled the body over onto its back. She was breathing heavily and shaking, and not just from adrenaline. She had allowed herself to be distracted by the sheer force of her target's personality—he was as evil as his father had been, of that there could be no question, the malevolence had radiated off the man in black waves—but he was a spellbinding speaker, and Tracie had been drawn in.

The mistake had nearly cost her life.

She forced herself to concentrate. There would be plenty of time later to castigate herself for her potentially lethal lapse in judgment—always assuming, of course, she made it out of here alive—but for now there was still work to be done.

Tracie stared at the corpse, shaking her head in amazement. The likeness of this man to the images she had seen of the 1940s-era Adolph Hitler was striking, even more so up close than when she had observed the man from a distance. If she had seen a photo of Adolph Hitler II today, she would have had no reason to believe he was anyone other than The Führer himself. Had this man lived, he would have been the most successful weapon in the New Nazi Party's arsenal in terms of recruitment and propaganda.

To Tracie Tanner, though, he represented nothing more than a checkmark inside a box. She was one step closer to mission completion.

The corpse's eyes were open and staring straight up at the ceiling, and although his heart no longer pumped blood through the twin bullet wounds, his nightshirt had nearly soaked through with it. The white cotton clung to his chest, sticky from blood.

A gold chain hung around the dead man's neck, and Tracie felt a lightning bolt of excitement shoot through her. She had almost given up hope of finding the relic that stood at the heart of this mission—the Amber Room treasure key—but now, it looked as though the key may have fallen right into her lap.

And it made sense that it would be here. A man with Hitler's arrogance and overarching confidence would never have entrusted an item worth upwards of three hundred million dollars to anyone else's care.

He would have insisted on keeping it close.

Probably very close.

Probably around his neck, hanging on a gold chain.

Tracie knelt and lifted the chain and raised her eyebrows in surprise. What she had thought was a single strand of gold rope, thick and glittering, was in reality a pair of identical chains.

They separated when she lifted them, and she began pulling them out from under Hitler's shirt. Whatever was hanging from the chains was large and relatively heavy, and offered considerable resistance against the weight of the blood-soaked nightshirt.

She tugged harder and a moment later they popped free. She held Hitler's head off the floor with one hand and lifted the chains clear. Dangling at the end of each was a large gold skeleton key, complete with tiny boxes threaded through with copper wiring at the end of each tine.

The keys looked identical.

And it all became clear.

Of course.

The door to the hidden vault containing the Amber Room treasure was secured by a *pair* of booby-trapped locks, not just by one single lock.

It stood to reason. Even with Berlin falling down around him in 1945, even as he prepared for a desperate dash to freedom that would likely result in death, Adolph Hitler Senior would never have trusted a lowly Nazi soldier with the only access to hundreds of millions of dollars. He would have wanted a failsafe, and by keeping one of the two keys to the locked vault, he would have ensured no one could access it until *he* decided the time was right.

She could see it all clearly in her mind's eye. To open the vault and render the booby traps—bombs, probably—useless, it would be necessary to turn both keys at the same time. It was one of the measures for safeguarding nuclear weapons that had been in place for decades: A single operator, working alone, could not produce a nuclear strike; the weapons were accessible only to at least two people working together.

It was simple and brilliant.

And if her theory was right, she now had in her possession *both* keys to the Amber Room treasure. But her mission was to cripple Phoenix, and although eliminating the two Hitlers represented a good start, it would all be for nothing if she were unable to escape this compound. A Hitler-less Phoenix would still be formidable if allowed to access three hundred million dollars.

And Tracie knew she had to be running out of time.

Hitler's bodyguard would be back any second.

She was surprised he hadn't already returned.

She slipped the pair of identical gold chains over her head and dropped the blood-soaked keys down the front of her blouse. They were tacky with drying blood and she could feel them sticking to her skin and she grimaced in distaste.

The sound of heavy footfalls pounding the dusty ground drew Tracie's attention away from the keys and back to the task at hand: staying alive. Someone was moving fast, and that someone was approaching Adolph Hitler Junior's cottage.

It could only be one person.

Tracie bent and shoved her hands under the corpse's armpits. Lifted Hitler's upper body and began dragging him across the floor toward the stuffed chair the bodyguard had apparently been using while his boss slept. Hitler Junior had not been a particularly large man, but he was nothing more than dead weight now—literally—and pulling him against the drag presented by the lush Oriental rug installed in the living area was a chore.

The footfalls clomped up the wooden steps of the farmer's porch as Tracie reached the chair. A pair of clipped knocks on the door were followed almost immediately by a voice, concerned and slightly out of breath: "Mein Führer? Are you alright? Do you need help, sir?"

Tracie lifted the body as high as she could with her petite frame. She was shaking and panting from effort, stress and adrenaline. She heaved Adolph Hitler Junior into the chair, wishing she had had the foresight to lock the front door. It wouldn't have kept the bodyguard out but could have given her a few extra precious seconds, time that very well might represent the difference between living and dying.

"Mein Führer! Please answer me!" The bodyguard knocked a second time, two quick raps with his knuckles, and from the rising tension in his voice she knew a third knock would not come. His sense of propriety had kept the man out of his boss's cottage thus far, but duty was about to override propriety.

Hitler's body slumped to the side and Tracie straightened it. Her goal was to make the corpse look like a man taking a well-deserved rest, although even if successful, the fiction would only last a fraction of a second—nobody "rested" with the amount of blood soaking this man's shirt. He had died with his eyes open, and now they stared straight ahead, directly toward the still-closed front door as if in rapt fascination.

Across the room the knob rattled, and Tracie pictured the bodyguard weighing his responsibility for protecting Adolph Hitler's life with the certainty of severe punishment that would follow if he entered without an invitation and the Führer was simply changing clothes or sitting on the john.

She crossed his legs at the knee and slipped behind the chair, gun drawn.

And waited for the door to open.

30

November 19, 1987
3:05 a.m.
Phoenix Compound
Langenberg, Federal Republic of Germany

She didn't have to wait long. She had barely dropped into a crouch, gun held in two hands against the chair's right wingback, when the door burst open and the bodyguard entered.

"I am sorry, Mein Führer, but I—"

A pair of combat-boot-clad footfalls told Tracie the man had taken two hasty steps into the cottage and then frozen at the bizarre sight of his boss, Adolph Hitler Junior, apparently relaxing in a stuffed chair while his precious Phoenix training camp burned to the ground around him.

The shock would only last a second, though, and then the man would take in the sight of the blood-soaked nightshirt and Hitler's sightless, staring eyes and reality would set in.

And Tracie would lose her only advantage.

She could not allow that to happen. She eased around the edge of the chair, gun first, and trained her weapon on the bodyguard. His eyes widened almost comically. He hadn't thought to draw his weapon, obviously hadn't believed his boss could be in any real danger inside a camp filled with loyalists, surrounded by an electrified fence and protected by sentries armed with automatic weapons.

He would now pay for that error in judgment. "Remove your pistol from its holster. Hold it by the handle with just your thumb and forefinger. Then drop it on the floor at your feet and kick it away."

The man didn't move. His mouth had dropped half-open and he looked as though he simply could not comprehend what was happening.

"Last chance," Tracie said. "Do as I say or die."

Very slowly, the guard unsnapped the black leather holster at his hip. He lifted his gun and held it to the side. The he dropped it onto the floor and offered up a half-hearted kick that moved the gun maybe a foot across the carpeted floor.

Maybe less.

She would have to keep a very close eye on this man.

"Now reach back and close the door."

"No."

"Excuse me?"

"The minute I close this door, you are going to shoot me, just as you shot the Führer. I will not make it easy for you to do so."

Tracie snorted. "If I wanted you dead, you'd be bleeding out on the floor already. Today's your lucky day, Fritz, because I want you alive. But I don't *need* you alive. That's a critical difference. So if you don't close that door, right now, I'll shoot you in the forehead where you stand."

She could almost see the gears turning in the bodyguard's head. *Do I have time to scream for help?* •

After a moment he reached the appropriate conclusion. He felt behind his body with his right hand and gave the door a shove. It slammed closed and they were alone.

"Very good," she said. "You're not exactly a soccer star, are you?"

Confusion clouded his eyes. Good. If her hastily devised plan for escape was to stand any chance of working, she needed to keep this man confused and off-balance.

"That kick," she said by way of explanation. "Any three-year-old could have moved the gun farther than you did. It's almost as though you weren't really trying."

The guard's eyes narrowed but he said nothing.

Tracie nodded to her left, toward the wall separating the sitting room from Hitler's Junior's bedroom. "Move over there and face the wall. Stand perfectly still or I'll put a bullet in your brain."

The bodyguard reluctantly did as instructed. He clearly thought he was about to die, Tracie's assurances to the contrary notwithstanding, and that was to her advantage also.

He reached the wall and stopped, face inches from it.

"Now, spread your legs and lace your hands together on top of your head."

"This is ridiculous." The man twisted, making a sudden move toward Tracie, and she squeezed off a round, risking the sound of one more gunshot, banking on the hope that everyone with a weapon was at the south end of the camp fighting the fire. No one had come running after the gun battle with Hitler; maybe her luck would hold out for a few more minutes.

And, really, she had no choice. It was critical she keep the bodyguard under control.

The slug thudded into the wall next to the man and he jumped as if tagged with a live wire. Then he froze in mid-step. He turned reluctantly back toward the wall and spread his legs as instructed, then lifted his hands to the top of his head and stood perfectly still.

"Much better," Tracie said, rising to her feet and stepping past the chair. "Move one centimeter in any direction and the next bullet goes into your head." She was behind him in three steps and she quickly patted him down, searching for a backup gun or knife and finding nothing.

The verification that the man was unarmed did little to calm her nerves. Hitler had hidden a gun behind a potted plant and had nearly taken her out with it; there was no way of knowing how many other weapons might be stashed away in here.

And time was rapidly running out. Even if the latest gunshot had gone unnoticed by anyone outside, when neither Hitler nor the bodyguard returned to the scene of the fire in the next couple of minutes, more soldiers would begin to wonder what had happened to their boss. They would come to investigate and this time they would likely not come alone.

And Tracie would be trapped.

She had to be out of here before that happened.

"Here's how this is going to go down," she said. "Pay attention, because I don't have time to say it twice." She shoved her gun barrel against the back of the man's head for emphasis and he flinched but said nothing.

"You're going to pick up that phone over there next to your dead Führer. You are going to notify the front gate that you have to leave the camp to coordinate with fire rescue, which is on its way. Then we're going to walk to one of the vehicles parked outside your headquarters. You're going to drive out of here while I sit behind you with my weapon trained through the back of the seat on your spine. If you can't get us out of the compound, I'll pull the trigger and you will either be dead or wish you were."

"That will *never* work," the guard said contemptuously. "We would never ask for outside help with a fire or with anything else."

"Then come up with something better. But make it believable or the next time you leave this room it'll be zipped inside a body bag."

"I could say the same of you."

He was right. If he chose not to cooperate, Tracie could kill him but she would be no closer to escaping the camp.

"Your choice," she said without hesitation. "Start walking toward that phone or I execute you right now and move on to Plan B." *If only I had one.*

The man exhaled forcefully and then turned away from the wall, moving slowly, being careful not to do anything that could be interpreted as threatening. "You'll never get out of here," he said again, but he continued moving.

"You let me worry about that," she said. "Just pick up the phone and give the performance of your life."

He lifted the handset off the cradle. Tracie jabbed her gun into his ribs and said, "If you try to pass along any kind of signal to your buddies at the front gate, you know what's going to happen, correct?"

He glared at her but remained silent.

"Good," she said. "Make the call."

The bodyguard stared for a moment longer and then dialed one number, lifting the handset to his ear.

After a brief pause, he spoke into the phone. "This is Statzer. Open the front gate, I must leave immediately."

Muffled sound came through the earpiece. Tracie could hear the garbled words but could not decipher them.

She didn't need to. It was obvious the sentry was protesting the absence of the proper protocol for someone leaving the camp.

"Don't worry about it," Statzer barked. "Just do as you are told. Do not force me to put the Führer on the line. He is very busy right now and you won't like what happens to your future in this organization if I have to interrupt him."

He listened a moment longer and then said, "That is not your problem. Just ensure the gate is open when I approach in my vehicle. I'll be there in five minutes." Tracie prodded him with her weapon. He jumped and glanced down at her, and she rotated the gun barrel in a *hurry up* gesture.

He returned his attention to the telephone and said, "Make it three minutes." Then he looked again at Tracie. She nodded and he replaced the receiver on the cradle.

"Very good," she said. "Now let's go."

He spread his hands in confusion. "You expect to simply walk out the front door of the Führer's quarters and not be seen?"

"That's exactly what I expect, unless a bunch of your fellow Nazis come running to see what's taking their messiah so long to arrive at the fire. Outside of the gate guards, everyone who matters—meaning everyone with a gun—is on the other side of the camp trying to keep this place from becoming nothing more than a smudge in the middle of the forest."

The guard shook his head but didn't protest further. It was obvious he expected Tracie to be accosted by a passing soldier the minute they walked out the door, but if it was her desire to die in a hail of bullets, he wasn't about to stop her.

He moved across the room, Tracie a half-step behind, her gun pressed to the middle of his back. When they arrived at the front entrance, Hitler's personal bodyguard snatched a key hanging off a peg in the wall, and then threw the door open and marched onto the porch. The authoritative *clack-clack-clack* of his boots provided a clear contrast to the distant shouts of panicked soldiers completely unprepared to fight a fire without someone telling them what to do and how to do it.

Tracie didn't die in a hail of bullets.

No one was around to shoot her.

As far as she could tell, no one was even around to see her. The nurses she had observed watching the fire from the middle of the access road were long gone, and the area surrounding the two Hitler residence cabins was deserted.

Statzer cursed under his breath, his frustration obvious. He continued moving, though, crossing the porch and descending the stairs.

"Which car is yours?" Tracie said.

"None of them are mine," he said. "They belong to Phoenix."

"Don't fuck with me. You know what I mean."

"The key I grabbed belongs to the Führer's personal vehicle."

"Lead the way."

The bodyguard stalked along the gravel path toward the Phoenix headquarters building. Gravel crunched underfoot and a light breeze fluttered Tracie's hair around her face. The fresh air smelled sweet after the bitter, coppery stench of blood and death inside Hitler's cabin.

Tracie removed her gun from Statzer's backbone but didn't dare holster it. He had turned on her once and she knew he was waiting for an opportunity to do so again. So she walked a step behind him with the weapon held in her right hand, pressed against her outer thigh. The distance between them would allow her enough time to raise the gun and squeeze off a shot if he reversed course and came at her.

She hoped.

A half-dozen vehicles sat empty in a small lot front of the headquarters building, all midsized Mercedes Benz sedans, all sporting similar anonymous-looking silver paint jobs. They had clearly been purchased or stolen with one goal in mind: to draw as little attention as possible on the rare occasions a Phoenix staff member left the relative safety of the Nazi compound and ventured into hostile territory.

Statzer approached the car closest them and unlocked the driver's door. He began lowering himself into the seat and Tracie stepped behind him, forcing her body into the space between the open door and the car's frame, determined to prevent him from slamming the door closed and trapping her outside.

She reached behind his left shoulder and unlocked the rear door.

Opened it and slipped inside.

Then she lowered herself to the floor behind the driver's seat, wondering how clear the line of sight might be between the headquarters building and the guard shack. Undoubtedly the sentries were equipped with binoculars, and she was sure the first thing they had done following Statzer's unusual phone call was to pick up their binoculars and train them on the interior of the camp. If they had seen her leave Hitler's cabin and follow the Führer's bodyguard into this car, in the middle of the night and with the compound burning to the ground, it would further lessen the already microscopic odds of her escaping alive.

But there was nothing she could do about any of that now. She had developed the best escape plan she could, and the only thing left to do was follow it through to its conclusion.

Whatever that might be.

"Now what?" Statzer said. The answer was blindingly obvious and Tracie knew he was stalling for time.

"Now you start the car and drive through the front gate. If it doesn't open, you die. If anyone approaches from any direction, you die. And so on, and so forth. You know the drill. Get moving."

The engine rumbled to life, and a moment later the bodyguard began backing out of the parking spot. He spun the wheel and hit the brakes.

Shifted into drive and accelerated out of the lot.

Turned toward the front gate.

Approached slowly and stopped.

And everything went to hell.

31

November 19, 1987
3:15 a.m.
Phoenix Compound
Langenberg, Federal Republic of Germany

"Move it," Tracie said. "If the gate hasn't opened yet, just hit the gas and ram it. Force your way through."

No response.

"I said go!" she hissed.

Statzer said, "You will never get out of here alive." His voice was resigned but calm, and Tracie realized what had happened just as the sound of approaching footfalls reached her ears. It was what she had feared from the moment she forced Statzer to call the sentries at the front gate. Some kind of code word was required any time they were ordered to open it, even when the order originated from a high-ranking Phoenix staff member.

And Statzer hadn't used it.

Without that code word, the guards were instructed never to open the gate.

No matter what.

It was still closed, and would remain so. Statzer was willing to die for his cause. He had never planned on allowing Tracie to leave the Phoenix compound. In seconds, at least one armed sentry would reach the car, and the moment he spotted Tracie crouched on the rear floor, her fate would be sealed.

It probably already was.

But she wasn't giving up without a fight. She moved instantly, relying on training and instinct and, hopefully, whatever was left of the element of surprise. She shoved herself off the floor and lifted her gun to eye-level while swinging it to the right. Squeezed the trigger once, concerned only with blowing out the rear window, knowing her odds of intentionally hitting anything through the glass were virtually nil.

The gun roared and fire belched from the end of the barrel and Tracie's ears, which had only just begun to recover from the percussive blast of the shots fired inside Hitler's cabin, started to ring and ache. The window shattered, turning milky white and spraying safety glass outward like a bomb had exploded inside the car.

She ignored the pain in her ears, ignored the distraction of the shattering glass, ignored everything except her desperate search for the approaching guard. She was dimly aware of Statzer beginning to turn toward her from the front seat. Hitler's bodyguard had been immobilized for a moment by the blast of the gunshot but in a split-second he would be all over her.

She squeezed off a second shot designed to keep the approaching sentry on the defensive, and then without taking her attention off the outside of the car, bent her left arm and pistoned it in Statzer's direction. The sickening crunch of bone-on-bone contact told her she had scored a direct hit, and if her ears hadn't been ringing, she knew she would hear the sound of the Nazi's nose shattering.

Blood spurted, arcing outward, and Statzer instinctively slapped his hands to his face. Probably no more than two seconds had passed since the car rolled to a stop in front of the security fence, but Tracie knew she was almost out of time.

She swung her gun hand across her body again, slamming the butt of the Glock into Statzer's face a second time, now feeling bones break in his fingers.

Hopefully the injuries would be enough to subdue Statzer for a little longer, because she was out of time and could no longer afford to be distracted by him. The gate guard had taken cover after Tracie's two gunshots, but he recovered quickly, and now the shadow looming through the broken window told her he was there.

A slug blasted into the car, fired hurriedly and haphazardly by the rattled sentry. It buried itself into Statzer's neck, and just like that, Tracie no longer had to worry about the driver. The sentry's shot had been rushed and panicked and the guard had unwittingly helped Tracie out, maybe even saving her life.

For the moment.

She ducked low, using the vehicle's steel frame to protect herself. Then she reached back and opened the rear door and rolled out of the car, dropping onto the dusty access road with a bone-jarring thud.

The same elbow that had just broken Statzer's nose cracked painfully against the ground and Tracie gasped but never stopped moving. She reversed direction and rolled beneath the Nazi's still-idling car.

Her right arm grazed the exhaust pipe, burning the skin, and she gasped again but kept rolling.

Positioned herself along the right side of the car between the front and rear tires.

Raised her weapon in both hands.

And spotted the gate guard's combat boots. Tracie moved slightly farther to the right, exposing a bit more of herself but gaining a view of the man's entire body.

He had only been a couple of feet away from the car when he fired his single shot into the interior, but he must have leapt instinctively backward after seeing Statzer's body slumped over the steering wheel. He was maybe eight feet from the car now, but beginning to approach again, moving slowly, holding his pistol in front of his face and sweeping it from side to side.

He knew she had disappeared from the car, but not where she had gone. At any moment, her location would occur to him. It was the only place she *could* have gone after rolling out of the car, and were it not for the stress and surprise of the situation, he would already have realized it.

She raised her weapon and shot him between the eyes.

The soldier didn't stagger backward. Didn't scream. He dropped straight down, landing in a crumpled heap next to the car.

From the south side of the camp, Tracie could hear garbled shouts and an authoritative-sounding voice issuing orders. The shouts seemed to be getting louder, which meant her luck had finally run out. Someone had heard the last two gunshots, or perhaps had seen the gunfight at Statzer's vehicle from a distance.

Tracie scrambled out from under the car, her injured arm burning in agony, and sprinted around the front to the driver's side. She glanced toward the rear of the camp as she did, and silhouetted against the raging blaze were a group of Nazi recruits sprinting in her direction.

The car's rear door was still standing open and she slammed it closed, then yanked open the driver's door. She filled both fists with the now-dead Statzer's uniform, grabbing him under the armpits, and dragged him from the car before dropping his body onto the access road.

Then she slid into the front seat and slammed the door closed. The steering wheel was slick with Statzer's blood, and her left hand slipped in it as she shifted the transmission into drive with her right.

Once in gear, she placed both hands on the wheel and jammed the accelerator to the floor. The car leaped forward, the growl of the engine transforming instantly into a high-pitched whine. The Mercedes sedans were heavy and powerful, and gravel and dirt sprayed from the rear wheels like machine-gun fire.

Tracie smiled thinly as the men leading the charge from the south side of the camp were peppered. Two of them fell to the ground, writhing in pain, but the rest kept coming. Some of the more operationally aware soldiers had drawn their weapons and were even now firing in her direction.

The chain-link security gate loomed in the windshield and Tracie braced for the collision that was about to come, ducking low and maintaining a secure grip on the steering wheel with both hands. She locked her elbows together so that her arms were positioned vertically over the wheel. She wished she had taken a half-second to secure the seatbelt but it was too late to worry about that now.

A second later the Mercedes slammed into the gate, engine screaming, and Tracie was thrown forward at the sudden deceleration. Her head impacted the wheel, her face crashing into her arms, blood exploding from her nose at the impact, mixing with Statzer's and dripping to the floor.

The car rocked and screeched as the gate's metal tines snapped apart, sliding across its steel body like grasping fingers desperate to keep Tracie contained inside the Phoenix compound. A bullet imbedded itself in the dashboard just to her right, thudding into the wood paneling.

And then she was through. She had kept the accelerator glued to the floor, and the big Mercedes began picking up speed again, barreling away from the Phoenix compound.

Without slowing, Tracie lifted herself upright. The car was angled toward the trees of the forest surrounding the Phoenix camp, and she flicked the wheel to the left to maintain the road, the engine still screaming. The needle on the speedometer passed forty kilometers per hour, then fifty, and then sixty, and still Tracie coaxed more horsepower out of the engine. Within seconds, the remainder of the vehicles parked outside the Phoenix headquarters building would be filled with armed soldiers, all with one mission: to capture or kill the infiltrator.

She aimed to be long gone when that happened, and she divided her attention equally between the windshield and the rear view mirror until reaching a crossroad three kilometers southwest of the camp.

Still no headlights behind her.

She picked a random direction—left—and yanked the wheel hard, barely slowing for the ninety-degree turn. The Mercedes screeched through the intersection and she buried the accelerator again, the car's rear end fishtailing, tires screeching in protest.

Two kilometers later she slowed. Traffic was minimal, and continuing her breakneck pace now would only get her killed or jailed for reckless driving.

She maintained a sedate speed all the way to the CIA safe house.

32

November 19, 1987
4:05 a.m.
Phoenix Compound
Langenberg, Federal Republic of Germany

"There's an old munitions factory west of Wuppertal," Stallings said, his voice crackly and faraway-sounding through the satellite phone's earpiece. "The place was abandoned following the conclusion of World War II and has been falling steadily further into disrepair ever since."

Tracie had wasted no time contacting the CIA chief after escaping the Phoenix camp. There was none to waste. She assumed that the command structure at Phoenix—what was left of it— would make every attempt to secure the Amber Room treasure the moment they discovered Adolph Hitler Senior and Junior assassinated and the odd-looking skeleton keys missing from Junior's body.

How much securing would be possible by a suddenly decimated Phoenix, especially minus the all-important Amber Room keys, Tracie didn't know, but she didn't plan to find out, either. Who was to say there weren't two more keys out there somewhere? Who was to say Phoenix wouldn't organize a hasty stakeout of the storage site in an attempt to murder Tracie and regain control of the keys?

After all she had seen over the last couple of days, Tracie wasn't willing to eliminate any possibility.

The first few minutes of the conference with Stallings had gone exactly as Tracie expected, with the acerbic spymaster stingy in his praise of her for completing her mission, and unimpressed by the news that she had secured the key taken from the Soviet operative's Kaminecke Hotel room after his murder.

Everything changed, however, when she added the bombshell that she had recovered a *second* key, similar to the first in that it contained identical tiny boxes rigged with copper wiring.

The boss's voice perked up, and his caustic manner fell away. He was suddenly all business.

"You have possession of both keys at this time?" he asked.

"That's what I just said."

"Then your assignment has just been amended."

"Let me guess," Tracie said. "I'm to attempt to locate the site of the Amber Room treasure."

"Finding the site will not be a problem," Stallings said with virtually no hesitation. "We think we know exactly where the treasure is located. I feel confident we've *always* known exactly where the treasure was located."

Tracie realized she wasn't the least bit surprised. "You just didn't feel the need to share that knowledge with me."

"I never hid that information from you."

"You said you thought you had a general idea of the treasure's location. That's much different than what you just said."

"You're splitting hairs, Tanner. There was no need to share that knowledge with *anyone*, including you. It was useless—as was our knowledge of the first key's location—unless and until we could gain possession of the second key. We've known all along, as have the Soviets, presumably, that the treasure site was booby-trapped by the Nazis when they stashed the loot there in the 1940s. They rigged it with explosives designed to incinerate the treasure—not to mention the people attempting to access it—if any attempt was made to open its storage locker without use of two custom-made skeleton keys.

"The two keys currently in my possession."

"Correct."

"So if you already know where the treasure is being stored, and the only thing preventing the CIA from accessing it is the lack of the second key, then…"

"That's right. I want you to visit the Amber Room."

"Why me? Isn't that something that should be handled by someone a little higher up on the food chain?"

"When it comes to extracting the treasure, sure. But I'm still basing everything on decades-old intelligence reports that may or may not have been accurate when they were filed. And even if they *were* accurate, who knows what may have happened in the intervening time. Perhaps someone came into possession of the keys years ago and moved the treasure. Perhaps…"

His voice trailed away, and Tracie knew exactly what he was thinking. Suddenly Aaron Stallings's willingness to send a single lowly field operative to examine three hundred million dollars' worth of treasure made perfect sense.

"Perhaps," she said, completing the director's unspoken thought, "in the forty-some-odd years since the booby-traps were planted, the explosives have degraded, and the whole damn thing is going to blow up in the key-holder's face."

Stallings cleared his throat and was silent for a moment. Then he said, "That outcome is highly unlikely. Those keys, and the explosives they are designed to defuse, were crafted by some of the most accomplished engineers at the Nazis' disposal, men who worked on the German nuclear program, and had a hand in developing their U-boat program and other weapons systems. I don't doubt for a second that the explosives are just as reliable today as they were back in 1945."

He spoke confidently, but Tracie had dealt with Aaron Stallings long enough to know when he was bullshitting her. This was one of those times. There was absolutely no way to know whether any of what he said was true.

She sighed deeply. "So where do we have to go?"

"What do you mean, 'we'?"

"Well if there are two keys, presumably the system must be accessed by two separate key-holders. I won't be able to do it by myself. I'm going to have to take Gruber with me, unless you want me to wait while you send another operative."

"No," he said firmly. "Any delay is unacceptable. Hitler had possession of the second key for decades. It's reasonable to assume he had engineers craft a copy after escaping Berlin and moving to Argentina. It's unlikely his son would have had time to do the same thing with the key stolen from the Soviet operative, but too much is at stake to take anything for granted. You need to secure that treasure absolutely as soon as possible."

"Then it's going to have to be Gruber."

Stallings sighed heavily, his mistrust of the man obvious. Tracie didn't share her boss's concern, however. Gruber had made mistakes, obviously, but since her arrival in West Germany, he had proven himself capable, at the very least.

"Fine," Stallings said. "Take Gruber with you. But keep a close eye on him, and remind him in no uncertain terms that you are still in charge."

"You won't have to worry about Gruber."

"I hope not," he said. "Your assignment is now to ensure the treasure is, in fact, still located in the specially reinforced container the Nazis stashed in a tunnel beneath the Wuppertal munitions factory. If so, you will secure the tunnel and notify me by satellite phone, then stand watch over the Amber Room until a determination is made regarding how to proceed."

"Until a determination is made? What is that supposed to mean?"

"That's not your problem, Tanner. Just complete your assignment. Immediately is not soon enough. I expect to hear from you ASAP."

"Understood," she said, annoyed. "I'll just need the location of the munitions factory, and Gruber and I will get started right away."

He passed along the directions and then broke the satellite connection without another word.

33

November 19, 1987
8:20 a.m.
Wuppertal, Federal Republic of Germany

"My career is over, isn't it?" Gruber looked across the Opel's front seat at Tracie, his penetrating blue eyes troubled.

It was an awkward moment. In all probability what he was asking was true. And the fact that he was asking it meant he knew it was true.

"Everybody makes mistakes," she said carefully. "Especially in the field. One thing I've learned is that no op ever goes the way you think it will."

"Of course," he answered. "I understand that. But this whole mess is my fault. I allowed the Soviet to kill Newmann and steal the key right out from under my nose, and I then allowed the Soviet to be murdered and the key taken *again*."

"I was here by then," Tracie said. "That outcome is on both of us."

Gruber shrugged. "Not really. You had just arrived, and were within minutes of successfully recovering it. Had the Soviet lived another quarter-hour, you would have done exactly that."

"You're missing the big picture."

"And what is the big picture?"

"The Phoenix camp was already built and staffed. Even though it was unfinished, it obviously had been under construction for some time. Phoenix was in the process of recruiting and training soldiers. Hitler and Hitler Junior were here in Germany, away from the safety of their home in Argentina. What does all that tell you?"

"That their plan had been put in motion months ago."

"Exactly. Months ago, if not years ago. You had nothing to do with any of that. Even if you had done your job perfectly, someone would still have had to infiltrate the Phoenix compound and eliminate Adolph Hitler and his son. And they would have had to do it soon."

Gruber nodded somberly and stared through the windshield.

"And there's something else," Tracie continued.

What's that?"

"Say we had been successful in recovering the key from the Soviet operative. Say we had gotten to him before Phoenix did. What do you suppose would have happened next?"

He thought about it for a moment, the Opel bumping slowly over a remote trail north of Wuppertal that looked as though it hadn't been maintained in any significant way since 1945. They had already passed two signs warning that the road was restricted to official personnel only. They had ignored both.

Finally Gruber turned his head and met Tracie's gaze. "Phoenix would have come after us."

"That's right. And since my *handler*"—the emphasis she placed on the word made clear her disdain for Aaron Stallings—"refused to divulge information regarding the strength of Phoenix, or the existence of a younger Hitler, or *anything* relevant to the op until he had no other choice, we would have been sitting ducks."

"We probably would be dead by now."

"We likely would have been killed within twenty-four hours of the Soviet's murder. And we would never have seen it coming."

Gruber grinned, a little of his former cockiness returning, at least for the moment. "You're saying we literally dodged a bullet."

"That's what I'm saying."

Gruber's smile faded and he said, "None of this changes the fact that I'm going to be out of a job when this is all said and done."

"I'll vouch for you when I get back to Langley. I'll do whatever I can for you. You deserve another chance."

"Thank you," he said. "After the way I treated you when you

arrived in West Germany, it's more than I have any right to expect. And I really appreciate it. But you and I both know it's not going to matter. I'm as well aware of Aaron Stallings's reputation as everyone else in the CIA. The man's not known for his forgiving nature."

"Sometimes he surprises you," Tracie said. "I can't deny he's detestable, but if he feels he can use you productively, he's not above offering a second chance. I'm living proof of that fact."

"Maybe," Gruber said doubtfully. "But I haven't heard from my handler since this fiasco started. That can only mean one thing: I'm getting burned."

"Not necessarily. Stallings is running this op personally. He's been pulling the strings ever since he sent me here. So it makes perfect sense that he would have relegated your handler to the back seat. The CIA director doesn't want any more eyes on Wuppertal than absolutely necessary until he knows the full situation at that munitions plant."

Gruber didn't look convinced, but he let the matter drop and Tracie was glad. Nothing she had told him was a lie, not exactly. But she also knew that Gruber was correct in his assumption that in all likelihood he would never again work in the field for the CIA.

She had tried to convince him otherwise not just because she didn't want to see him suffer—which was true as far as it went—but also because she needed him focused on the situation at hand. There was virtually no chance she could access the Amber Room treasure alone, and they were walking blind into an unknown scenario. Their chances of surviving the next few hours might just come down to clear thinking.

A distracted Gruber was a man who could get not just himself killed, but Tracie as well.

The road curved around obstacles and wound up and down hills, deep in the German forest. The sky was clear overhead and somewhere above them the sun shined brightly, but the thick canopy of leaves and twisting branches allowed precious little illumination to reach the ground. The air felt heavy, portentous, as if warning her not to continue.

Gruber seemed to notice as well. "How much longer do you

think it is before we get there?" His voice sounded weak and uncertain, a direct counterpoint to the self-assured man she had met upon her arrival in country.

"I think we're almost there. The Nazis would have kept the Amber Room close, if only so they could monitor it attentively."

He nodded and kept driving, and less than thirty seconds later the remains of the Wuppertal munitions plant came into view. The building was large and rambling, a concrete block monstrosity that the surrounding forest had already begun the process of reclaiming.

Massive cracks ran along stress points in the construction, entire wings beginning to droop and fall away from the main building. Weeds ran rampant through what at one time must have been a courtyard fronting the main entrance, some of them nearly half Tracie's height. Vines crisscrossed their way up the exterior walls in random patterns, some of them disappearing through smashed-out windows in the lower two floors.

Most of the building's facade was taken up by a series of garage doors, all metal, all of them closed and chained, most dented and rust-covered. *There must be three dozen doors here,* Tracie thought. This was clearly the loading dock, where the manufactured munitions had been loaded onto trucks for delivery to the German Army.

A parking lot spanned the entire length of the plant, its pavement crumbling. Huge swaths of macadam had rotted away completely, replaced by dirt and crabgrass and weeds. The lot was empty, of course. The entire property gave off an air of desperation and abandonment. There would be no reason for even the most suspicious of observers to believe a treasure worth hundreds of millions of dollars might be contained here.

Gruber downshifted and eased into the decrepit parking lot. He had no choice but to drive slowly; the lot was in such deplorable condition that any speed over a couple of miles per hour would have put him at risk of breaking an axle or blowing a tire. Or both.

"Where to?" he asked.

Tracie thought for a moment. The administration area was clearly located on the north side of the plant. Whereas the vast majority of the building was constructed of cement block, bland and utterly lacking in personality, the area to the far left was marginally nicer: red brick and glass. The glass was long gone, the windows now boarded up and barred, and harsh weather conditions had severely damaged the brick walls, but she believed this section of the plant would constitute their best bet.

"The main entrance," she said. "Stallings claims there are dozens of tunnels running under the city of Wuppertal, of which more than one pass beneath this building. Various tunnels are accessible from various points throughout the structure. But the one we want is most likely located beneath the former plant manager's office. Supposedly, a high-level Nazi from this area named Erich Koch installed the facility manager into his position for the sole purpose of safeguarding the Amber Room treasure. The manager's appointment created a stir among Nazi military leaders, because the guy had absolutely no experience running a munitions plant. All their complaints were ignored by Koch and also by Adolph Hitler himself, though, which makes sense."

Gruber braked to a stop as close to the plant's entrance as possible. He turned to Tracie and said, "Makes sense? How?"

"Think about it. The treasure disappeared shortly after the Nazis looted it from the Russians in 1941. At that point, the war was going well for Hitler. Life was good in the Third Reich. He would have been willing to accept slightly lower-than-expected production from one munitions factory in favor of placing a man he trusted implicitly in a position where he could guard such a valuable treasure. When the tide began turning against him later in the war, his attitude may have been totally different. But by then, the treasure was ensconced here and his priorities had shifted drastically. Moving the Amber Room at that point would have been far down on his to-do list."

She shrugged. "It makes sense in theory, at least. I guess we'll find out soon enough whether the theory is proven out by reality."

Gruber killed the engine. A stillness as complete as any Tracie had ever experienced dropped over them. No birds sang in the distance, no small animals rustled the thick underbrush. No crickets chirped. Even the air was dead calm. Only the ticking of the cooling engine disrupted the silence.

They opened their doors and stepped out of the car. "How do you know all this?" Gruber asked.

"Research," Tracie said. "The flight over the Atlantic was a long one, and the information about Koch and this munitions plant was buried deep inside the intel I received from Stallings. There was no mention of the Amber Room being here, of course, but the fact that the Nazis had put a man with zero experience in the field of weapons manufacturing in charge of a key munitions plant in the middle of what was going to be a long war stuck out like a sore thumb to me. It didn't make sense."

"So when Stallings told you the location the intelligence community believes is holding the Amber Room…"

Tracie nodded. "It all came together."

"I'm impressed," Gruber said.

"Don't be." Tracie shrugged again. "Like I said, the trip here was long and boring. There wasn't much else to do than study my paperwork."

He let the subject drop, but Tracie knew exactly what he was thinking: maybe if he had paid as much attention to detail, he wouldn't be about to fly back to Langley with his CIA career hanging in the balance.

Gruber sighed. "What do we do now?"

"Now we go find three hundred million dollars."

34

Tracie bent back inside the car and lifted out a backpack stuffed with supplies. She turned toward the abandoned building and stared at it through narrowed eyes. In keeping with the condition of the rest of the structure, the front entrance had deteriorated badly. The twin wooden doors hung drunkenly, prevented from dropping to the ground only by a thick chain, which had been threaded through the handles and padlocked.

Gruber followed her glance and frowned. "Maybe we should just go through a window," he said, "rather than expending all of the energy required to break through those doors."

"No," Tracie said. "It would take at least as much time and energy to cut through the bars covering the windows as to break down the doors. And once we were finished, we'd still have to cut through or remove the plywood sheets that have been nailed into place."

Gruber looked unconvinced.

"I know the wood looks thick," she said, "but look at how those doors are hanging. We might be able to get away with cutting through the chains and pushing the doors off to the side. And if that's the case, I'd rather use the entrance. I'd be willing to bet the manager's office is located right off the main lobby. Let's find out."

She handed the backpack to Gruber and reached one more time into the car's rear seat, pulling out a large bolt cutter. Then she turned and strode toward the front of the empty, hulking building.

It was a short walk, but by the time they reached the entrance, Tracie realized the doors were in even worse condition than she had originally thought. They weren't the glass, steel, and aluminum construction typical of modern industrial doors. Rather, they were constructed entirely of thick, reinforced wood, with what once had been a single small window cut out of each, approximately at eye level. As with the rest of the facility, the glass had long since been shattered out and now a pair of small holes, one per door, was all that remained. The holes were so tiny they hadn't even been boarded up.

The padlock securing the chains was large and forbidding, but decades of exposure to the German elements had caused it to become badly corroded. The shackle was now fused to the padlock's body, and even had she possessed the key—which she didn't—Tracie knew it would have been useless.

She placed the jaws of the bolt cutter around the shackle and eased the handles together. The tool went through the rusty padlock like a warm knife through butter, and the lock fell to the ground with a heavy thud, rust flakes fluttering away on the heavy air.

The doors creaked and groaned but stayed put. They leaned inward like a pair of drunks supporting one another after last call. The hinges had corroded away over the years and Tracie could see there was nothing actually securing them to the building.

She stepped away from the doors and placed the bolt cutter on the ground, then looked up at Gruber. "You grab the handle on the left," she said, "and I'll take the one on the right. I think if we pull at the same time, the doors might just fall away from the entryway."

He nodded and grabbed his handle. There was one on each door, large iron monstrosities that would have looked at home in a medieval castle. Rust had attacked them, like it had attacked the padlock, but they were thick and heavy and in no danger of corroding away any time soon.

"Whatever you do," she said, "don't let the doors fall on you. Give a good pull and then use your momentum to keep going out of range of the doors as they fall."

"Will do," Gruber answered. "Just tell me when to pull."

"On three," Tracie said.

She gripped her handle firmly and began counting, and when she reached three, heaved back on the handle with all the strength she could muster out of her one hundred five pounds. The door resisted initially, seemingly out of sheer inertia, and then began dropping away from the building.

Gruber was bigger and stronger than Tracie and had been able to exert more torque. His door crashed to the ground first, kicking up dust and dirt when it fell. Tracie's hit the ground a split-second later with the sound of rotted wood splitting and cracking and breaking apart.

"You okay?" she asked, and Gruber nodded.

She stepped carefully over the smashed remains of the doors and entered the ancient munitions plant. The air inside felt musty, stale. Although all of the plant's windows on the first floor had been boarded up, some of those boards had begun to rot away, and small gaps in the windows allowed a bit of light to filter through and into the building. There hadn't been many windows to begin with, though. Long stretches of the plant featured nothing but concrete block after concrete block, and ventilation inside the structure had been minimal.

It felt more like an ancient dungeon than a World War II-era factory. Gruber flicked on his flashlight and Tracie did the same. They played their beams slowly around the interior. Dust and rat droppings littered the worn linoleum floor, and aside from bits of trash scattered randomly, the foyer was empty.

Doorways to what were obviously three staff offices lined the wall to the left, and more than a half-dozen corridors stretched off into the inky blackness from left to right beyond the offices. The section of the foyer where they now stood had probably been a reception area, although if a desk had once stood here it was now long gone.

"If your intel is accurate," Gruber said, "the manager's office would have to be one of those three." He trained his flashlight beam on the trio of doorways lined up on the left side of the foyer.

Tracie nodded. "Presumably the facility manager would have had the biggest office, so it should be fairly easy to determine which was his. Worst case, we go one by one and examine all three."

She crossed the foyer in the direction of the offices, the dank mustiness increasing with each step. She stifled a sneeze and wished they had thought to include respirators or dust masks with their supplies.

Too late now.

She selected a door at random, deciding to examine the offices from left to right. She had thought Gruber would follow, or perhaps select one of the other two offices to explore, but instead he began crossing the lobby floor. He stopped at one of the corridors and shined his light through the entry before whistling softly.

"Fiona," he said. "Come here, you've got to check this out."

Her heart began beating a little faster. It couldn't possibly be this simple, could it? Could the Nazis have pulled the Amber Room treasure up out of its subterranean hiding place, only to leave it in the middle of a munitions plant before simply abandoning it?

She turned on her heel and crossed the lobby, joining Gruber at the oversized doorway. Aimed her flashlight through the door.

There was no treasure stored in the manufacturing area of the plant; at least, none that she could see. But the sight that greeted her tempered her disappointment a little and she raised her eyebrows in surprise. The factory floor looked exactly as it must have more than four decades earlier. If not for the thick layer of dust covering every surface, it almost appeared as though the workers had shut production down for the weekend, or to go home overnight, and as soon as they began arriving for their shifts, the factory would roar to life once again.

All the machinery was there, and looked more or less intact. Long conveyor belts ran from one end of the floor to the other. Cranes hung suspended over the belts, chains dangling from their jaws as if awaiting the start of another workday.

Giant furnaces lined the far wall, open doors ready to melt iron or lead or whatever other metal was being used to manufacture Nazi weaponry. Machinery was everywhere, scattered about the factory floor in a seemingly random manner, for unknown purposes. Hand tools—sledgehammers, hacksaws, etc.—littered the workspace.

The Nazis had abandoned the munitions plant in the face of advancing Allied forces with virtually no cleanup, perhaps walking out the doors in the middle of a shift at the appearance of Allied troops. There must have been little warning, and for their part, the Allies had simply boarded up the facility, securing it as best they could before moving on.

And it had sat like this for forty-two years.

Why the West German government had never cleared the facility of its machinery and torn the place down was a mystery, although the plant's isolation and the new government's desire to distance itself as much as possible from the stain of the Nazi legacy probably had a lot to do with it.

Tracie realized she was holding her breath, and she blew out forcefully before inhaling the musty air. The sight was ghostly and chilling. How many lives had been lost to the bombs manufactured here? How many Allied soldiers had suffered agonizingly from the output of this very factory floor before going to the grave? How much death and misery had this plant caused?

"Let's get back to work," she said, her voice shaking slightly.

35

November 19, 1987
9:10 a.m.
Wuppertal Munitions Plant
Northwest of Wuppertal, Federal Republic of Germany

All the furniture had been removed from what Tracie believed to be the plant manager's office with the exception of one chair. It was constructed entirely of wood and looked solid but extremely uncomfortable. Its heavy base featured four rollers, making the chair easy to move, and it had been shoved off into the far corner of the room.

Which made the trap door in the middle of the floor impossible to miss.

The door was oversized and perfectly square, easily six feet by six feet. It had been fitted to the concrete floor with hinges on one side and a gap on the other large enough for a 1940s plant manager—or 1980s CIA operatives—to slip a hand under and lift. The trap door had been installed so that when closed, it fit flush with the rest of the floor. When covered with, say, an Oriental rug and a desk, it would have been invisible, while still reasonably accessible to the manager, or to any Nazi bigwig who might wish to examine the tunnel's contents.

Maybe even the Führer himself.

The trap door was, of course, padlocked closed, but the locks would provide little resistance to a bolt cutter, and once again,

Tracie wondered why the Allies wouldn't have spent a little time exploring the unexpected find they had undoubtedly made after wresting control of the facility from the Nazis.

Then she thought about the sheer chaos that must have been present in early 1945, of Allied troops advancing deep into German territory, taking ground and moving relentlessly forward, anxious to press their advantage and rid the world of the scourge of Nazism once and for all after seven long years of war.

In all likelihood, Allied leaders on the ground would have had little interest in a Nazi munitions plant, secret trap door or no secret trap door, other than to secure it and ensure it could no longer provide the means of killing and wounding Allied troops. If Stallings's intel was correct regarding the existence of dozens of tunnels crisscrossing the earth under Wuppertal, leaders responsible for the Allied advance into Germany had likely just ignored the trap door, thinking it nothing more significant than another means of escape for a nervous Nazi plant manager.

Or maybe the tunnel *had* been examined, and then new locks installed as the Allies churned forward.

Tracie and Gruber looked at the trap door and then at each other, and she said, "Go back outside and grab the bolt cutters. Let's get this done."

Thirty seconds later he was back.

"Have at it," she said, and Gruber bent over the door. It was secured by one padlock on each corner opposite the hinged end. These locks had been protected from the elements and they looked as forbidding in November 1987 as they probably had back in the 1940s.

They were no match for the jaws of the bolt cutter, though, and in seconds Gruber had sliced through the shackles and removed them.

Together, the operatives slipped their hands into the space built into the floor and lifted. The trap door swung open easily, its hinges unaffected either by the passage of time or the accumulation of dust and grime in the office.

Tracie and Gruber eased the door to the floor and bent over the now-gaping hole. An iron ladder had been affixed to the tunnel wall, the first rung hanging just below the base of the floor.

The setup looked remarkably similar to the escape route she had discovered at the Phoenix safe house despite the fact the two tunnels had been constructed decades apart. The air flowing up from underground felt cool and moist, and Tracie could see that the bars had become heavily corroded over time.

The hole was pitch-black, as dark as an overcast night, and the ladder disappeared into it like a magician's trick. Tracie gazed skeptically at the iron, trying to gauge the extent of the corrosion, picturing the bars giving way as she and Gruber climbed down into the pit.

"I'll go first," Gruber said, sensing of her concern. "If the ladder breaks, you can pull me back up with our rope and we'll find a different way into the tunnel. There has to be more than one access point."

He didn't address the issue of how Tracie would be able to pull a man nearly double her own weight out of a deep hole with no tools and no way to gain leverage. She knelt at the trap door and grabbed the uppermost rung of the ladder in both fists and then yanked hard.

Nothing happened. The ladder felt solid. But she knew the force she had been able to exert on the iron bar was nothing compared to the stress that would be placed on it when Gruber began climbing down into the tunnel.

She sighed.

Shook her head.

"I don't like this," she said.

"It's not like we have any choice," Gruber pointed out. "You have your orders, and unless you want to end up unemployed, like I'm about to be, we have to find a way into that tunnel."

"I know. I still don't like it."

They stared at each other in the darkness, each face lit by the other's flashlight.

"Fine," Tracie said resignedly. "Let's see what happens. We'll tie a rope around your waist and I'll—"

She stopped speaking mid-sentence as Gruber turned his flashlight back toward the trap door. He stepped into the hole and eased his weight onto the first rung of the ladder.

"Hey!" Tracie said. "That's not safe. Just stop for a second while we plan this out."

He didn't listen. He stepped to the second rung, placing one booted foot on it and easing his weight down gingerly. The iron bar held and he grinned up at Tracie. "See? No problem."

"Jesus, that was foolish," she said, irritated. "You could have fallen to the bottom of that hole and broken your back. Hell, you still may."

Gruber shook his head. "Listen," he said. "This job was my life, and I'm soon to be unemployed. I've learned that when you have nothing left to lose, you have nothing to fear."

"You're not going to get fired, Gruber. You'll still have a job when you go home."

"Maybe. Maybe not. But even if I have a job, but it's not going to be *this* job. They'll put me behind a desk analyzing data, or they'll make me train recruits, or something else equally distasteful. You know Aaron Stallings a hell of a lot better that I do, but even I've heard enough about the man to know that he'll never let me operate in the field again, and that's all I've ever wanted to do."

She opened her mouth to argue, to tell him anything was possible, that after a short hiatus spent paying his dues he might find himself a field operative again.

Then she reconsidered and said nothing. He was right, so what was there to say? By allowing the Soviet operative to swipe the Amber Room key right out from under his nose, when monitoring it had been his only job in Wuppertal, Matthias Gruber—or whatever his real name was—had sealed his fate, professionally speaking.

Tracie more than probably anyone else in the CIA knew that to be true. She had seen Stallings's vindictiveness, had been on the other end of his ruthlessness. In many ways she was still suffering from both, operating once again in the field but unacknowledged as an agency employee, still officially relieved of duty on charges of insubordination, making her the most secret asset in an agency dependent upon secrecy above all.

She sighed deeply and changed the subject. "How does that ladder seem? Does it still feel secure?"

He flashed another smile and left unspoken the fact that he knew exactly what she was thinking.

"Feels fine to me," he said. "Nice and solid."

"Keep going then. Hang onto the sidebars on the ladder as you move down, and take each step very slowly. Ease your weight onto the rungs until you can determine whether they'll hold you. If any of them feel less than solid, come back up and we'll—"

Gruber waggled his eyebrows and disappeared into the darkness, not moving slowly *or* carefully. He flung himself down the iron ladder into the tunnel like a twelve-year-old boy playing explorer.

Tracie shook her head and tamped down on her annoyance. Haranguing Gruber now would accomplish nothing and might serve to make him even more reckless. Instead, she watched the beam of his flashlight bouncing and shaking as he descended. A moment later the light steadied and she knew he had reached the tunnel's base.

"Come on down and join in the fun!" he said brightly. "No reason for me to be the only one enjoying all these spiders and snakes."

"Wonderful," Tracie grumbled as she slipped into the hole and onto the ladder. "I can't wait to get started."

36

November 19, 1987
9:25 a.m.
Under the Wuppertal Munitions Plant
Northwest of Wuppertal, Federal Republic of Germany

"Just kidding about the snakes and spiders," Gruber said as Tracie stepped off the ladder and onto the hard-packed floor. "I'm sure they're here, but I guess I must have scared them away. For now, at least."

She glowered at him, knowing he couldn't see her face in the near-total darkness but doing it anyway. She held her tongue—again—and aimed her flashlight down the tunnel. The decades-old excavation appeared arrow-straight, at least as far as she could see, which wasn't far at all. The beams from their two lights were overmatched, seeming to wither and die, swallowed up by the black passageway.

What she *could* see didn't inspire much confidence that they could safely complete their mission. The tunnel walls had been reinforced during construction using bricks and mortar, but the relentless subterranean moisture over the last four decades had weakened the structure to the point where cave-ins had begun occurring, the earth breaking through the seal of bricks and causing side walls to crumble inward.

The tunnel was still passable only because it had been dug so wide. Its width was even greater than the six-by-six opening in the factory floor above. It had been excavated far more completely than would have been necessary for a simple escape route, the size making perfect sense if Aaron Stallings's intel regarding the treasure was accurate.

The Amber Room panels were large—Tracie didn't think exact measurements had been included in her intel packet, leading her to believe the exact measurements weren't known—but she had seen photographs of the room that had been taken prior to its looting in World War Two, and she knew a tunnel limited in size would not have permitted the panels to be transported below ground.

She flashed her light upward and winced at what she saw. Thick wooden beams had been used to support the ceiling, six-by-six timbers spaced a few feet apart as far as she could see down the length of the tunnel. The beams had degraded over the years even more than had the brick-and-mortar tunnel walls.

Some hung at odd angles from the ceiling, having rotted badly enough to break completely apart. Others, although still intact, bowed downward, sagging nearly to the breaking point from gravity and the incredible pressure exerted by the tons of earth suspended over their heads. Massive spider webs hung from the support beams, pulsing thick and silver and glossy in the uneven light.

"Apparently we found the hiding place for all those spiders I mentioned, Quinn." Gruber said. His tone was light but Tracie could feel the tension behind his words. "And from the looks of those support beams, I might not have to worry about losing my job, because we may not get out of here alive."

"Knock it off, Gruber. The damn tunnel has lasted this long, there's no reason to think it's going to cave in now." Tracie was whistling past the graveyard, though, and she knew it. Worse, she knew that Gruber knew she knew it.

There were actually plenty of reasons to believe the tunnel could collapse at any moment. It had presumably sat undisturbed for more than forty years, and even the slightest change in conditions below ground now could have disastrous consequences. The vibration caused by two people climbing down an iron ladder, for example, or the inevitable dislodging of soil as they clambered over and around cave-ins, or any of a hundred other variables related to their disruption of the delicate conditions, could easily result in them being trapped underground or buried alive.

"Standing here contemplating our fate isn't helping anything," she finally offered. "Let's go find that treasure." She aimed her flashlight down the tunnel and began trudging slowly into the darkness.

Gruber, who hadn't answered, hesitated only a moment and then fell in behind her. They wound their way forward, moving to the far right side of the tunnel and climbing over dirt piles that had resulted from long-ago cave-ins, before repeating the procedure on the opposite side of the tunnel ten or twelve feet farther along.

Furtive scurrying sounds betrayed the presence of rats, but although she played her light around as completely as she could, Tracie was unable to find even a single one. She imagined hundreds or even thousands of rats burrowing a network of tunnels behind the crumbling brick walls, further weakening the structure, and shuddered involuntarily.

Twenty feet farther along they came to a cave-in bigger than any they had encountered thus far. The support beam overhead had shattered and enough earth had fallen into the tunnel to render it impassable. The only thing preventing the tunnel from being totally blocked was a thin strip at the very ceiling, a gap of no more than six inches separating the pile of dirt from the top of the passage.

But that wasn't the worst part. The worst part was that a boulder had fallen through the ceiling and into the tunnel. It balanced precariously about a third of the way down the pile of earth, and was plenty large enough to crush either of them should it break free and begin sliding or rolling down the pile.

"What now?" Gruber said softly.

"Now we dig."

Tracie knelt and opened her backpack, shining the light inside, searching for the collapsible shovel she had included with her supplies. There was one inside Gruber's backpack as well, and after a moment—and accompanied by a heavy, theatrical sigh—Tracie's temporary partner dropped to his knees and began rummaging through his pack, reluctantly following her lead.

She pulled her shovel free a moment before Gruber did the

same with his. The removable pieces had been folded together and held in place by a large elastic band. After pulling off the band and snapping the pieces into place, they would have a pair of small but rugged spades.

Fifteen seconds later Tracie began attacking the pile, working quickly but as gently as possible given the hard-packed nature of the dirt. The possibility of a cave-in brought on by the vibrations of their work continued to worry her, but moving enough of the pile to allow them to slither through and continue down the tunnel would take vigorous effort; there was simply no way around it.

Shovelful after shovelful, she lifted the moist earth free of the pile and scattered it behind them, tossing it along the tunnel floor. Next to her, Gruber did the same. They worked without speaking, heavy breathing and the occasional grunt the only sounds.

Tracie kept a wary eye on the boulder, but for the time being it showed no signs of dislodging. It had fallen into the dirt toward the left tunnel wall, so Tracie and Gruber concentrated their efforts on the right side, as far away from it as possible.

Ten minutes of steady digging lowered the pile several inches. Ten more and Tracie guessed they were close to having sufficient clearance to pass. She stepped back and bent over, hands on her knees, breathing heavily.

Gruber had stopped digging to take a break. He spit on the floor and between panting breaths said, "Remind me again why in the hell I ever wanted to do this job?"

"Glory," she replied. "Oh, and the everlasting gratitude of your superiors in Washington."

Gruber burst out laughing.

Tracie almost shushed him, concerned about causing further cave-ins, but decided against it. Whatever his deficiencies as a covert operative, and despite the fact he came across as a slimy womanizer, the man meant well, and his previous statements to her had made clear the fact that he was torturing himself over his failure in the field. A little laughter would do wonders for him.

Besides, she had to admit the sound lifted her spirits as well. She was at least fifteen feet underground, surrounded by rats and insects and probably snakes and who knew what else, working in secret for a boss who didn't give a damn about her, knowing if she died down here beneath a crumbling abandoned German factory, no one would ever know what had happened.

Precious few besides her parents would even notice she was gone.

So let Gruber laugh. It would do wonders for him, but it wasn't the worst thing in the world for her, either.

His laughter died away and he wiped his eyes on his shirtsleeves. "You're okay, you know that, Quinn?"

"Right back atya," she said.

"So…now that we're bonding and getting to know each other and all, does this mean you'll sleep with me when we get out of here?"

"Jesus, Gruber, do you ever give up?"

"You can't blame a guy for trying. Besides, my daddy always told me you can't catch a fish if you don't throw your line in the water."

"Your pole's not coming anywhere near me, got it?"

He burst out laughing again and Tracie found herself giggling like a teenager. *This might be the most surreal moment of my life,* she thought. *Thousands of miles from home, chasing buried Nazi treasure and fending off the advances of a handsome but disgraced spy.*

She realized with a start of surprise that she was exactly where she wanted to be. She loved her job. Despite the constant loneliness and unrelenting danger, the heartbreak and the isolation and the gunshot wounds and the sociopathic boss and the unfair firing and everything else she had endured—*and I'm not even thirty yet,* she thought with another giggle—she loved her life.

She wouldn't trade it for anything.

Not for a million dollars.

Not even for three hundred million dollars.

"Let's get moving before this marvel of Nazi engineering falls down on top of us," she said.

37

There was now enough room to squeeze between the top of the dirt pile and the tunnel's damaged ceiling, but just barely. Tracie went first, clawing her way up the big mound, which was now unstable, the result of being chopped at and dug out by a pair of shovels after sitting undisturbed for perhaps a decade or more.

She was nearly to the top when the loose dirt gave way and she found herself sliding back toward the ground, out of control. Gruber was standing directly below her, though, and he stopped her momentum, grabbing her with one hand on her upper right leg and another on her butt. He gave a firm shove and she was able to climb/claw/swim her way upward again, this time reaching the top thanks to the added momentum Gruber had provided.

She cracked her skull on a support beam and barely noticed. She had climbed straight into one of the thick spider webs hanging from the ceiling, and she flailed her hands and arms, brushing the webs out of her hair and off her face, feeling her stomach begin to turn. She had stared down men with guns, single-handedly rescued the sitting U.S. secretary of state, gone toe-to-toe against deadly Soviet operatives, but this was worse than all of those things put together.

Tracie hated spiders.

She realized she was moaning involuntarily and clamped her mouth shut.

From below, Gruber said, "Thanks for the free feel."

"You're welcome, but I'm still not sleeping with you," she answered. She swallowed hard, choking back the bile that had threatened to spew out her mouth, doing her best to ignore the massive spider web.

She took a deep breath and then rolled onto her belly. Her upper body hung toward Gruber, and she extended her arms.

"Take my hands," she said, "and I'll support you while you climb."

"First I get to cop a feel and now we're holding hands," he said. "I consider this extremely promising."

"You're relentless, aren't you?"

"It's part of my irresistible charm." He reached up with both arms and they locked hands, each grabbing the other's wrists.

"Now, climb," Tracie said, and as his legs churned against the loose dirt, she began squirming backward, counting on gravity to take over and provide enough leverage to assist in getting Gruber's much bulkier body up and over the mound. His face scraped the side of the pile as he climbed and she could hear him spitting dirt and coughing, but he continued moving.

When he reached the spot where she had begun sliding backward, his feet slipped exactly as hers had done. He was too heavy and she was too light, and she felt herself being pulled toward the top of the pile again as he fell back toward the tunnel floor.

She shook her left hand free of his right and reached up, hoping to jam her hand against the ceiling support beam and halt their wrong-direction momentum. For a half-second nothing happened, and then white-hot pain exploded through her hand as her knuckles cracked the beam and took the brunt of not just her own weight but Gruber's as well.

She grunted and cursed.

Forced her elbow to stay locked.

All she wanted to do was bend it and take the pressure off and relieve the pain that had exploded in her hand, but she refused to yield.

Refused to give up.

Their movement stopped.

For a moment nothing happened. They hung suspended, Gruber on one side of the pile, Tracie on the other, panting and cursing and trying not to think about how many knuckles she had just broken.

"Well?" she said through gritted teeth. "Are you going to climb or are you going to take another break?"

His answer was to kick his toes into the pile in an attempt to gain traction. He moved upward a few inches, then a few more, each gain increasing the pressure against her hand and arm, both of which were now burning.

Sweat poured down her face, even in the damp cool of the tunnel, and she could feel the grip of her good hand beginning to loosen on Gruber's wrist. "I'm losing you," she gasped, her resolve weakening. The pain was immense and the task seemingly impossible. How much could one person take?

Finally, with one manic burst of energy, Gruber pistoned his feet against the pile like a man racing a bicycle, and at the same time, he yanked upward against Tracie's right hand, pulling hard with no warning.

The pain exploded and she screamed, forgetting the risk of cave-ins, forgetting her fear of spiders, forgetting everything except the dozens of fiery nails being hammered into her injured left hand.

And still she kept her elbow locked.

Gruber blasted over the top of the pile, his momentum carrying him forward like a freight train, and he cracked his skull against the support beam exactly as Tracie had done, and then he flopped over the top of the pile, the relentless pressure against her hand finally falling away. She fell backward, tumbling down the far side of the pile, caring about nothing besides cradling her hand to her chest.

She hit the tunnel floor and cracked the back of her head on the hard-packed ground and the pain was negligible when measured against the agony radiating outward from her left hand. The fire raced from her knuckles in one direction to the tips of her fingers, which she could not feel, and in the other direction up her forearm all the way to her elbow.

"Quinn!" Gruber called, and scrambled down the pile, hitting the floor next to Tracie in a shower of dirt and pebbles and, in all likelihood, more spiders. "Quinn, are you hurt? What happened? How the hell did you pull me up like that, anyway?"

"I'm still not sleeping with you," she mumbled, rolling from her side onto her back and then forcing herself to sit up.

"Jesus Christ, Quinn," he said, ignoring her comment. He had yanked his flashlight from his waistband and now he shined the beam down at her injured hand, an expression of horror clouding his handsome face. "Your hand. What the hell did you do to your hand?"

She tried to smile and managed a wince. "I jammed it against the support beam to stop our momentum when you began falling back down the dirt pile. Unfortunately I couldn't open my fist in time, so instead of my palm striking the timber, it was the back of my hand."

"Jesus Christ," he said again. "Why didn't you let go?"

"Well, that wouldn't have accomplished anything, would it? I'd still be injured and you would be stuck on the other side of the pile."

"Jesus Christ." It seemed to be all he could manage. "Look at your hand. You need medical attention."

For the first time, Tracie allowed herself a glance at her injury. It was gruesome. Blood flowed heavily, her skin ripped and torn, and the chalky greyish-white of exposed knucklebones peeked through the skin flaps in several places.

"You see any doctors around here? Maybe an infirmary somewhere up inside that wreck of a Nazi ammo factory?"

"Of course not," Gruber said, showing annoyance for the first time. "And that's exactly why we need to get you out of here and to a hospital."

"Agreed. And we'll do that the minute we complete our mission."

He stared at her, jaw hanging open. "Complete our mission? With you bleeding to death? You're insane, do you know that?"

"Flattery will get you nowhere. I'm not sleeping with you."

He shook his head in disbelief, unsure of what to say or do.

She said, "I'm not going to bleed to death, Gruber. Get real. My hand's been ripped open, it's not like I severed my carotid artery. We'll bandage it up and then you can drive me to the hospital after we get out of here."

She had tried to keep the pain out of her voice but couldn't quite manage it. It quivered and shook, and she could feel herself slipping into shock. The fire continued to rage in her hand, the knuckles a furnace, flames racing up her fingers and arm.

On the bright side, Gruber seemed to have given up on arguing. He shook his backpack off his shoulders and began rummaging through it for the few medical supplies they had packed before leaving their Wuppertal safe house. After a moment he lifted out an ace bandage and plastic bottle of rubbing alcohol.

"This isn't going to work," he said. "The bandage isn't even long enough."

"We'll make do. Just dump the alcohol over my hand and wrap it up."

"This is going to hurt something awful."

"Thanks for the warning. Get on with it."

Gruber sighed heavily and unscrewed the plastic cap. Then he lifted it and said, "I'm sorry about this, Fiona." In one motion, he poured the contents over Tracie's hand even as she held it cradled against her chest.

The pain blasted into the stratosphere.

It doubled.

Tripled.

She wouldn't have thought it could get any worse than it already was, but it did. The liquid seared and burned, it was gasoline poured over a campfire.

She screamed again, the sound of her anguish booming down the tunnel and echoing back to them. Her vision wavered, the two flickering flashlight beams fading to pinpricks in the dark tunnel as consciousness threatened to desert her. She panted. She lowered her head almost to the hard-packed ground, willing herself not to pass out.

Seconds ticked by that felt like hours, and then Tracie felt herself return—more or less—to the land of the living. The fire continued to blast through her hand, stinging and throbbing, the pain dwarfing even that of getting shot, something she had experienced more than once.

"Bandage it up," she said weakly. "I'd do it myself, but wrapping one-handed would take time we don't have. Phoenix is in disarray right now with the elimination of Adolph Hitler and his devil-spawn son, but once the organization's remaining leaders recover enough to start thinking clearly, this will be the first place they come."

Gruber nodded. He reached out and moved her arm gently away from the protection of her body. Then he reached under her hand and began straightening her fingers. The bones ground together and electric shocks blasted through the waves of fire already burning through her injury.

"No," she gasped. "Leave the fingers bent. You're going to do more damage if you try to straighten them. Just stop the bleeding and protect the area as much as possible. We'll leave the real medical stuff to the professionals after we get out of here."

Tracie's flashlight had fallen to the ground when she tumbled down the dirt pile, and its beam illuminated Gruber's face at a crazy angle. Most of his features were covered in shadow, but she could still clearly see the skepticism in his expression.

"What?" she said.

"I don't even know if the bandage is long enough to effectively stop the bleeding. You really did a number on that hand."

"Believe me, I'm not likely to forget that any time soon," she said. "Just do the best you can. Sitting here talking about it isn't getting us anywhere."

Without another word, Gruber placed the rolled-up bandage under her palm and began paying it out, rolling it around her hand, over the fingers and knuckles and then under, over and under, again and again.

The pain had begun to recede, just a bit, but now the fiery agony returned, and Tracie felt her gorge rising, and she turned her head and vomited on the ground, splashing herself and Gruber with stomach acid and partially digested food.

Gruber never said a word. He continued to wind the bandage around her injury, over and over.

38

"Sorry about puking on you," Tracie said weakly.

They sat side by side on the tunnel floor, propped up against the dirt pile they had just cleared at such a high cost. The Ace bandage had been long enough to fully cover the injury, but Gruber's concerns about stopping the bleeding seemed well founded. Tracie could already see a dark maroon smudge beginning to soak through.

"No problem," he answered. "I figured it was just your way of reinforcing your message to me."

"What message is that?"

"That you're not going to sleep with me."

Tracie chuckled. It was the best she could manage at the moment; a full-fledged laugh was out of the question.

Her breathing had returned more or less to normal, though, and while the pain in her left hand was still there, throbbing and noxious, she knew it was as manageable as it was going to get. She simply had to wall it off, compartmentalize it, acknowledge it and then move past it. She had done exactly that before, many times, and she would do it again today.

"Let's keep going," she said, "before this tunnel collapses

once and for all and we end up sleeping together down here permanently."

"Sounds good to me," he said. "The sooner we get this done and get out of here, the happier I'll be, even if it bring me that much closer to getting my head chopped off back at Langley."

He looked over at Tracie. "I mean that figuratively, of course. Although you know Stallings pretty well. Maybe he'll do it literally, too."

She pushed herself to her feet, trying to ignore the pain in her hand and mostly succeeding. "Stallings is a teddy bear," she said. "You just have to know how to handle him."

"Teddy bear," Gruber repeated. "From what I've heard, he's more like a rabid, rampaging killer grizzly."

"I suppose that characterization would work, too," she said as she began trudging forward. She prayed there were no more hidden surprises waiting for them in the darkness, but doubted that prayer was going to be answered.

"How much farther do you think it could possibly be?" Gruber asked. "I mean, the Nazis buried the treasure underground in a secret location, probably known only to a select few. What would have been the advantage in hauling it farther down the tunnel than was necessary?"

It seemed a rhetorical question, since Tracie would have no way of knowing the answer any more than Gruber would. He was walking next to her with his head down, eyes on the tunnel floor. He looked exhausted and dispirited. The joking persona he had exhibited just seconds ago had disappeared.

"If I say I have a hunch that we're getting close, would you believe me?"

"Not really."

"Then look for yourself." She rotated her flashlight toward him and waited for him to raise his eyes from the ground, then nodded toward the tunnel ahead. She aimed her light into the darkness and heard the sharp intake of breath as Gruber followed the beam.

An iron storage locker loomed in front of them, perhaps twenty feet farther down, barely visible in the weak light. The structure was massive. It virtually filled the tunnel. The sides of the container cleared the walls of the subterranean passageway by mere inches, and there was even less room than that between the top of the container and the ceiling support beams.

The structure had been painted black, and even though splotches of rust and corrosion had begun eating through the paint and into the iron, the dark paint job had rendered the storage container nearly invisible until they were almost on top of it.

Very visible, however, were two large red swastikas. They had been painted on the section facing Tracie and Gruber, one on either side of an oversized set of double doors.

"This is it," Gruber whispered.

"Looks like it," Tracie agreed, the pain in her injured hand momentarily forgotten as they stood side-by-side facing the relic.

"That thing is huge. How the hell did they get it down here?"

She shook her head. "Either they brought the materials in separately and then constructed the container underground, or maybe they dug a hole in the forest behind the munitions plant and lowered the container into the tunnel in one piece, then re-covered the hole."

"Jesus Christ," Gruber said, returning to what seemed to be his default expression when under extreme stress.

"Actually," Tracie said, "that would answer your question about why the Nazis placed it so far from the tunnel entrance: they needed a location that was isolated in order to manage the excavation without anyone figuring out what was going on."

"These were the Nazis under Adolph Hitler," Gruber said. "They could simply have forbidden anyone to approach the area, and then guarded it with men under orders to shoot onlookers on sight. That would have done the trick."

"I'm sure that's exactly what they did," Tracie answered. "But we're talking about an estimated three hundred million dollars' worth of stolen loot. Even translated into 1940s dollars, it would have been a staggering amount of money. They wouldn't have wanted to take any chances with it, and—I never thought I would say this about Nazis—I can understand their concern."

"Let's get in there and make sure it's actually the Amber Room being stored inside, and not Adolph Hitler's collection of Eva Braun lingerie or his Beatles record collection."

"The Beatles didn't come along until almost twenty years after the end of World War II."

"You know what I mean," Gruber said. He began approaching the double doors. "Let's open this baby up so we can get the hell out of here and get you to a hospital."

"Not so fast," Tracie said.

"What are you talking about? We're within minutes of completing our assignment, and you're in the process of bleeding to death, and now you want to take it slow?"

"I told you already, I'm not going to bleed to death from a hand injury. And believe me, nobody in the world could want to get up and out of this moldering gravesite any more than I do. But the whole reason *we're* here and not Aaron Stallings or the U.S. secretary of state or maybe even President Reagan himself is because the container is supposed to be booby-trapped, remember? And since Adolph Hitler Junior had both keys in his possession, on chains around his neck like they were the most important things in the world, I take the threat of explosives very seriously, and so should you."

"Fine," he said. He stopped walking and faced Tracie, who still hadn't moved. "Then how do you want to approach this?"

"We should examine the exterior of the container as closely as we can. First we need to determine the location of the two locks that fit the funky skeleton keys. Then we should locate the explosives if possible, and see if there's any way of bypassing them before we attempt to access the treasure. My fear is that after all this time, tampering in any way with that big hunk of iron—even with keys—will result in us blowing our own heads off."

"Well, I can answer half of your first question already. Look." He shined the beam of his flashlight straight at the container, where a cast iron plate had been welded to the narrow space between the closed double doors. The plate ran from the top of the container to bottom, and in the middle was a lock.

The lock was clearly designed to accept one of the two customized skeleton keys.

Gruber was much closer to the container than Tracie, and now she stepped forward to examine the lock. At first glance it appeared quite basic. But closer examination revealed small square cutouts added to the openings, and even in the dark and more than forty years after the container's construction, Tracie could see the tiny copper threads that had been built into the squares.

Clearly the threads on the lock were designed to line up with the similar copper threads built into the keys. Presumably those connections, when matched, would nullify the explosive charges wired into or on the container. Using any key other than one of the specially crafted pair, or attempting to force the doors open or cut into them with a torch, would set off the charges.

It's a terrifyingly simple design, Tracie thought, *and a deadly one.*

"Horrifying, isn't it?" Gruber spoke quietly, seemingly reading her mind.

"It sure is. But I suppose we should have expected no less from the people who condemned six million human beings to death simply because they were different."

Gruber nodded and remained silent.

Tracie said, "Okay, let's think about this. We have the key that will allow us to bypass the explosives. Hopefully. But I doubt the Nazis manufactured two of these keys—and then kept them separated for forty years—simply because they wanted to have a spare hanging around just in case Hitler lost one. They made two keys as a failsafe, so no one could access the Amber Room without both."

Gruber sighed. "Let's start looking."

He crouched in front of the door and began running his flashlight beam along the lower edge of the container, moving clockwise. When he reached the corner he moved up the right edge.

Two people searching the same area would be pointless, so Tracie moved away from the container and concentrated on the tunnel wall to her right. Finding the big storage locker had diverted her attention from the injury to her hand, and while the pain had never fully receded, it had faded into the background for a couple of blissful minutes.

Now it was back with a vengeance, determined to remind her it wasn't going anywhere.

She breathed deeply and blew the breath out and tried to concentrate on the task at hand. She began moving slowly away from the container in the direction from which they had just come, concerned that they may have passed the second lock without noticing it while in the process of working their way here. The Nazis could have placed the second lock anywhere, as its only function would be to render the explosives inert through the process of the two custom keys being inserted in their separate locks at the same time.

If her theory was correct, though, the entire operation would be dependent upon that precise synchronization of key insertion, which would mean the key holders would have to be in close proximity in order to coordinate their actions, or risk blowing themselves up through less-than-precise timing.

The second lock had to be right under their noses.

She turned and began examining the other wall, exasperated. Maybe her theory was all wrong. Maybe it wasn't necessary for both keys to enter both locks at the same time. If that were the case, the second lock could be upstairs in the manager's office.

It could be anywhere.

She cursed under her breath and then froze. Despite the intense pain still radiating through her left hand—and most of the arm as well—she smiled.

There it was.

39

November 19, 1987
10:45 a.m.
Under the Wuppertal Munitions Plant
Northwest of Wuppertal, Federal Republic of Germany

The lock had been mounted on the tunnel wall directly across from Tracie's location. It was nothing more complicated than a four-inch by four-inch iron box bolted onto the brick wall. The box had been painted the same matte black as the storage container, with a customized keyhole cut into the front that matched the one on the container exactly, right down to the tiny filaments fabricated into the odd little box cutouts on the keyhole.

But the bricks and mortar to which the box had been bolted so many years ago were no different than the bricks and mortar throughout the rest of the dank, moist underground passageway: they had long since begun to crumble. The box hung crookedly, suspended over the tunnel floor by a single remaining corroded bolt. The other three were gone, presumably disintegrated.

Tracie didn't bother to alert Gruber to the fact she had found the second lock. He was busy examining the space between the storage unit and the brick wall on the right side of the container. She was grateful for a little time to inspect the box herself, without the pressure of her partner pushing to insert the keys immediately and get the mission over with.

She reached under her filthy blouse at the neck and lifted the chain containing one of the two skeleton keys over her head. Then she held the key against the lead-plate box front, examining the fit. Without inserting the key into the lock it was impossible to be certain, but it looked as though the boxes fashioned on the ancient keys were a perfect match for the ones on the receptacle.

She nodded, satisfied that they were on the right track. She drew in a breath to let Gruber know she had found the second box, but before she could get the words out, he called to her. He was now on his hands and knees on the other side of the container, shining the light into the narrow gap between it and the tunnel wall.

"Quinn, check this out."

She slipped the chain back over her head, sliding the key under her blouse and then walking to the vault.

She dropped into a crouch behind him. "What did you find?"

"It looks like the Nazis actually planned ahead when they wired the explosives to this giant tin can. Take a look."

He stood and moved aside, allowing Tracie enough room to lift her flashlight and peer into the narrow space. Roughly a third of the way down the side of the container a hole had been drilled into the brick retaining wall. Heavy rubber wiring insulation extruded from the hole. The insulation snaked from the hole in the wall to the side of the container, where it disappeared inside via a similar opening.

"This is how they wired the explosives," she said. The rubber was dried out and cracked, the result of four decades spent in much less than ideal conditions, but from what little Tracie could see, none of the actual wiring had yet become exposed.

"It looks that way," Gruber agreed. "But wiring implies electricity, and there's no way the wreck of a facility falling down above our heads still has working electricity. The place probably hasn't had power since the late 1940s. We should be able to disregard the damned explosives. They're harmless."

"Don't bet on it," Tracie said, shaking her head.

"What are you talking about? You expect me to believe the power is still on in this place?"

"No, of course not. But maybe there's a generator somewhere out there in the forest. Or maybe there are a couple of car batteries wired to the thing, supplying enough power to detonate the explosives."

"Are you kidding me? Generators? Car batteries? The Nazis lost the war more than *forty-two years ago*, Quinn! There's not a car battery in the world that could last forty-plus years."

"Jesus, Gruber, use your head!" Tracie's hand was burning and her skull pounding where she had smacked it against the tunnel ceiling. She was exhausted and dispirited and tired of Gruber's bull-in-a-china-shop demeanor.

"I'm not talking about forty-year-old car batteries," she snapped. "That guy you were supposed to be watching, Newmann, what do you think he was doing here in Wuppertal all these years? Hanging around holding a key? Passing the time taking random walks in the forest? It was more than that, Gruber. He was placed here by Phoenix after the war, with a specific mission assignment. Don't you think it's reasonable to assume he might have been tasked with maintaining a generator or a set of batteries in addition to holding a goddamned key?"

At the mention of Newmann, Gruber's head snapped back as if he had been slapped. His voice hardened and he said, "Supposed to be watching? That was a cheap shot, Quinn."

"I'm sorry, Gruber. It's not my intention to be cruel. But it's been a long few days and I'm trying to keep us from getting blown into next week. We have to consider every angle, and I think it's a very real possibility that there is enough of a charge running through this wiring to detonate whatever explosives the Nazis placed on or inside this box. Whether the explosives themselves are still viable is anyone's guess, but I can't come up with a single good reason to assume they're not, can you?"

"No," he admitted. "I guess not. And your apology is accepted. Thank you. I suppose I ought to stay on your good side, what with you being so close to Aaron Stallings and all. You might be the only thing standing between me and the unemployment line once I get back to the states."

Tracie smiled in the darkness. Matthias Gruber was alternately maddening and charming, and while those personality swings made for a less-than-ideal field operative, he struck her as sincere and straightforward, a guy who honestly tried to do a good job but sometimes didn't know how. That last issue could be the kiss of death for an operative, though, and the thought occurred to her that keeping Gruber out of the field might be the best thing the CIA could do, both for his continued health and for the good of the agency.

But she wasn't about to tell him that. She had had more than a little recent experience with career disappointment and had no desire to contribute to someone else's.

She shined the light up the side of the vault, moving gradually, and then again up the side of the tunnel wall. Nothing. No clusters of explosives had been attached to the wall or the outside of the container, which made sense. The Nazis would not have wanted to leave them exposed, where if the tunnel were discovered, an enterprising ordnance disposal expert might successfully bypass the explosives.

They were all locked away inside the container. The insulated wiring running from behind the wall proved as much. There was no way of accessing the bombs. *It's probably just as well,* Tracie thought. *I'm no explosives expert, and if I let Gruber take a shot at disarming them I have a feeling we'd be dead in seconds.*

"I guess it's time to get to work," she said. "Let's open this thing up and see what's inside."

"Aren't you forgetting something?"

"What?"

"We still need to find the second lock."

"Nah, I found it just before you called me over here."

"You weren't planning on telling me?"

"No, Gruber. I wasn't planning on telling you. I was going to send you home and then utilize my twelve foot long arms to open both locks at once. The fact that my left hand is completely useless might have caused me a few problems, but I'm sure I would have figured something out."

"A little touchy, aren't you, Quinn?"

"My hand feels like someone's inside it with a blowtorch trying to burn his way out, and as a general rule, I'm against getting blown to bits and then buried underground before dinner. So, yes, I suppose you could say I'm a little touchy."

"Point taken. So how do we proceed?" Tracie could hear the

smile in his voice when he answered. She had been an only child, but she imagined this would be what it was like to have had a brother deriving great joy from pushing his sister's buttons.

"We proceed by each of us taking a key. We insert the keys into the locks at the same time and then turn them, and hope like hell we live to see the next couple of seconds."

"As plans go, it seems less than surefire."

"You were the one who wanted to disregard the explosives a few moments ago," Tracie pointed out.

"Touche."

She stood and stretched. The cool, damp tunnel air had tightened her muscles, and her joints cracked and complained. It served as another reminder—as if she needed one—that while she would still be considered a young woman by most, in the eyes of the intelligence community she was rapidly approaching the end of her useful life as a field operative.

It was not a comforting thought.

She pushed the notion to the back of her mind and said, "Pick a lock, Gruber. You want to do the one on the wall back there," she nodded behind her, "or the one on the container door?"

"Container door," he said without hesitation. "I want to be the first person to lay eyes on the Amber Room in almost half a century."

"Assuming it's even in there," Tracie said. "What if we went through all this only to open the doors and find nothing but Al Capone's vault?"

"Al Capone's vault? What are you talking about?"

"Jeez, Gruber, don't you watch TV? Or is all your free time spent romancing women?"

"I think you know the answer to that question."

"I suppose I do."

"Well? What's the deal with Al Capone's vault?"

"About a year-and-a-half ago, a bunch of secret tunnels were discovered under a hotel Al Capone had been living in until his arrest in the 1930s. A vault had been hidden inside one of the tunnels, much like this one. The vault was unsealed and opened on live national TV by Geraldo Rivera, the journalist."

"And what was inside?"

"Nothing. Just a few empty bottles and some trash."

Gruber chuckled. "That would be ironic. But I don't think even the Nazis, as crazy as they were, would go to the trouble and expense of burying a giant iron container and then wiring it with explosives, only to leave it empty."

"I guess we'll find out," she said. She lifted the two chains from around her neck and handed one of the keys to Gruber, picking randomly.

"It doesn't matter which keys we use?"

"They look exactly the same, and so do the locks."

"I hope you're right."

"You and me both," she said under her breath as she walked to the box hanging on the tunnel wall.

She held the key against the lock with her right hand while placing her flashlight between her left arm and her body. Holding the light in her injured left hand would have been impossible. Then she rotated her body toward the container.

The beam of light showed Gruber standing in front of the double doors, his key at the ready. Her stomach was in knots and tension filled the darkened passageway. The air was electric.

"Ready, Gruber?"

"Ready, Quinn."

"On the count of three, we slide the keys in and turn, got it?"

"Got it."

"Okay." She took a deep breath, then started counting. "One… two—"

"Hey, Quinn?"

"What?" she answered, annoyed. She had damned near thrust the key into the lock.

"Thanks for believing in me."

"You're welcome, Gruber. Now don't interrupt me again unless you're having a stroke or something."

"You got it, boss."

"One…two…three." She jammed the key into the ancient Nazi lock and turned it in one motion, waiting for the roar and the blinding flash of light that would tell her they had failed, a split-second before ending their lives.

Nothing happened.

The key squealed and complained after four decades without lubrication, but it turned in the lock.

A few feet away, Gruber's did the same.

He looked up at her, his eyes shining with anticipation.

Then he reached up and pulled on an iron handle that had been welded to the door.

40

The door swung slowly open and Tracie's flashlight beam lit up the interior of the storage container.

And there it was.

The Amber Room treasure.

Panel upon panel of wall coverings had been neatly aligned, each one at least four feet wide by eight feet high, all of them covered in clear plastic tarpaulins. The panels featured mirrors and exotic filigree designs and were dripping in gold, encrusted with diamonds and precious stones.

Tracie's breath caught in her throat as the light refracted crazily off the treasure. *Three hundred million dollars,* she thought. The number had seemed absurd when she first heard it, the estimated value an impossible sum of which to conceive. And now, with the treasure in front of her, the panels intact and spectacular, the concept seemed even more difficult to grasp, rather than less.

Gruber peeked around the door and inside the container, and then turned his head toward Tracie and grinned. "What do you say we grab a couple of panels and hit the road?"

"Very funny. Our mission's complete, Gruber. Here's what we're really going to do: we're going to close the doors and secure the locks. We're going to retrace our steps out of here and let the big-shots figure out what to do next. That's why they make the big bucks. This is way above our pay grades."

"I know, I know," he said. "Just joking. But let's take a few minutes to admire this stuff before we go running off. We're the first people to lay eyes on the Amber Room in nearly a half-century."

He waggled his eyebrows and grinned again and leaned against the heavy iron door, which was standing roughly two-thirds open. The addition of his weight caused it to begin moving again.

Toward the front wall of the container.

Skeleton key still sticking out of the lock.

It was about to be smashed between the door and the wall.

"Gruber, no!" Tracie shouted.

He reacted quickly, removing his weight from the door and flashing a hand out to stop its backward motion.

But it was too late. It hit the wall with a BONG that echoed through the tunnel.

Then it rebounded toward Gruber, who caught it just as the exposed portion of the key fell to the tunnel floor. The force of the collision had caused it to snap off inside the lock.

A flash of white light from somewhere inside the container seared the image of Gruber into Tracie's retinas. He was semi-crouched in front of the open door in an instinctive attempt to shield his body from what he knew was coming.

Tracie heaved herself backward down the tunnel as a sizzling noise came from inside the container. It sounded like an electrical short circuit, and for the briefest of moments she thought they might be okay.

Then came the explosion. It roared from inside the iron vault, the flash of white light becoming a bright orange blaze in an instant. Her body struck the tunnel floor and she rolled, desperate to put as much distance between herself and the explosive charge as possible, lifting her arms to her head to protect her skull from the projectiles she knew were about to rain down.

And they did.

The front of the storage unit blew off, huge chunks of jagged iron whistling down the tunnel, somehow missing Tracie's prone body and then thudding into the dirt pile she had worked so hard to climb over. A piece of four-by-four ceiling timber fell next to her shoulder, nearly crushing her skull before embedding itself into the hard-packed dirt of the tunnel floor.

An instant later, a sting of pain as bright as the light from the explosion ripped through the back of her head and she realized the timber *had* struck her on its way past, and it *had* torn out a piece of her skull, and she wondered how badly she was bleeding as she stopped rolling, her progress halted by some unknown object holding her head down into the dirt.

It must be the support timber, she thought as panic threatened to overwhelm her. *Good God, the timber has crushed my skull and pinned my head to the floor. I'm going to bleed to death down here, I'm going to die and no one will ever—*

Stop it! She commanded herself. She banged her left hand against the tunnel floor and the pain in her head was overwhelmed by the pain in her hand, a wave of fire that radiated outward and served to focus her attention on something other than dying in a secret Nazi tunnel. *Get ahold of yourself and think. You survived the initial blast, now you have to figure out how to survive the cave-in.*

And it was a cave-in, a big one. Dirt had begun dropping into the tunnel, tons and tons of dirt showering down like rain, blocking out the light from the explosion and dampening the sound of the chaos until all she could hear was the heavy rumble of falling earth.

And then there was silence, the only sound Tracie's moans.

41

November 19, 1987
Approximately 11:10 a.m.
Under the Wuppertal Munitions Plant
Northwest of Wuppertal, Federal Republic of Germany

Tracie lay motionless on the tunnel floor, amazed to still be alive but fearful that any vibration at all might negatively affect the unstable earth and cause further cave-ins.

How the hell had she survived? The fact that the storage container had been constructed with virtually no clearance between the iron walls and the side walls of the tunnel must have caused the explosion to concentrate its greatest force upward toward the surface and outward from both ends, like a pipe bomb blowing off its end caps.

She had been standing almost flat against the tunnel wall as she turned her key and then again as she rolled she had snugged up against it. This had removed her from the path of most of the chunks of iron as they rocketed up the passageway.

It was the only explanation she could think of.

And right now the issue of how she had survived was irrelevant. The fact was that her head was injured and pinned to the ground, and surviving the initial blast wasn't going to matter unless she could figure out how to stop the bleeding in her head and protect her injured skull and then—

Wait a second.

If her skull was so badly injured, where was all the blood?

Her head was pressed against the tunnel floor, meaning her eyes were *right there*, and she should be able to see blood pooling on the dirt and soaking into the earth. She should have a front-row seat for the bleed-out, an up-close-and-personal view of her lifeblood as it drained away.

But she didn't see blood.

None.

Her right arm was trapped under her body, and she shifted her weight as much as she could, lifting her arm clear and raising her good hand toward her head. She placed her fingers against the back of her neck and eased her hand upward, moving slowly, expecting to feel a crater of splintered skull bone, thick with blood.

Nothing.

She forced her hand to continue upward along the back of her head and in another inch her fingers tangled themselves in her hair, which had become matted and snarled. She'd been wearing an old Washington Senators baseball cap and it had been torn off her head in the explosion, lost somewhere among the debris and the tons of fallen earth.

She pushed harder against her snarled hair and the pain in her head returned. It was nothing like what she had felt immediately following the explosion, but it was there, and the truth began to dawn on her.

My skull's not damaged at all, she thought wonderingly. *The chunk of timber landed on my hair as it embedded itself into the ground next to me head. The pain I felt was the wooden beam ripping out my hair. I'm not going to bleed to death!*

The flash of elation faded quickly as Tracie realized that although she was in no immediate danger of dying—barring a second cave-in, which remained a very real possibility—she was still alone in the tunnel and trapped, unable to move, likely facing a long, slow, tortuous death. Her hair was holding her in place against the tunnel floor. In many ways what she faced would be worse than the quick extinction she had somehow avoided and that Gruber must have experienced.

The feeling of panic began to return and Tracie forced herself to slow down and think. She would not remain trapped. She would rip her hair from her head by the roots if that was what it took to free herself.

She pulled her hand away from her head and let it drop to the tunnel floor. Pushed against the dirt and tried use her hand as a lever, to force her body upward. Tugged her head, attempting to pull free.

But it was no use. She felt a flash of pain as her hair pulled taut against her head but there wasn't enough clearance between her skull and the tunnel floor to generate any momentum.

She breathed deeply, working hard to forestall the panic that was lurking in the back of her mind.

Think, dammit.

Then she smiled despite the pain in her hand and her head, despite the shock of losing Gruber and the fear of dying alone fifteen feet underground. She knew what to do. If she hadn't been so stunned by the sudden explosion it would have occurred to her immediately.

She snaked her good hand along the ground toward her lower body as she scrunched into the fetal position, knees together and folded in toward her chest. Lifted her right pant leg up her calf toward her knee. Grasped her combat knife and lifted it clear of its sheath.

Then she bent her arm at the elbow and began hacking away at her hair, working quickly but carefully to avoid stabbing herself in the skull. *Wouldn't that be ironic,* she thought. *Survive the cave-in after thinking my skull was crushed, only to bleed to death after slicing my own head open.*

Her eyes watered as each slice of the knife pulled her hair tight against her skull. She didn't mind the pain. Rather, she relished it, each stroke of the knife a reminder that she was still alive.

Still kicking.

A half-dozen strokes later she was free.

She rolled to her knees, pivoting her body to peer down what was left of the tunnel toward the storage container. She had maintained a death grip on her flashlight, instinctively knowing that in the unlikely event she survived the explosion she would stand no chance at escaping the tunnel without it.

She flicked the light on and gasped.

The container was gone, replaced by moist black earth that had dropped onto it seemingly in a solid mass. It was as if the tunnel had been dug to a point five feet from Tracie's prone body and then had been abandoned.

She crept forward in shock, fearful of another cave-in but unable to stop herself from moving toward where she knew the storage container—and Gruber—to be.

I hope the explosion killed Gruber, she thought. *Because the prospect of being buried alive…*

Tracie shook her head and turned away from the fresh earth. Gruber was gone, and any more time spent contemplating the gruesome nature of his death would make her *own* death down here that much more likely.

She stood and took and step.

Froze as the sound of a muffled cry drifted through the tunnel.

No way. It can't be. I'm imagining it.

She shook her head and took another step and then heard it again. It was not her imagination. Gruber was alive. How that could be, she had no idea, but she had seen plenty of death in her lifetime and in not a single case had a corpse cried out.

"Gruber?" she whispered, immediately shaking her head with the realization that he would never hear a whisper. He would have been lucky to hear her pathetic attempt were he standing right next to her, never mind buried under tons of dirt and rubble.

She turned in a circle, using her flashlight to reveal the devastation of the tunnel. Beams hung from the ceiling, the brick side walls had collapsed. The portion of the tunnel that had survived the cave-in was narrow and ill defined.

God help me, Tracie thought, and then she raised her voice and half-spoke, half-shouted, "Gruber! Are you okay?"

A half-second delay, and then the response. "I-I'm bleeding, Quinn. I'm trapped."

"Stanch the bleeding the best you can, Gruber. I'm going to dig you out." She spoke the words knowing their futility. There was no way she could dig out a man buried under tons of earth with no tools and one good hand.

"Forget it, Quinn."

"I'm damned well not going to forget it," she answered angrily.

"I'm not leaving you there to die. How did you survive the blast, anyway?" She asked the question partly to keep his mind off his situation and partly because she simply couldn't fathom the fact that he could have been that close to the blast site and still be breathing.

"One of the panels wedged itself just above my body, between the storage container and the falling dirt," he said. His voice was shaky and fading, she could hear it getting weaker. He was going into shock. "There's a narrow gap underneath it. That's where I am."

"I'll get to you as quickly as I can. Hang on, Gruber, do you hear me? That's an order."

"I told you, forget it. I'm dying."

"And *I* told *you* you're not going to die. Hang on." She knelt against the fresh earth and began shoveling scoops backward, one small handful at a time, knowing it was hopeless but doing it anyway.

"You're not hearing me," Gruber said. His voice wavered like a ninety year-old man's. "My leg is gone. A piece of iron took it off above the knee. I'm bleeding out, Quinn. I've got a couple of minutes. Maybe less."

"No!" Tracie answered. "No! That's not acceptable. Hang on, I'm coming. Do you hear me, Gruber? I'm coming to get you out of there." She continued to dig as the tears began to fall, rolling down her cheeks and plopping into the dirt below. "I'm not leaving you there to die."

"Quinn, listen to me. Stop. You could have a bucket loader to dig with and I'd be gone long before you could get to me. It's okay. I'm not in any pain, just feel a little cold, and that will be gone soon, too. I've just got one question for you, Quinn."

"What is it?" She tried to keep the tears out of her voice when she answered. It was the least she could do for the dying man, but she failed miserably at the attempt.

"Will you sleep with me now?"

42

November 19, 1987
Approximately 11:15 a.m.
Under the Wuppertal Munitions Plant
Northwest of Wuppertal, Federal Republic of Germany

"I'll sleep with you, Gruber, just keep breathing. Hang on for me."
She tore at the soil with her hand and ripped off a fingernail and
barely noticed.

Silence.

"You hear me, Gruber? Yes, I'll sleep with you. Tell me all the
things we're going to do when we sleep together."

Silence.

"Gruber! You hear me? Answer me!"

Silence.

43

November 19, 1987
Approximately 11:20 a.m.
Under the Wuppertal Munitions Plant
Northwest of Wuppertal, Federal Republic of Germany

Tracie wasn't sure how long she cried. The concussive blast of the explosion had smashed her watch, or maybe it broke while she was clawing at the fresh earth in her frantic—and futile—attempt to get to Gruber following the cave-in.

She wasn't even sure *why* she cried, or at least why she cried so fiercely. This wasn't the first time another operative had died on a mission, and in all likelihood it would not be the last.

Maybe next time it would be her.

Hell, maybe this time it would still be her. She wasn't out of the woods yet, not by a long shot. She had the length of the tunnel to fight her way through and who knew how much damage the Nazi explosives had caused down the line?

But the tears kept coming, making furrows down her filthy face and dropping onto her clothing, and out of nowhere the reason occurred to her.

She was crying because this was her fault. This death had been entirely avoidable, and the fact that Gruber had fallen victim to his own impetuous nature did nothing to change the fact that it should never have happened in the first place.

I shouldn't have given him the choice of locks to open, Tracie

261

thought bitterly. *I should have taken the lock closest to the explosives. It's my fault just as much as it is Gruber's that he's dead. It's not like I hadn't seen plenty of examples of his carelessness. Hell, the reason I was sent here in the first place is because he couldn't handle his assignment.*

Gruber's dead because of my poor judgment.

Mine.

I'm to blame.

*   *   *

After a while—ten minutes?...ten hours?—the tears stopped of their own accord. There were none left to cry. Tracie felt hollowed-out, defeated, an exhaustion that was every bit as much mental and spiritual as physical. She had switched off her flashlight to save the batteries and the resulting darkness seemed utterly appropriate to the occasion.

"I'm sorry, Gruber," she muttered into the darkness. "I let you down and I'm sorry." She spoke so softly she could barely hear the words herself; they certainly weren't going to carry through the tons of dirt piled between her and the storage container.

But the volume at which she spoke no longer mattered.

Tracie rose to her feet and switched on her flashlight. The result was a weak and flickering beam, and she realized with no surprise whatsoever that either the light had been damaged in the explosion or the batteries were failing.

She might well be plunged into darkness before escaping the tunnel.

*   *   *

The blockage that she and Gruber had passed only at great cost while working their way to the Amber Room—Tracie wouldn't know how high a cost until her hand had been thoroughly examined back at Langley, assuming she survived—represented even more of a challenge on the way out.

As she had feared, the explosive blast further damaged the ceiling supports and caused more earth to spray into the passageway. The narrow gap that had existed between the top of the dirt pile and the tunnel ceiling was now gone. The corridor was completely blocked.

She sighed and climbed the pile as far as she could, then flicked off the flashlight and started digging. Every few minutes she checked her progress, pausing for a short break and flicking on the light before resuming her work. For a long while she didn't seem to be making any.

Her fear was that as she removed dirt from the cave-in, more would fall from above, dooming her to a Sisyphean struggle that would end only when she ran out of energy.

Or oxygen.

Or will.

The Nazis had obviously provided for air circulation when constructing the tunnel, but who was to say that the ductwork wasn't by now completely blocked?

The thought spurred Tracie on, and she forced herself to continue working when her arm burned and her shoulder ached and she wanted nothing more than to climb to the bottom of the pile and curl up into a ball.

But doing so could be fatal, and she kept digging. One by one the fingernails of her right hand were ripped off, falling victim to rocks embedded in the dirt, or pieces of the iron storage unit that had been blasted the length of the tunnel, or the hard-packed earth itself.

The passage of time became elastic. With no watch to provide context to her struggle and no sun—or moon, as by now it was just as likely nighttime as day—to track across the sky, it became impossible to guess how long she had been at work.

Not that it mattered. Time was relevant only to the extent that she didn't want to outlast her air supply, and that consideration was beyond her ability to control.

She alternated between hopelessness and the certainty that if she worked hard enough and kept at it long enough she would survive.

Finally she punched through to the other side, a puff of air flowing through an opening so small she could not even see it yet. The airflow was so minimal it could not even legitimately be considered a breeze, but it was there and it was real. It tickled her bloody fingers and provided hope to her flagging spirit.

She celebrated with a momentary sob of relief and then got back to work, digging and enlarging the opening, working without any further breaks until she had excavated a hole just large to allow passage for her shoulders. Her mini-tunnel was located in the upper left corner of the cave-in, between the ceiling and what remained of the tunnel wall, perhaps twelve inches wide by twelve inches high.

Tracie paused before crawling through. She was dirty and tired and in pain, and perhaps as devastated in spirit as she had ever been. She turned and aimed her flashlight—it was still working, although the quality of the light was nothing like what it had been at the beginning of the subterranean journey—back at the solid wall of earth standing between her and the Amber Room.

And her now-dead temporary partner.

"See ya on the other side, Gruber," she said softly. "I'm sorry I let you down."

Then she turned back and slithered through the hole, sliding headfirst down the other side of the pile until she came to a painful stop amid fallen chunks of ceiling supports, bricks and other unidentifiable rubble.

The massive boulder she had been so concerned about a thousand years ago when they were working their way toward the Amber Room, the one that had been perched precariously a third of the way down the dirt pile, had disappeared, apparently buried under thousands of tons of fresh earth.

"Small favors," Tracie muttered. Dirt had forced its way into her mouth as she tumbled down the pile, and now she dug out the biggest pieces—clods the size of strawberries but not nearly as sweet—with her fingers and spit out the rest.

And her flashlight failed. Without warning the beam of light disappeared, and even though the equipment failure was anything but unexpected, for a moment Tracie froze in her tracks, her pulse skyrocketing and adrenaline pounding through her system.

Relax, she thought. Barring any further serious damage from the explosion, all she needed to do was pick her way around smaller cave-ins until reaching the entryway beneath the plant manager's office, and then feel around for the iron ladder bolted to the wall.

Simple.

Unless there's more damage.

She forced the thought away, along with the accompanying image of herself trapped in the darkness, lost and unable to find her way out, rats chewing at her exposed skin when she became too weak to fight them off.

Keep moving.

She tamped down on the panic and worked her way forward. She discovered to her surprise that the damage to this end of the tunnel seemed to have been relatively minimal. The unseen obstacles she was forced to pick her way around seemed no more daunting than she remembered them being while she and Gruber were moving in the other direction.

Her mind wandered. She was moving slowly but her brain was racing. She thought about the Amber Room, and its supposed value, and about whether the fact that a man had died in the quest to retrieve it added to that value or subtracted from it.

She thought about Marshall Fulton, to whom she felt a strong attraction and whom she had dated a few times but had mostly kept at arm's length, concerned about starting a relationship when her own future was so uncertain.

She thought about Aaron Stallings, and about D.C. politicians and bureaucrats to whom the Amber Room represented not a rare and important historical artifact, but rather a prize, monetary and strategic, to be bartered and leveraged in their unending quest for more power and greater influence.

She thought about the man she had known as Matthias Gruber. That hadn't been his real name, of course, any more than Tracie's real name was "Fiona Quinn." But that was how she had known him, and it would be how he lived on in her memory.

She was so absorbed in her racing thoughts that she was actually surprised when she reached the beginning of the tunnel. Her head banged on the iron ladder, in virtually the exact spot she had already bruised on the tunnel ceiling support, and she didn't care at all. She sank to her knees in relief, blurting out thanks to a God she wasn't even sure she believed in.

44

Climbing out of the tunnel was simple once she had made her way back to the ladder.

Once above ground and inside the plant manager's office, Tracie lifted the hinged door with her "good" hand, which was now missing fingernails and dripping blood. She dropped the door into place over the tunnel entrance, and then sprinted to the Opel.

She had no car key, of course. That was in Gruber's pocket, buried under the tons of earth now covering whatever was left of the Amber Room. But Tracie didn't let that minor inconvenience slow her down.

She picked up a chunk of crumbled pavement and hurled it through the passenger window, shattering the safety glass. Unlocked and opened the door. Swept the glass out onto the parking lot as best she could and then bent down under the steering column, searching for the ignition and battery wires.

Hotwiring the Opel was a simpler task than she expected. The ignition and battery wires were readily available, and within seconds she had yanked them out of their harnesses. She pressed the leads together and the engine bucked and complained before grumbling to life.

Less than thirty minutes later Tracie was back inside the safe house, and less than thirty *seconds* after that she was on the secure satellite phone to CIA Director Aaron Stallings.

She didn't bother cleaning up before making the call.

She still had no idea what time it was.

She didn't care.

The connection crackled and popped, and then Stallings picked up. "You want to explain to me why you always have to call in the middle of the night, Tanner?"

"It's nice to talk to you, too, sir."

"Don't be a wiseass. I have a meeting first thing in the morning with key members of the House Appropriations Committee, and going in there on less than a good night's sleep is not the recipe for ensuring a healthy budget. And you know what a healthy budget means?"

"What's that, sir?"

"It means *you* continue to get paid."

"Well, I'm sorry to interrupt your beauty sleep, sir, but a lot has happened in Wuppertal, and I thought an immediate update was warranted. Please accept my apologies if I was wrong about that."

The sigh came through the receiver loud and clear. "I'm up now," Stallings said resignedly. "You may as well hit me with it. I assume the Amber Room is, in fact, contained inside the tunnel beneath the munitions plant northwest of Wuppertal. Even you would know better than to call in the middle of the night if you hadn't found anything."

"It's under there all right."

"Well? Is it secure?"

"Yes and no."

"Yes and no? What the hell does that mean?"

"It means that nobody's going to get to the Amber Room anytime soon. Not without a backhoe and other heavy construction equipment, anyway. And even if they do, I don't know that there'd be anything left to excavate."

The impatient petulance left Stallings's tone. "What happened?"

Tracie ran through an abbreviated version of the events as they had taken place under the abandoned factory. She didn't bother including her own injuries in the narrative. For one thing, Stallings wouldn't care, and for another, there were more important issues to discuss.

She spoke without interruption, and when she finished, the CIA director was silent for a moment. Then he said, "I told you Gruber wasn't to be trusted."

"It was my fault, sir. I should have taken the lock closest the explosives, and I should have placed Gruber at the lock closer to the tunnel entrance."

"Obviously." The comment was brief and acerbic and, Tracie thought, devastatingly accurate.

In most cases she would have been quick with a sarcastic reply, something to reinforce to the bully of a CIA director that she wasn't intimidated by him, that she didn't care what he thought of her, that she was doing her job out of service to her country and respect for the chain of command, not because she valued his opinion in any way.

But this time there was no sarcasm to be had. No retort to toss out, no put-down, no remark that could lessen the effect of Aaron Stallings's one word comment.

It hurts, Tracie thought, *probably more than the physical injuries do.*

Good.

The pain was no more and no less than she deserved. A man had lost his life because of her miscalculation. Her poor judgment. His actions had been rash and had led directly to his death, but she was in charge, and she had had plenty of opportunity to observe firsthand Gruber's penchant for carelessness.

And still she had allowed him to stand directly in harm's way.

She deserved Aaron Stallings's scorn and disgust. And it was nothing compared to the scorn and disgust she felt for herself.

Tracie realized she hadn't spoken for several seconds. She cleared her throat and wiped the back of her "good" hand across her eyes. Her vision had gotten suddenly blurry, and she could feel the dirt smudging her cheeks as she wiped away the tears that had begun to form.

"Tanner," Stallings said before she could speak.

"Yes, sir?" *Here it comes. He's going to tear into me and I deserve every word.*

"Nobody can anticipate every eventuality in the field. You know that as well as I do. Hell, maybe better than I do, considering

I haven't worked in the field in almost forty years. You made a mistake. It happens. You aren't responsible for Gruber blowing himself up in that tunnel. Gruber was. Only Gruber. Do you understand me?"

"Yes sir." It was all she trusted herself to say. Any more and she knew there would be no way to keep the pain and guilt out of her voice.

"Give yourself a break, Tanner. You know how this business works. Gruber was about to be pulled out of the field for the very reasons that led to his death. It wasn't your fault."

"But—"

"That's enough, Tanner." The tone coming through the sat phone's receiver was unlike anything she had ever heard out of Aaron Stallings. It sounded more like the gentle rebuke a grandfather might give, or a kindly uncle, than anything that had ever come from the ruthless manipulator who had ruled the CIA with an iron fist for decades.

"Yes sir."

"Now, we need to consider the implications of this."

"I know, sir. That's why I called. How are we going to prevent Phoenix from attempting to access the Amber Room treasure despite the explosion, and how are we going to recover Gruber's body?"

"Phoenix will not be an issue."

"Sir?"

"West Germany's Federal Intelligence Service is in the process of rounding up and arresting the surviving members of Phoenix even as we speak. They will be charged with treason against the Federal Republic of Germany and will no longer be capable of anything other than rotting in German prisons."

"But…once the bodies of Adolph Hitler Senior and Junior are discovered, this thing is going to explode. It will be immediately clear that they were assassinated, and—"

"The bodies aren't going to be discovered, Tanner. Ever. To the rest of the world, Adolph Hitler Junior never existed, and Hitler Senior died in April of 1945, exactly as everyone thought all along."

"I don't understand."

"The first thing I did after your notification that both Hitlers had been eliminated—even before I called my counterpart at FIS and filled him in on the Phoenix camp—was to contact our agency cleanup team in the area. The bodies of both men have been removed and will never be found."

"How did they—"

"They're very good at what they do, Tanner, just like you are. They were forced to eliminate several Phoenix members in the process of removing the Hitler corpses, but that's nothing to worry about. The FIS will suspect CIA involvement when they find the dead Phoenix members, of course, given the fact that I tipped them off to the whereabouts of the camp. But they know better than to ask too many questions, especially considering the outcry they will face among West Germany's political class if word of Phoenix—and its purpose—ever leaks out. I will be sure to stress to the FIS that as long as they play ball with me, they have nothing to worry about on that score. If they don't, they know what will happen. I'm confident they'll make the right choice."

Tracie was silent for a moment, and not just out of wonder at the compliment Stallings had just off-handedly thrown her way. She had worked with the man closely now on several assignments, and for all his faults, his ability to pull strings and influence global events—even when those events were occurring halfway around the world—never ceased to amaze her.

Finally she spoke. "What about the second issue, sir? How are we going to recover Gruber's body without giving away the location of the Amber Room?"

"We're not."

"Excuse me?"

"We're not going to recover the body, Tanner. It's going to remain buried along with the Amber Room, until such time as the United States Government makes a determination on how to proceed with regards to the hundreds of millions of dollars' worth of treasure now buried in that tunnel. Even if the Amber Room panels were blown to bits, they still retain at least some of their value."

This was the Aaron Stallings Tracie had grown to know and detest. The shrewd, calculating puppeteer was back. "But sir, Gruber's family deserves—"

"No, Tanner, they do not. Gruber's family understood the risks that accompanied his acceptance of CIA fieldwork assignments, just as yours understands the same. He was not a soldier who perished on the battlefield. He was an intelligence officer working undercover in a foreign land. The situations are dissimilar, and traditional rules of combat do not apply. Is that understood?"

She bit back the retort that tried to force its way out. She wanted to argue but couldn't, because for as much as the thought horrified her, she *did* understand.

Instead, she changed the subject. "What about the tunnel entrance, sir? Even though the factory is abandoned, and even though it's located in the middle of nowhere, sooner or later someone's going to stumble on the hinged door on the floor of the plant manager's office. There's no lock on it anymore, and there's nothing covering it, and—"

"The flooring is being replaced even as we speak. It will match the rest of the ancient plant exactly, and within a few hours, no one but the agency will know the tunnel entrance was ever there."

Once again he's way ahead of me, she thought.

"Now," Stallings said. "We need to get you back to Langley to have your injuries assessed and treated. I'll send the Gulfstream for you tomorrow. Just get to Hahn Air Base by early afternoon and you'll be back in the States by late tomorrow night."

"Thank you, sir."

"You're welcome, Tanner."

"But sir, if you don't mind me asking…"

"What is it now? I've got to get back to sleep. I already told you I have an important early meeting."

"How did you know I was injured? I never mentioned it."

The CIA director barked out a laugh. It sounded a lot like a pistol shot. "You always get injured, Tanner. Always. It's part of what makes you, you. Now get back here and get healthy. We're going to need you out in the field again sooner rather than later."

The line clicked dead and for the first time since the underground explosion, Tracie Tanner fully realized the extent of her exhaustion. She still didn't know what time it was and still didn't care. Her safe house bed was calling, and she didn't have to be at Hahn until tomorrow afternoon.

She knew she should clean and dress her wounds.
She knew she should arrange transportation for tomorrow.
She knew she wasn't going to do either thing.
She stumbled to her bed and fell under the covers, fully clothed and filthy. She was asleep in less than a minute.

Tracie Tanner will return soon in her fifth action-packed thriller. To be the first to learn about new releases, and for the opportunity to win free ebooks, signed copies of print books, and other swag, take a moment to sign up for Allan Leverone's email newsletter at AllanLeverone.com...

Reader reviews are hugely important to authors looking to set their work apart from the competition. If you have a moment to spare, please consider taking a moment to leave a brief, honest review of *The Hitler Deception* at Amazon, Goodreads, or your favorite review site, and thank you!

Also from Allan Leverone

Thrillers:

Parallax View: A Tracie Tanner Thriller
All Enemies: A Tracie Tanner Thriller
The Omega Connection: A Tracie Tanner Thriller
Final Vector
The Lonely Mile
The Organization: A Jack Sheridan Pulp Thriller

Horror/Dark Thrillers

Mr. Midnight
After Midnight
Paskagankee
Revenant: A Paskagankee Novel Book Two
Wellspring: A Paskagankee Novel Book Three

Novellas

The Becoming
Flight 12: A Kristin Cunningham Thriller

Story Collections

Postcards from the Apocalypse
Uncle Brick and the Four Novelettes
Letters from the Asylum: Three Complete Novellas

WHITE-HOT SUBMARINE WARFARE
BY
JOHN R. MONTEITH

www.braveshipbooks.com

WHO IS HUNTER? WHO IS PREY?
WHO WILL SURVIVE?

ROBERT BIDINOTTO

In a world without justice, sometimes
you have to make your own...

CUTTING-EDGE NAVAL THRILLERS
BY
JEFF EDWARDS